WILLIAM
THE CONQUEROR

Richmal Crompton was born in Lancashire in 1890. The first story about William Brown appeared in *Home* magazine in 1919, and the first collection of William stories was published in book form three years later. In all, thirty-eight William books were published, the last one in 1970, after Richmal Crompton's death.

'Probably the funniest, toughest children's books ever written'
Sunday Times on the Just William series

'Richmal Crompton's creation [has] been famed for his cavalier attitude to life and those who would seek to circumscribe his enjoyment of it ever since he first appeared'
Guardian

Books available in the Just William series

Just William
More William
William Again
William the Fourth
Still William
William the Conqueror
William the Outlaw
William in Trouble
William the Good
William at War

WILLIAM
THE CONQUEROR

RICHMAL CROMPTON

FOREWORD BY CHARLIE HIGSON

ILLUSTRATED BY THOMAS HENRY

MACMILLAN CHILDREN'S BOOKS

First published 1926
This selection first published 1984 by Macmillan Children's Books

This edition published 2011 by Macmillan Children's Books
a division of Macmillan Publishers Limited
20 New Wharf Road, London N1 9RR
Basingstoke and Oxford
Associated companies throughout the world
www.panmacmillan.com

ISBN 978-0-330-54519-8

1 3 5 7 9 8 6 4 2

A CIP catalogue record for this book is available from
the British Library.

Printed and bound in the UK by CPI Mackays, Chatham ME5 8TD

CONTENTS

FOREWORD

I came to William Brown late in life. I was forty-odd, and had never read the books or seen any of the TV series, but I had three boys of my own and was always looking for ways to keep them entertained. They had an older cousin, Marlon, who handed down to them a battered cardboard box stuffed with cherished old cassette tapes. Surprisingly, apart from a couple of Masters of the Universe stories, they were all Just William tapes. I say surprisingly because, as might be surmised from his name, Marlon was a modern London teenager through and through, cynical, streetwise and surly. His dad assured me he had loved the tapes, but somehow I didn't think my own kids would be interested. All they seemed to like were computer games and bizarre impenetrable American cartoon shows. How could they could possible relate to some schoolboy from the 1930s? But I put a tape on for them one night and left them to it.

Ever since then my two youngest boys have gone

to sleep every single night to the sound of Martin Jarvis reading Richmal Crompton's ageless stories. They must have heard those tapes hundreds of times – no, thousands. The originals are worn out, replaced and updated from the huge library available. I don't know if the boys even hear the words any more, or if they have simply developed a Pavlovian response to Martin Jarvis, whose voice transports them to a safe and comforting world of tea parties, scraped knees and an endless sunny summer's afternoon that has lasted ninety years.

Listening with the kids on car journeys and in hotel bedrooms, I've grown to love the stories just as much as they have. The only problem is that when I read the originals I can't get Martin Jarvis's voice out of my head, and can't imagine how Richmal Crompton thought the boy should sound. Martin Jarvis is William Brown.

And I understand now why the stories cast such a spell over my own kids. They are boys and William is a boy, and Marlon was a boy, and boys are the same the world over and have always been the same, and probably always will be. And we never grow up. William is essence of boy. He has everything a boy could want – a dog, a stick, a penknife, a gang, a den, trees to climb, stones to throw, sweets in his pocket . . . Also, in these stories there's a war on, sheer bliss for an eleven-year-old boy, so there's shrapnel to collect, soldiers to admire, parachutists to spot, spies to thwart. There is no death and hardship and horror, but the William stories are nevertheless quite tough. William and his gang are always getting into punch-ups and some of his exploits would be quite alarming to a namby-pamby, overprotective modern parent. Today William would probably be put into therapy and made the subject of a documentary on Channel Five. Except, of course, William always gets away with it. Despite the trail of chaos and anarchy he leaves behind, he always ends up as the only thing that any boy has ever wanted to be. A hero.

Charlie Higson

CHAPTER 1

ENTER THE SWEEP

WILLIAM and the sweep took to one another at once.

William liked the sweep's colouring, and the sweep liked William's conversation. William looked up to the sweep as a being of a superior order.

'Didn't your mother *mind* you being a sweep?' he said wonderingly, as the sweep unpacked his brushes.

'N-naw,' said the sweep, slowly and thoughtfully. 'Leastways, she didn't say nothin'.'

'You don't want a partner, do you?' said William. 'I wun't mind being a sweep. I'd come an' live with you an' go round with you every day.'

'Thanks,' said the man, 'but p'raps your pa would have somethin' to say.'

William laughed bitterly and scornfully.

'Oh, yes, *they'd* fuss. *They* fuss if I get a bit of mud on my boots. As if their ole drawin'-room carpet mattered. Have you any little boys?'

'Yus, three,' said the sweep.

'I s'pose *they'll* all be sweeps,' said William gloomily, feeling that the profession was becoming overcrowded.

'Come *out* of that room, Master William,' called cook, who, in the absence of William's parents, took what William considered a wholly unjustifiable interest in him.

William extended his tongue in the direction of the voice. Otherwise he ignored it.

'I'd meant to be a robber,' went on William, 'but I think I'd as soon be a sweep. Or I might be a sweep first, an' then a robber.'

'Come out of that *room*, Master William,' called cook.

William simulated deafness.

'I'd like to be a sweep an' a robber an' a detective an' a soldier, an' some more things. I think I'd better be them about a year each, so's I can get 'em all in.'

'Um,' said the sweep. 'There's somethin' in that.'

Cook appeared in the doorway.

'Didn't you hear me telling you to *come* out of that room, Master William?' she said pugnaciously.

'You can't expect me to hear you when you go shoutin' about in the kitchen,' said William loftily. 'I just heard you *shoutin*'.'

'Well, come out of this room, anyway.'

'How can you expect me to know how it's done if I

don't stay to watch? Wot's the good of me goin' to be a sweep if I don't know how it's done?'

'What's the good of me covering up all the furniture if you're going to stay here getting black as pitch? Are you coming out?'

'No,' said William exasperated, 'I've *gotter* stay an' learn. It's just the same as Robert goin' to college – my stayin' to watch the sweep. Wot's the *good* of me bein' a sweep if I don't learn? Folks prob'ly wun't pay me if I didn't know how to do it, and *then* what'd I do?'

'Very well, Master William,' said cook with treacherous sweetness, 'I'll tell your pa when he comes in that you stayed in here with the sweep when your ma said most speshful you wasn't to.'

William reconsidered this aspect of affairs.

'All right, Crabbie,' he said grudgingly. 'An' I hope that I jolly well *spoil* your chimney when I'm a sweep with not knowing how to do it.'

He wandered round the house and watched through the window. It was a thrilling performance. He was lost in roseate dreams of himself pursuing the gloriously dirty calling of chimney sweep when the sweep appeared with a heavy sack.

'Where shall I put the soot?' he said.

William considered. There was a nice bit of waste ground behind the summer-house. He looked carefully round to make sure that his arch-enemy cook was nowhere in sight.

'Jus' here,' he said, leading the sweep round to the summer-house.

The sweep emptied the sack. It was a soft grey-black pile. William thrilled with the pride of possession.

'That's *mine*, isn't it?' he said.

'Well, it's not *mine*,' said the sweep jocularly. 'You can 'ave it to practise on.'

He left William smiling proudly above his pile.

From over the wall behind the summer-house William could see the road. He waved his hand effusively to the sweep as he passed on his little cart.

'I say,' called William.

The sweep drew up.

'Does the horse an' cart cost much?' said William anxiously.

'Oh no,' said the sweep. 'You can get 'em dirt cheap. I'll lend you this 'ere of mine when you go into the business.'

With a facetious wink he drove on, and William returned to the contemplation of his pile of soot.

Soon a whistle that he knew roused him from his reverie and he peeped over the wall.

Ginger, William's lifelong friend and ally, as

THE SWEEP EMPTIED THE SACK. WILLIAM THRILLED WITH
THE PRIDE OF POSSESSION. 'THAT'S MINE, ISN'T IT?'
HE SAID.

earnest and freckled and snub-nosed as William himself, was passing down the road. He looked up at William.

''Ello,' said William, with modest pride. 'I've gotter bit of soot in here.'

But Ginger had a rival attraction. 'They're ratting in Cooben's barn,' he said.

William weighed the attraction of ratting and soot, and finally decided in favour of ratting.

'All right,' he called, 'wait a sec. I'll come.'

He completely forgot his soot till tea-time.

Then, as he was going out of the house, he met Mr and Miss Arnold Fox coming in. They were coming to call on Mrs Brown. Both were very tall and very thin, and both possessed expansive smiles that revealed perfect sets of false teeth.

'Good afternoon, William,' said Mr Fox politely.

'Afternoon,' said William.

'A rough diamond, our William,' smiled Mr Fox to his sister.

William glared at him.

She laid her hand on William's head.

'Manners maketh man, dear William,' she said.

She then bent down and kissed William.

Mr Arnold Fox took off his hat and playfully extinguished William with it. Then he laid it on the hall table and went into the drawing-room, leaving William boiling and enraged on the doorstep.

That reminded William of his soot.

William and Ginger sat lazily upon the wall watching the passers-by. Absent-mindedly they toyed with handfuls of soot.

They were cheered by the sight of Mr Arnold Fox going down the road – his forehead beneath his hat suspiciously dark.

'That'll teach *him*. *He'll* take some washing,' said William.

'Look!' said Ginger, excitedly, leaning over the wall.

Along the road came three children in white, Geoffrey Spencer and Joan Bell with her little sister Mary. Geoffrey Spencer, in a white sailor suit, walked along mincingly, holding Joan Bell's little bag-purse for her. Mary, toddled along holding her elder sister's hand.

William admired Joan intensely. Occasionally she condescended to notice his existence.

'Hello!' called William. 'Where you going?'

'Posting a letter,' said Geoffrey primly.

'Come in an' play,' said William, 'we've got some soot.'

'No,' said Geoffrey piously. 'Mother said I wasn't to play with you.'

'You're so rough,' explained Joan with a little fastidious sniff.

William flushed beneath his soot. He felt that this reflected upon his character. He was annoyed that anyone, even so insignificant as Geoffrey, should be forbidden to play with him.

'Rough!' he said indignantly. Then, 'Well, an' I'd rather be rough than an ole softie like you – you an' your ole white suit!'

'Come along, Joan,' said Geoffrey with a superior smile. 'I'm not going to talk to him.'

William rolled white, angry eyes in his black face.

'Yah-boo, softie!' he called over the wall.

Yet he was depressed by the proceeding, and even Ginger's suggestion of trying the effect of the soot on the bed of arum lilies did not revive him much. However, the effect was certainly cheering. So they moved on to the white roses and worked with the pure joy of the artist on them till they heard the dulcet tones of Joan and Mary and Geoffrey returning from the spot. Then they went back to the wall. Joan was growing bored with Geoffrey. She looked up almost longingly towards William's grimy face.

'Where *is* your soot, William?' she said.

'Jus' here,' said William. 'It's jolly good soot.'

'I'll come an' *look* at it,' she said condescendingly.

'I won't come in an' play. I'll come in an' *look* at it. You can go on home, Geoffrey.'

Geoffrey debated with his conscience. 'I won't come in,' he said, ''cause mother says he's so rough. I'll wait for you out here.'

So hand-in-hand Joan and Mary came round to the back of the summer-house. William and Ginger proudly introduced them to the soot.

'Ith lovely,' said Mary. 'Leth – leth danth round it – holding handth.'

'All right,' said William genially. 'Come on.'

Nothing loth, they joined hands and danced round it. Joan laughed excitedly.

'Oh, it's fun,' she cried. 'Faster.'

'Father!' cried Mary.

They went faster and faster. William and Ginger with the male's innate desire of showing off his prowess began to revolve at lightning speed.

Then came the catastrophe.

Plop!

It was Mary who lost her balance and fell suddenly and violently on her face into the heap of soot.

Joan, with feminine inconsistency, turned upon William, stamping her foot.

'*You* did it! You nasty, rough, horrible boy!'

'I *didn't*!'

'You *did*!'

'He *didn't*!' said Ginger.

'He *did*!'

'He *didn't*!'

Meanwhile Mary had arisen from the soot heap — hair, eyes and mouth full of soot, soot clinging to her dress.

Her voice joined in the general uproar.

'Oo — it taths nathy, it taths nathy — oo — oo.'

Joan wept in angry sympathy.

'See how *you* like soot in your mouth, you nasty boy!' she screamed at William, seizing a handful of soot and hurling it at William's face.

That was the beginning of the battle.

Geoffrey, hearing the noise, came nobly to the rescue, to be received by a handful of soot from Ginger. It was a glorious battle. Ginger and William fought Geoffrey, and Joan fought everyone, and Mary sat on the soot heap and screamed. They threw soot till there was practically no soot left to throw. A butcher boy who was passing and heard the noise came in to arbitrate, but stayed to participate. Sheer lust of battle descended upon them all.

Then came sudden sanity. In stricken silence they gazed at each other.

Joan seized Mary by the hand. She glared round at them all from a small black face framed with grimy curls.

IT WAS A GLORIOUS BATTLE. GINGER AND WILLIAM
FOUGHT GEOFFREY, AND JOAN FOUGHT EVERYONE, AND
MARY SAT ON THE SOOT HEAP AND SCREAMED.

'I *hate* you all!' she said, stamping a small black
foot.

'*Hate* you all!' screamed Mary, whose tears were
making white tracks down her black face.

'It wasn't me,' said Geoffrey eagerly and
ungrammatically.

'I hate *you*,' said Joan, 'worse than anybody — worse than William and worse than anyone, an' I'm going home to tell mother — so there.'

'Tho' there,' wailed Mary in concert.

With outraged dignity and clinging soot on every line of her figure, Joan led Mary from the garden.

It was more than Geoffrey could bear.

He followed them sobbing loudly, his white suit a cloudy grey-black.

Joan's voice floated out on the twilit air.

'An' I'm *goin*' to tell mother — *you'll* catch it, William Brown.'

Ginger looked round uneasily.

'I'd best be going, William,' he murmured.

Dejection descended upon William.

'A'right.'

Then he looked at Ginger and down at himself.

'Funny how it gets all over you,' he said, 'and don't it make your eyes look queer?'

'Am I's bad as you?' said Ginger apprehensively.

'Worse,' said William.

'Will it come off with cold water?'

'Dunno,' said William.

'I'll give it,' said Ginger, 'a jolly good *try*. What'll your folks say?'

'Dunno,' said William.

'Well, goo'night, William.'

'Goo'night,' said William, despondently. Dusk had fallen.

He crept round to the back door, hoping to slip up the back stairs unobserved. But the cook's strident voice came from the library.

'Mrs Bell wants you on the telephone at once, please'm. It's something about Master William.'

William beat a hasty retreat to the laurel bushes. Then, hearing footsteps on the drive, he stood on tiptoe and peered out. He met the horrified gaze of the housemaid, who was returning from her afternoon out.

With a wild yell she ran like an arrow towards the back door.

'Oh lor! Oh lor!' she called. 'I seed the devil. I seed 'im in the garding.'

William among the laurel bushes smiled proudly to himself.

Then he sat down cross-legged in his retreat, black face on black hands, gleaming white eyes gazing dreamily into the distance.

He was not building castles in the air; he was not repenting of his sins; he was not thinking about future retribution. He was merely deciding that he wouldn't be a sweep after all. It did taste so nasty.

CHAPTER 2

A BIRTHDAY TREAT

'WHAT we goin' to do this afternoon?' demanded William of his boon companions, the Outlaws.

They felt that as far as the morning was concerned they had pretty well exhausted the resources of the universe. They had fished in the pond with bent pins, which were attached to the end of strings which were attached to the end of sticks, and they had caught a large variety of water weeds and one sardine tin. Douglas said that he caught a fish which escaped before he could draw in his line, but this statement was greeted with open incredulity by the others.

'A jolly big one too,' said Douglas, unconsciously following in the footsteps of older adherents to the piscatorial art.

'Oh, yes,' said William sarcastically, 'so big that none of us could *see* it. If it was as big as what you say it is why din' you tell us, then we could have had a look at it?'

'I din' want to scare it away,' said Douglas

14

indignantly; then with a faint emulation of William's sarcasm, 'Fancy you not knowin' that. Fancy you not knowin' that fishes get scared of you shoutin' an' yellin' about. I'm not s'prised that you only catch ole tins an' things that can't hear you shoutin' an' yellin' about. I should think all the fishes for miles round've got headaches the way you've been shoutin' an' yellin' about. I know the one I caught looked's if it'd got a headache with it.'

William was taken aback by this outburst, but he quickly recovered.

'Oh, yes, I dare say it looked pretty funny alto-gether, the one you caught. I'm sure if you caught a fish at all it was a pretty funny one.'

'D'you say I *din't* catch a fish?' said Douglas furiously, squaring up to William.

'I say no one *saw* your ole fish, 'an you oughter ask your mother to buy you a pair of spectacles s'as you can *see* what *is* fish an' what's your own 'magination.'

Ginger and Henry sat on the ground to watch the fight. It was not a long one, because Douglas lost his footing soon after they had begun and fell into the pond and was rescued by William, and the excitement of this proceeding dimmed the memory of Douglas's alleged 'catch'.

Then Henry thought that he saw a rabbit on the edge of the wood, so the Outlaws invaded the wood in a body with Jumble, William's mongrel, at their head. Jumble hunted imaginary rabbits with yelps and barks and futile rushes, and the Outlaws urged him on with war-whoops and cries of 'Good old Jumble! Fetch him out.' Jumble caught and dismembered a leaf after pursuing it with wild excitement from tree to tree in the breeze, worried a clump of fungus, pricked his nose badly on a holly bush, and retired to bark defiance at it from a safe distance.

Tiring of rabbit hunting, the Outlaws climbed trees, and when Ginger had torn his coat and Henry split his trousers with the effort of attaining dangerous heights, they abandoned that occupation. They 'tracked' each other with much ostentatious secrecy and noisy 'silence' and crawling about on stomachs and sibilant whispering and 'Sh's' and stepping upon twigs and exclamations. Finally they were chased into the road again by a furious keeper and were given a ride in a farm waggon by a passing labourer, who was blessed with a good nature and rather liked the dare-devil looks of the Outlaws.

William, drunk with ecstasy, drove and narrowly escaped precipitating the equipage into the ditch, and Ginger, while experimenting how far he could lean out at the back without falling, overbalanced and fell into the road. He climbed back cheerful and unhurt, if somewhat dishevelled.

Arrived at the village, they descended with much exuberant thanks and made their way to the disused barn that was the scene of most of their activities.

There they had a shooting match with the home-made bows and arrows that they kept concealed at the back of the barn. After breaking the window of a neighbouring cottage by accident they fled to the other end of the village, where they watched the blacksmith shoeing a horse. Ginger, to his great delight, was allowed to hold the hammer for a minute. This made him rather uppish, and his subsequent boasts of the honour thus paid him annoyed the other Outlaws so much that they all sat upon him (literally) in the ditch till he promised as well as his mouthful of mud would allow him not to mention it again.

It had been, on the whole, a thoroughly satis-factory morning. A similar afternoon was hardly to be hoped for, but the Outlaws were notoriously optimistic.

'What we goin' to do this afternoon?' repeated William.

A look of despondency came over Ginger's face.

'Gotter stay in at home,' he said mournfully.

'Why?' said the Outlaws.

'Gotter naunt comin' to stay. She's not comin' till tea-time, but they say they want her to see me clean, so I gotter stay in clean all afternoon.'

There was a murmur of indignation at this inhuman cruelty.

'Jus' like grown-ups,' said William bitterly.

'What's your aunt like?' said Henry with interest. 'Sorter one who gives decent tips?'

The Outlaws always 'went shares' in tips, and therefore each one took a personal interest in the visits of the other members' relations.

'Never seen her before,' said Ginger disconsolately. 'Don't know what she's like.'

'Sure to be awful,' said Douglas unfeelingly.

'But we don' mind that if she gives a decent tip,' added Henry.

'Oh, no,' said Ginger bitterly. '*You* don' mind. *You've* not gotter sit all afternoon clean an' doin' nothin', have you? Oh, no, I'm sure *you* don't mind.'

'She might poss'bly be nice,' said William, without much conviction.

'Oh, yes. She might,' said Ginger still more bitterly. 'S'easy for *you* to talk, isn't it? *You* don' mind. Oh, no! An' she might be nice. Oh, yes, you'd talk like that if it was *your* aunt what was comin' an' *you* what had to sit clean all afternoon, wun't you?'

When roused, Ginger could emulate William's sarcastic manner rather well . . .

The afternoon passed happily enough. William, Douglas and Henry practised lassoing Jumble in the back garden of William's house. Jumble enjoyed the game immensely. The lasso never caught him, but occasionally he caught the lasso and worried it zestfully. When, however, they had by mistake lassoed a flower pot on to and through the glass of a cucumber frame, the Outlaws very quietly left the precincts of William's home and spent the rest of the afternoon sliding down a battered hayrick in one of Farmer Jenks' fields, and bringing down a considerable portion of hay with each descent. At intervals they thought of Ginger sitting in solitary cleanliness and boredom in his family's drawing-room waiting for his aunt.

'Poor old Ginger!' said Henry, as he descended from the hayrick with a bump.

'She'll have come by now p'raps,' said Douglas.

'Hope she's rich,' said William cheerfully.

'Let's go'n look at her,' said Henry.

The idea appealed to the Outlaws, and they set off at once for Ginger's house.

Dusk was falling when they reached it. They crept round to the back of the house, where they knew that Ginger's drawing-room window was. There they crouched among the ivy and peered cautiously into the lighted window.

The first thing they saw was Ginger dressed in his best suit, made unfamiliar with gleaming cleanliness of face and collar, sitting on a chair opposite the window. The first thing they noticed was that he was not looking bored. He was, in fact, beaming delightedly, though he had not yet seen his friends . . .

Then the eyes of the Outlaws wandered across to Ginger's aunt. She was sitting in front of the fire. The Outlaws' eyes and mouths grew wide as they watched. Their noses were pressed flat against the window pane. For Ginger's aunt was young and radiantly pretty.

'Crumbs!' gasped William ecstatically.

Ginger found himself unusually and unexpectedly popular the next day.

'Hello, Ginger!'

'G'mornin', Ginger.'

'How's your aunt, Ginger?'

Ginger at first suspected sarcasm in this question, then realised with surprise that there was none.

'V'well,' he said laconically; 'she's a jolly lot better than I thought she was going to be.'

'Nicer than you thought she was goin' to be!' repeated William sternly. 'You're jolly well not to talk like that about her. You don' *deserve* her, that's what it is; you don' *deserve* an aunt like wot she is. You—'

'You don't know anything about her,' said Ginger amazed and indignant.

'Oh, *don*' I?' said William. 'I bet I *do*. I bet I know

all there is to know about her. I bet I know she's beauteous an' good an' – an' – good an' – an' – beauteous—'

'Here!' interrupted Ginger pugnaciously. 'What you talkin' like that about her? She's not your aunt. She's mine.'

'I'll fight you for her,' said William.

'A'right,' agreed Ginger, taking off his coat.

They fought and William won.

'Now she's my aunt,' said William complacently, as he put on his coat and felt tenderly and proudly a fast-swelling eye with his grimy hand.

'Well, you can call her your aunt,' said Ginger, 'but the fac' remains she's my father's sister.'

'But I've fought you for her,' said William indignantly.

'A'right,' agreed Ginger. 'I said she was your aunt all right, but 'f you want her to be your father's sister you'll have to get your father to fight my father for her, an' even then I don' see—'

'Let's have her for all our aunts,' suggested Douglas pacifically.

'It's her birthday next week,' added Ginger, 'while she's staying with us.'

'I say!' said William, as though struck by a sudden brilliant idea, 'let's get up a sort of treat for her.'

'Crumbs!' said the Outlaws. 'Yes, let's.'

'What'll we have?' said Henry brightly. 'A picnic?'

'No,' said William decidedly. 'The only decent picnic places are trespass places, an' prob'ly she can't run's fast as what we can 'f anyone comes.'

'Let's act something,' said Douglas.

'Don't forget she's my aunt,' said Ginger proudly. 'I mean William's aunt,' he corrected himself as he met William's eye. 'William's aunt an' my father's sister.'

'What'll we act?' said Henry.

'Oh, anythin'. 'S easy's easy to act. Jus' make somethin' up or do somethin' out of a book.'

'Means learnin',' said Ginger despondently. 'Jus' like lessons. Might's well be doin' hist'ry or g'ography as learnin' actin' stuff.'

'We needn't learn it,' said Douglas. 'We can jus' make it up as we go along.'

'Well, you know what *that's* like,' said Ginger sternly. 'You oughter, anyway, 'cause we've done it. You jus' dunno what to say when it comes to the time, or someone else says the thing you wanted to say, an' you int'rupt each other an' get fightin'. It wun't be much of a birthday treat for my aunt. I mean William's aunt an' my father's sister.'

'Well, let's do it dumb show, then,' said Douglas, 'let's act without speakin'. Jus' move our arms an' legs about an' things like that an'—'

He stopped. The Outlaws were looking at William.

Upon William's freckled, homely countenance was dawning an expression that those who knew him recognised as inspiration. At last he spoke.

'I know!' he said. '*Waxworks?*'

'Crumbs!' chorused the Outlaws in delight. '*Waxworks?*'

'What'll we be?' said Henry. 'People out of history?'

''F you know enough history to go actin' it you can,' said William scathingly.

'Well, we could have someone bein' murdered or hung or somethin'. It'd be sort of excitin'.'

'Well, who was murdered or hung?'

'Er – Henry VIII.'

'No, he wasn't, then. He was the one what had seven wives.'

'You're gettin' a bit muddled. That was the man goin' to St Ives.'

'No, it wasn't neither. It was Henry VIII.'

'Anyway, we're not enough to do Henry VIII an' seven wives.'

'Yes – one of us could be Henry VIII, an' another could be the seven wives. We could have a label round his neck with "Seven Wives" wrote on.'

'Well, we're not goin' to. We'd rather have someone bein' murdered some way.'

'Well, let Henry VIII murder his seven wives.'

'Oh, do shut *up* about Henry VIII. Who *was* murdered in hist'ry?'

'Charles the something.'

'Charles the First – we did him last week. His head was chopped off an' he said he was sorry he took such a long time dyin' of it an' keepin' everyone waitin'.'

'Hangin'd be easier for a waxwork,' said William thoughtfully, ''cause their head wouldn't have to come off. They could jus' give a deep an' holier groan an' close their eyes . . . Yes, we'll have who-did-you-say-it-was bein' hung for one. We'll have to get a bit of string for it from somewhere an' we've gotter crown somewhere in our house what Ethel once had. We'll jus' have to practise it a bit, that's all. Ginger be who-did-you-say – the man, you know, in a crown an' a dressing-gown or a mackintosh or somethin' an' Douglas be the policeman with a bit of string hangin' him. Well, that's *that* one. We'll have to practise movin' jerky, that's all. We'd better not have any more history. She mayn't be much int'rested in hist'ry. She din't look's if sh'd be int'rested in hist'ry. She looked – awful nice.'

'What'll we have next, then?'

'Let's have somethin' funny. Let's have ole General Moult walkin'. I can do him.'

As a matter of fact, William could do the half strut,

half run that was General Moult's normal mode of procedure to the life.

'That oughter make her laugh,' he added complacently.

'An' what else'll we have?' said Douglas. ''S not much so far.'

'Well, we can't arrange a whole long performance in one *breath*,' said William sternly. 'We've gotter *think* a bit.'

There was a short silence tense with mental effort. Then Ginger said:

'I know, let's have Dick Turpin holdin' up a coach. I've gotter pistol an' some caps.'

'An' we could borrer a wheelbarrow for the coach,' suggested Douglas excitedly.

'Henry be Turpin Dick,' said William, 'an' Douglas his horse an' Ginger in the wheelbarrow an' me pushin' it. An' I'll do the talkin' in them all.'

'What else'll we have?' said Douglas.

'That'll do to start practisin' on,' said William; 'we can think of more things's we go on.'

Rehearsals in the old barn took place daily.

William's mother noticed vaguely that life seemed very peaceful, but she happened to be very busy herself and had no time to wonder what William was doing. She had become a member of the New Era Society. The New Era Society existed chiefly to educate the village and entice speakers down from London to speak on subjects of which the village knew nothing either before or after the lectures. The Society wanted the village to be 'in the swim'. The kindred expression 'at sea' aptly describes the feelings of most of the audience. The subject this month was 'Egyptology', and in the absence of the Secretary, Mrs Brown, William's mother, and Mrs Flowerdew, Ginger's mother, were arranging for the speaker.

Mrs Brown was relieved that William seemed suddenly so unobtrusive . . .

In the intervals of hanging Charles I and holding up the stage coach with strange jerky movements as demonstrated by William, the Outlaws dogged the footsteps of Ginger's aunt. They pursued her in a body with languishing eyes and bouquets of wild flowers which were generally also languishing. And, strange to say, Miss Flowerdew liked it. She received the drooping bouquets with profuse thanks. She listened with due and proper excitement to their tales of adventure, she went with Jumble to hunt rats in the barn. (Jumble was wildly excited, but a large number of flies were his net 'bag'.) They told her that they were arranging a surprise 'treat' for her birthday, and she received the news with delight.

'We're not goin' to tell you what it is,' said William, 'but it's goin' to be in the ole barn at half-past four, an' you can bring any fr'en's you like to it free.'

'How lovely!' said Miss Flowerdew. 'I simply don't know how I can wait till then. I'm sure it will be most exciting.'

'Oh, yes, it's going to be a jolly good show,' said William complacently.

During the week they had added to their repertoire Columbus discovering America and Jonah and the whale. William was Columbus and Henry, Douglas and Ginger, lying on the ground side by side, were America.

William's jerky dumb show of looking for America, shading his eyes and gazing into the distance and searching upon the ground near his feet until at last he came upon the three prone forms and sat down upon them heavily was considered by the troupe to be very good.

William was showman as well as actor. As Columbus, he wore his Boy Scout's costume and an old top hat of his father's to add distinction to the *tout ensemble*. As Jonah he wore (appropriately) a mackintosh and (inappropriately) an old boudoir cap of his sister's rescued from the rag bag. The latter was supposed to add a Biblical touch.

Henry, Ginger and Douglas, were the whale. The swallowing of Jonah was almost worthy of the Russian ballet – full of drama and movement and realism. Then the whale lying upon Jonah emitted deep groans, and Jonah finally emerged quite fresh and perky in his boudoir cap and mackintosh and swam away, leaving the whale still groaning loudly . . .

'It's goin' to be a fine show,' said William enthusiastically to Miss Flowerdew after a long and energetic rehearsal.

'Bother!' said Miss Flowerdew. 'I've just discovered that it's the same day as the New Era Lecture, but I'll cut that.'

'Oh, yes!' said William. 'I sim'ly can't tell you how good ours is goin' to be. You'll be awfully sorry if you miss it, an' it's bein' all done for you, too.'

'Oh, I'll come. Never fear!' said Miss Flowerdew.

Mrs Brown and Mrs Flowerdew had made all the arrangements for the New Era Society's lecture except with regard to the hall. There were two halls in the village, the Parish Room and the Village Hall, and there was some doubt as to which would be the better for the lecture, and the final arrangement of that had been left to Mrs Flowerdew. Mrs Brown had secured as speaker a Professor Smith.

The day of the lecture, which was also the day of Miss Flowerdew's birthday and the waxwork show, arrived.

'I don't yet know which room,' Mrs Brown said distractedly at breakfast. 'I wish Mrs Flowerdew would send a message.'

William was too much intent upon his own thoughts and plans to listen to his mother's jeremiads. He went out into the garden – moving his arms to and fro with eloquent gestures and murmuring, 'An' now, ladies an' gentlemen, kin'ly allow me to introjuce to you King Charles bein' hung in the tower by a policeman, like what he was in ole days . . . lifelike on' nat'ral . . . ladies and gen'l'men, kin'ly notice the policeman tyin' the string round his neck—'

He was interrupted by a tall, pale young man who came in at the front gate and said to him:

'Are you Mrs Brown's little boy?'

'Yes,' said William ungraciously.

'Well, Mrs Flowerdew says the Parish Room,' said the young man; and hastily departed.

Now, the young man did not speak very distinctly, and William's mind and heart were full of 'Miss Flowerdew'. As a matter of fact, William rarely thought of Ginger's mother as 'Mrs Flowerdew'. She was just 'Ginger's mother'. Also William's thoughts were full of his waxwork show.

William went off to the barn where the rest of the troupe were assembled.

'I say,' said William importantly, 'she must have invited a lot of fr'en's. I've just gotter message from her to say we're to do it in the Parish Room, not the ole barn. She must've got a *lot* of people to come an' watch.'

'Crumbs!' said the Outlaws, deeply gratified.

Then they fell to rehearsing with renewed energy.

Four-thirty arrived. The Parish Room was filled with a despondent-looking crowd of villagers whipped up by the energetic members of the New Era Society. The village was less anxious to be educated than the Society was to educate it. The speaker had arrived and had lunch with the Vicar. He and the Vicar were still talking earnestly in the Vicar's study. They were discussing the morals of the younger generation.

'Terrible,' sighed Mr Monks, the Vicar. 'The modern child is utterly devoid of those qualities of sensitiveness and humility and reverence that one used to associate with childhood. There is a boy in this very village – a boy of the name of William Brown—' he shuddered as at many painful memories.

'I say,' said Professor Smith, 'it's nearly half-past. Ought we to—'

'It only takes a minute across the field,' said the Vicar, 'we'll give them time to settle down. They're never punctual.'

And he went on talking with deep feeling about the boy of the name of William Brown . . .

The Outlaws arrived at the Parish Room and entered by the door behind the platform.

A Birthday Treat

'I say,' whispered Ginger, impressed, 'it's *full*. She must've invited a whole *lot* 'f 'em.'

'I can't see her, can you?' said William.

'No, but there's such crowds of 'em.'

'Well, we'd better not keep 'em waitin',' said William importantly.

And the Outlaws marched up on the platform.

A gasp of mingled horror and surprise and excitement went up from the audience.

The Outlaws were wearing the clothes they would need for the waxwork show. William wore his top hat and Scout's costume. Douglas was dressed in readiness for his policeman scene in a dressing-gown and a bread basket. Ginger, in readiness for Charles I, wore a tinsel crown and a shirt of his father's, and Henry, as the highwayman, wore a home-made mask and a paint-smeared overall several sizes too large for him – the property of his father, who fondly imagined it to be still hanging in his studio.

William looked around his paralysed audience. 'Ladies an' gen'l'men,' he began, 'this is a waxwork show, 'cause of her birthday, an' I'm doin' the talkin'. The first waxwork is me. I'm not dressed for it, but you can imagine me in a long coat an' I've got these things on for Columbus an' I've not got time to go changin' every time. Ladies an' gen'l'men, this is the *only* waxwork show of its kind in the world. We're

just goin' to begin an' if you'll kin'ly watch careful this
is General Moult walkin' along the road – lifelike *an'*
nat'ral. This is waxwork number one, ladies an'

'LADIES AN' GEN'L'MEN,' SAID WILLIAM, 'THIS IS THE
ONLY WAXWORK SHOW OF ITS KIND IN THE WORLD.'

gen'l'men. This is General Moult walkin'. Kin'ly all watch General Moult walkin'.'

William assumed the pompous strut well known to all the village, and slowly and jerkily progressed across the stage.

The spell was broken. The hall was full of murmurs of mixed consternation and delight, the delight predominating. In the second row sat Mrs Brown, her eyes full of helpless horror, fixed upon her son. In the

IN THE SECOND ROW SAT MRS BROWN HER EYES, FULL OF
HELPLESS HORROR, WERE FIXED UPON HER SON.

third row sat General Moult, his face purple with fury, his eyes bulging. A group of village youths at the back of the hall, reluctantly dragged in to listen to the lecture on Egyptology, began to cheer. William bowed, gratified.

'Ladies an gen'l'men,' he continued, 'our second waxwork is—'

'Crumbs!' whispered Ginger, looking at the open door behind the stage. 'The Vicar's coming with a man . . . he's goin' to come right up on to the stage. He's goin' to spoil it all.'

'No, he's not,' said William firmly. 'It's our show an'—'

Certainly the Vicar and the other man were coming up on to the stage. William, with admirable presence of mind, threw himself into the breach.

'Ladies an' gen'l'men, our nex' waxwork is Mr Monks comin' up on to the stage. Kin'ly notice Mr Monks walking up on to the stage.'

The hall was full of excited murmurs. The figure of the Vicar was seen to appear on the stage, as though in obedience to William's stage directions, and speak to William.

The murmurs in the hall were too loud to admit of anyone's hearing what the Vicar was saying to William. Everyone was talking excitedly. General Moult had found his voice, and was shouting:

'Impudence! Damned impudence! I'll tell his father. Confound his impudence! I say, confound—'

Mrs Brown was past all power of interference. She merely watched William with a helpless, fascinated look. Above the babel rose William's strident voice.

'Waxwork number *three*, ladies an' gen'l'men. Mr Monks talkin'. Mr Monks talkin' to me. Kin'ly notice Mr Monks talkin' to me, *ladies* an' gen'l'men – nat'ral *an*' lifelike.'

The youths at the back of the stage applauded frenziedly. William bowed. The Vicar began to lose his self-control. He hit the palm of his left hand with his right clenched fist as he expostulated. William imitated the gesture.

'Waxwork number four, ladies *an*' gen'l'men,' he shouted. 'Mr Monks doin' this. Kin'ly notice Mr Monks doin' this – lifelike *an*' nat'ral.'

Mr Monks caught hold of William's collar.

'Waxwork number *five*,' shouted William hoarsely. 'Mr Monks an' me goin' to have a fight.'

The audience had decided how to take the situation. It rocked with laughter. The youths at the back clapped and stamped. The Vicar, who was deeply attached to his sense of dignity, retired hastily.

'Now,' said William, who was slightly put out by the contretemps, 'we have King Charles discoverin'

America. I mean the other way round. Ladies an' gen'l'men, if you'll kin'ly notice—'

The Vicar and Professor Smith were interrupting him again. William turned upon them sternly, no longer trying to save the situation.

'We'd all be glad,' he said indignantly, ''f you'd kin'ly *stop* keep comin' up here 'n int'ruptin'. This is a birthday party an' all these people've come special to see the waxworks an' you keep comin' *spoilin'* things. 'F you want to watch we'd be glad 'f you'd go down to where the others is watchin' 'stead of comin' up here int'ruptin'—'

The Vicar was speechless with fury. Professor Smith was staring at William's strange attire with bewildered horror.

'But I've come here—' he began.

'You've come here to a birthday party,' said William sternly, 'if you've been invited, an' if you've *not* been invited we'd be kin'ly glad 'f you'd *kin'ly* go home 'stead of stayin' here int'ruptin'. Ladies an' gen'l'men, will you kin'ly notice—'

Mrs Brown had decided to relieve the tension by having hysterics, and the spell that bound the members of the committee of the New Era Society was broken suddenly. They surged upon the platform and surrounded William explaining, expostulating, scolding . . .

'But she said to come here,' protested William, 'it's her birthday party. All these is her fr'en's. It's a *party*. An' you've all gone 'n *spoilt* it int'ruptin'.'

He was finally convinced of the absence of Miss Flowerdew and of the mistake. But he was still pained and aggrieved.

'Ladies an' gen'l'men,' he said to his audience with great dignity. 'This waxwork show what you've seen the beginnin' of is goin' on in the ole barn across the field.' He had a sudden inspiration. 'The other part's jolly good – better than the bit what you've seen, an' is free an' open to all on payment of one halfpenny.'

Then with great dignity he led his troupe across the field to the barn where Miss Flowerdew sat in solitary patience.

The Parish Room settled down with an audible gasp and sigh. Mrs Brown, seeing that all was over, came out of her hysterics. General Moult ceased to shout and settled down to a fierce and sustained muttering. The Committee of the New Era Society came down from the platform to their places. The Vicar, pale and tense, took the chair. Professor Smith smoothed back his hair, took a deep draught of water, and began:

'Ladies and gentlemen, the earliest mention of Egypt in the Bible is under the name of Mizraim, which word, probably, is a plural form, testifying to the fact that Lower and Upper Egypt were regarded as distinct. The chief objects of cultivation in Egypt are millet, wheat, barley, dhurra, maize, peas, beans, lentils, clover, rice, sugar, etc. The philologist, D. I. Taylor, is of the opinion that the Egyptian alphabet, although incomplete, is one of the oldest known. Even at the time of the Eleventh and Twelfth Dynasties the hieroglyphic writing was a venerable system of vast antiquity—'

The hall was very dimly lighted, but Professor Smith began to have a vague suspicion that his audience was mysteriously thinning.

It was. Shadowy forms were creeping from the room and making their way in a furtive procession across the field to the old barn . . .

CHAPTER 3

THE LEOPARD HUNTER

MR Falkner had been staying at the Browns' house for a very long time.

He had written to Mr Brown to remind him of the fact that they had been at school together and to ask if he might pay him a short visit. Mr Falkner was like that. Also his idea of a short visit was not Mr Brown's.

Not that Mr Falkner needed much entertaining. He entertained himself. He talked. William had never met anyone who talked quite as much as his father's guest. Mr Falkner talked perpetually, and the subject of all his conversation was Mr Falkner. Mr Falkner was a never ending source of interest to Mr Falkner.

He talked about his exalted social position, his many and varied talents, his marvellous exploits, his ingenuity, his aristocratic friends.

'Oh, yes, the Duke and I are the greatest of pals. Always have been. The way the man pesters me to go and stay with him! But all my friends are the same. There's the Honourable Percy Wakefield − you've heard of him, of course? − I ran into him again last week. He simply wouldn't take "No". I managed to put him off at last. Quite a nuisance, these people. Simply won't let one alone.'

Politeness prevented Mr Brown from remarking that he did not grudge Mr Falkner to the Duke or to the Honourable Percy. Instead, Mr Brown sat, silent and oppressed, trying to read the evening paper which lay carelessly on the arm of his chair and to look as if he weren't doing so.

And Mr Falkner talked on.

Mr Falkner was small and rather stout, with a round face, a small blighted moustache, a glassy stare and a very squeaky voice.

During term time Mr Falkner did not trouble William much. William merely watched him curiously in his brief respites from school.

William practised diligently and acquired a very good imitation of Mr Falkner's squeaky voice and glassy stare. He practised them alone every evening in his bedroom.

At meals he rather welcomed the presence of Mr Falkner than otherwise. Mr Falkner's accounts of his varied exploits of dauntless bravery and dazzling cleverness seemed to induce in William's family a certain apathy of hopelessness which William thought a very proper attitude on the part of a family.

No one told him to go and wash his hands and

brush his hair again. No one made sarcastic remarks about his table manners. They simply had not the spirit. In fact, such is the humanising effect of a common misfortune, they almost felt drawn to him. They had thought that no family could be afflicted with an affliction worse than William. They had discovered their mistake. They had discovered Mr Falkner . . .

Then came the end of the term. The end of the term was a time of mixed feelings for William. On the one hand, there was the glorious prospect of the holidays. On the other hand, there was his report.

William's best friends could not assert that he was intellectual or industrious. He was a daring and capable leader. He was, at different times and in different moods, robber chief, pirate, Red Indian, explorer, castaway, desperado – but he was not at any time, or in any mood, a student. William's attitude towards the question was one of humility and self-effacement. He'd do without them. There were enough swots in the world without him.

So there was a certain monotony about William's reports. Masters who had a delicate shrinking from the crude and brutal truth wrote, 'Fair'. Those who had the courage of their convictions wrote, 'Poor'. The mathematical master, who was very literal, wrote, 'Uniformly bad'.

The horror and disgust of William's father at these statements was generally as simulated as William's penitence. They knew their respective roles and played them, but they had gone through the scene too many times to be able to put much spirit into the parts.

But this time Mr Falkner was there. Before Mr Brown could begin his set speech expressive of horror and disgust, he took the paper from him and began to comment on it squeakily.

'By jove, very different from the things I used to get. "Excellent" and all that sort of thing all over them. Some of them simply couldn't say enough. "Remarkable talent" and "Very industrious" and "Splendid work", and all that sort of thing. I remember the headmaster saying to my father one speech day, "Brilliant boy of yours, that!" Very keen-sighted man he was, too. Never made a mistake. I believe I was a great favourite at school. I've no doubt I'm still remembered there.'

'No, neither have I,' said Mr Brown.

'Yes,' bleated Mr Falkner, 'it's extraordinary how anyone at all above the average makes himself felt through life. So often I find that people who've only met me once remember me when I've quite forgotten them.'

Again Mr Brown had no doubt of it.

'Now, this boy of yours,' went on Mr Falkner,

'quite a good fellow, no doubt – well meaning and all that. But –' he tapped his hand upon the damning report – 'if anything below the average in intellect. I hope I don't annoy you by saying that.'

Mr Brown hastened to assure him that he didn't.

'We can't all be above the average, of course. But a boy like this wants a little friendly advice, that's all. I've no doubt that I shall be able to help him a good deal during the holidays. I always get on well with children. I could tell you most interesting stories about young friends of mind. A marked difference in them from the minute they know me.'

Again Mr Brown didn't doubt it.

'I'm sure that if I stayed here through the next term, you'd find a very different report at the end of it.'

Mr Brown thought that on the whole he'd prefer the same report and the absence of Mr Falkner, but with great exercise of self-control he remained silent.

'Very different indeed,' went on Mr Falkner. 'I wish I'd got some of my old school reports to show you. Really remarkable. I remember my form master saying when I left that the school would be a very different place without me.'

For the fourth time Mr Brown remarked that he'd no doubt of it.

During this interview William sat with his most inscrutable expression and stared at the guest unblinkingly.

The next day was the first day of the holidays. William wandered out into the garden after breakfast, and to his horror saw that the guest was accompanying him.

'Now, my boy,' squeaked Mr Falkner, 'tell me how many names of flowers you know.'

William cleared his throat sternly and threateningly and went on as though he had neither seen nor heard Mr Falkner.

'None?' bleated his companion. 'Come, come! Tut, tut! That's sad for a boy of your age! Where are you going? Out into the road? Very well. I'm at your service. I can join in all your little activities, you know. What do you like to do in the holidays? Stamp collecting, I've no doubt. Most instructive – and a little school work every day so as not to forget all you learnt last term? And a nice quiet walk sometimes for exercise. That's what you like, I've no doubt. That's what I liked when I was a boy. What were we talking about? Ah, flowers! Now, here in this hedge, you will see the Arum or Cuckoo Pint. Notice the large hood which is botanically termed a spathe. Notice also the spadix and the stamens—'

At the end of the road stood Ginger, Douglas and

Henry. Their faces dropped as they saw William's companion.

'Ha!' he said. 'These your friends, Willy? They're going to join us for the morning? Very well, little boys. Come along with us quietly. And what are we all going to do this morning, eh? I propose a nice little walk along the road, and you can all listen to what I'm telling Willy about the Arum or Cuckoo Pint. Notice, as I said the spathe and the spadix and the stamens. Don't drag your toes in the dust, little boy. Think of your kind father who pays for them. And don't whisper to each other when I'm talking. It's not polite; I like my little friends to be polite. Now, would you like me to tell you about the habits of the busy little ant?'

The Outlaws were nonplussed. They had meant to go to the old barn where they generally played, but they felt they could not go with – this. It would spoil the old barn for them for ever. And they couldn't escape it.

Mr Falkner's harsh, squeaky voice had a sort of hypnotising effect. It seemed to fill the whole world. It paralysed all their faculties. Once, in the middle of the discourse on the busy little ant, they caught each other's eyes; into their dejected faces came a gleam of hope, and they set off running. But their self-appointed 'friend' ran too. Despite his stoutness, he could run.

'A little run?' he gasped. 'Yes, certainly. Nothing like exercise – nothing like exercise. That will do now, I think, though.'

And so utterly were their spirits broken that they let that do. They slowed down.

'A rest here, I think. Now I'll give you a little practice in mental arithmetic. Let us see who can get the right answer.'

It was a nightmare of a morning for the Outlaws. They could not shake him off; they could not shut out the terrible sound of his voice. And there was his glassy eye. The ancient mariner was nothing to him.

He gave them a little lecture on History and another on Geography and another on Astronomy. He spoke to them at great length on Patriotism and Manliness and Industry and the British Empire.

'Well,' he said brightly, when he led them back to the Browns' house at lunch-time, 'I'm afraid I can't come out with you this afternoon, but tomorrow morning Willy and I will be with you early.'

The Outlaws stared at each other blankly for a minute, then Douglas, Ginger and Henry turned on William.

'Well,' they said sternly, 'you've given us a nice mornin'.'

'Nothin' to do with me,' said William. '*I* din' make him. *I* din' want him. You'd think you'd be *sorry* for me. You've only had him a mornin'. He's *stayin'* with us.'

'How long's he stayin'?'

'We don't know,' said William gloomily.

'Well, we'll wait for you tomorrow mornin', but if we see *him* comin' with you, we'll jus' run off alone.'

'You're cowards,' said William bitterly. 'Jus' cowards. That's what you are. *Cowards!*'

They parted moodily. William walked slowly up the drive, oppressed by the thought of tomorrow morning spent in the sole company of Mr Falkner.

In the morning-room Mr Falkner was talking to Mr Brown.

'No, I never grudge the time I spend with children. They always enjoy it so tremendously. You should have seen them hanging on to my words this morning. I expect they'll remember it all their lives. I shouldn't wonder if it proved to be the turning point of their lives in a way. I opened up fresh fields of interest for them on all sides. I showed them how fascinating the pursuit of knowledge can be. I *stimulated* them. There was a distinct difference in their expressions even at the end of the morning. More soulful somehow. I always have that effect on children.'

The Outlaws spent the afternoon together – but it was not a happy one. The shadow of Mr Falkner lay heavy over it. In William's mind was a nightmare vision of morning after morning spent alone with Mr Falkner. In the minds of Ginger, Douglas and Henry was a nightmare vision of morning after morning spent without William's inspiring leadership and company.

When William returned home, Mr Falkner was still talking to his father. He was talking about a mounted leopard skin which lay across the back of the sofa.

'Where was it shot?' he said.

'In Africa. By my brother,' said Mr Brown shortly.

'Quite easy things to shoot, leopards,' bleated Mr Falkner. 'Ridiculously easy, in fact.'

'You shot many?' said Mr Brown.

'Oh, yes – I've never actually counted how many. In Africa, you know – fact is, leopards *know* a good shot when they see him. Now, no leopard would dream of attacking me. I simply raise my gun, the thing turns to flee and I get him on the run. Never failed. I don't know what fear is. Simply don't know the meaning of the word. Never have. And they know it. Turn and run from me at once. Always. Invariably. Big game shooting is like knocking down skittles to me—'

It was late that evening when William came into the room, and said excitedly:

'The leopard's escaped from the circus at Offord. Ginger just heard down in the village. They're out trying to find him and shoot him. He's a wild leopard.'

Mr Brown turned to his guest.

'An opportunity for you, Falkner,' he said.

Mr Falkner turned rather pale.

'Ha! Ha!' he laughed nervously.

Mr Brown looked almost as if he were enjoying himself.

'You simply look at him, you know,' he said, 'and shoot him as he turns to flee.'

'Ha! Ha!' laughed Mr Falkner again mirthlessly.

'They *know* a good shot when they see one, you know,' went on Mr Brown, warming to his subject. 'No leopard would dream of attacking you, you know.'

'B-but I haven't got a gun,' said Mr Falkner with a ghastly grin.

'Oh, I've got one,' said Mr Brown. 'Loaded, too. I'll get it for you.'

Mr Falkner's jaw fell open loosely.

'I wouldn't dream of putting you to all that trouble,' he spluttered. 'Don't trouble. Pray, don't trouble.'

'No trouble at all,' said Mr Brown with beaming politeness as he went from the room.

Mr Falkner sat down and mopped his brow, smiling inanely. The hope that his host would not be able to find the gun shone like a beacon from his face. William sat in a corner of the room and watched him.

WILLIAM CAME INTO THE ROOM AND SAID EXCITEDLY:
'THE LEOPARD'S ESCAPED FROM THE CIRCUS AT OFFORD.
HE'S A WILD LEOPARD.'

Mr Brown returned with the gun.

'Here it is,' he said, 'quite ship-shape. Now, don't
let me detain you, my dear fellow. I'm sure a sportsman like you must be longing to join the fray.'

Mr Falkner took the gun gingerly. A pallid green
had replaced the usual roseate hue of his round face.

'B-but, suppose he comes here,' he said with a
sudden gleam of hope. 'H-hadn't I better stay and
p-protect you?'

'Not at all, not at all,' said Mr Brown heartily. 'We wouldn't spoil your sport for anything. We'd much prefer to think of you out there shooting it as it turns to flee from you. Why, you know, you've shot more than you can count.'

He pushed the reluctant sportsman to the front door.

'Good-bye, old chap – good luck!'

Then he returned to the dining-room. The slow and cautious footsteps of the big game hunter could be heard treading gingerly on the gravel outside, stopping every now and then to listen.

William had mysteriously disappeared.

'Well, I'm going to bed,' said Mr Brown. 'I've stood him every night for three months, and tonight I'm going to have a holiday. I don't care whether the leopard eats him or he eats the leopard. I'm going to bed.'

'And what shall I do – read?' said Mrs Brown.

'Come to bed, too, if you've any sense. You can leave the front door unlocked. He'll come back soon enough, you bet!'

Meanwhile the courageous hunter was creeping cautiously down the garden path. His idea was to creep round the garden several times, then return to the house with an account of his long and fearless but unsuccessful search for the leopard. But there was a cold sweat of fear upon his brow. Suppose the creature happened to be in the garden. Could, oh, could he get back in time? He kept one determined eye upon the front door as he prowled. He held the gun very cautiously. He hoped the beastly thing wouldn't go off. Nasty dangerous things, guns.

As he crept cautiously about he was composing his account of his adventure. 'I should think I traversed the whole village trying to come upon the creature without warning – before it could have time to escape. It's a most *bitter* disappointment to a sportsman like me to miss such an opportunity. The brute must have *felt* my coming and slunk off.'

Suddenly he was startled by a sound in the bushes behind him. The sound was between him and the house.

With a scream of terror he dashed away – down to the end of the little path.

At the end of the path was a summer-house and on to this the intrepid game hunter, who knew not the meaning of the word 'fear', clambered, panting and moaning and displaying in his ascent singular determination and lack of grace. He clung on with his hands while his legs dangled in the air. He tried to hoist himself up.

His legs waved wildly in the air. The little sound in the bushes was repeated.

The Leopard Hunter

With a quivering little scream, the leopard hunter hurled himself on to the roof of the summer-house. He sat down and began to rub his bruises. He had barked his shins. He had aroused echoes in his funny bones. He thought he had sprained both ankles, but he wasn't quite sure.

He had certainly got the skin off his knees. He examined them tenderly. He was rather surprised to find that he still had the gun. He had thrown it up to the roof before he began his climbing exploit. He gazed down through the darkness into the bushes.

'Go away, you brute,' he said sternly. 'Shoo! Shoo! Shoo!'

It didn't 'Shoo!' On the contrary, there came the sound of some stealthy creature creeping through the bushes. Twigs cracked. He could see the bushes move as the Thing approached.

'I told you to go away,' he squeaked hysterically from his roof. 'Go *away!* GO AWAY!' He flung out his arms in a gesture of dismissal, 'Sh!'

The Thing came on.

Perhaps it might be a cat or a dog, thought the hunter, and at the thought hope sprang afresh in his heart.

'Puss! Puss! Puss!' he said through the darkness.

There was no response.

'Good dog!' he panted. 'Rats! Cats! Fetch 'em out!

Come for a walk! On trust! Where's that bone? Good dog, then! Good dog!'

There was no response.

Something fairly large, not a cat or a dog, banged against the summer-house. Could it be a donkey or a sheep or a cow? Oh, *couldn't* it be a donkey or a sheep or a cow? He peered anxiously over the edge of the roof.

'Hee-haw!' he greeted the unknown with eager propitiation in his voice. 'Ba-a-a-a! Moo-oo-oo!'

For answer there came through the darkness a low growl. It certainly wasn't a cat or a dog or a donkey or a cow. It was certainly a leopard. He'd never heard a leopard's voice before (for the matter of that he had never seen a leopard before), but there was no doubt that this was a leopard's voice. Through the darkness came the sound of teeth chattering. They weren't the leopard's. Then the man on the summer-house began to think out plans. He leant over the edge and gave a ferocious growl. The growl that answered his through the darkness made his blood curdle.

'Oh-h-h-h-h!' he moaned. 'Oh-h-h! My holy aunt!'

The Thing was prowling round and round the summer-house. Mr Falkner saw himself suddenly as he might be in the morning light – a mass of whitened bones – or did the creatures eat you bones and all? The tears rolled down his fat cheeks at the thought.

Soon he realised that all was silent. Perhaps the creature had gone away again. He waited for what seemed hours. Still silence. Surely now he might creep back to the house. He lowered one foot cautiously from the roof. Then he gave a yell. Something had grabbed at it in the darkness. He wrenched it free and cowered on his roof rubbing it.

'Oh-h-h-h-h!' he moaned. 'Oh-h-h-h! My holy aunt!'

The agony of that night will live for ever in the memory of the leopard hunter. Most terrible was the moment when the leopard tried to clamber up the summer-house.

Sometimes there was silence for so long that the weary watchman almost fell asleep (he had given up all thoughts of escape), but no sooner did he doze than the creature below would arouse him by growls and bumps or threatening sniffs.

Mr Falkner was cold and miserable. Every bone in his body ached. And the creature would not let him rest. It growled on one side of his roof and drove him to the other. Then it growled on the other side and drove him back again. Many times did his moaning 'Oh-h-h-h-h-h!' fall upon the midnight air.

Mr Falkner had had no idea before that a night was so long. It was an eternity. He dared not strike a match to look at his watch in case the creature should spring.

But he was sure that it was longer than any other night had ever been. It was a phenomenon. It was like a month of nights. But at last the first faint rays of dawn appeared. They grew less faint. Mr Falkner's pallid, anxious, dishevelled countenance peered over the edge of his roof. He could hear no sound.

Then he saw it – saw it unmistakably – a leopard's head among the bushes. With a sudden spasm of

THEN MR FALKNER SAW, UNMISTAKABLY, A LEOPARD'S
HEAD AMONG THE BUSHES. HE TOOK HIS GUN.

desperate courage he took his gun, shut his eyes and fired. And he hit it. By a miracle he hit it. He saw it roll over among the bushes. Then all was still. He waited. After about half an hour he descended cautiously from his perch. He dared not approach his 'bag'. He had heard terrible stories of the ferocity of wild animals in their death throes.

He tiptoed slowly and furtively to the front door.

They all met at breakfast. Both Mr Falkner and William looked as though they had spent sleepless nights. But Mr Falkner, though pale, was his usual debonair self.

'Any luck?' said Mr Brown.

'Oh, yes,' said Mr Falkner carelessly, 'I got the brute. Found him in your garden, too. Came upon him

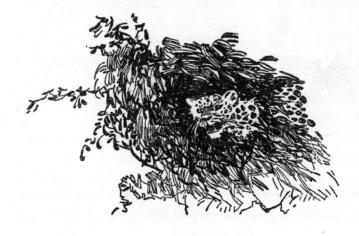

face to face in the path. He gathered to spring. I just stood and looked at him. Simply looked. He turned and began to slink away. Then I raised me rifle and fired – just as I told you. Perfectly simple with a sportsman of my calibre. Lucky it was I who met him. You'll find the body somewhere in the garden.'

They all trooped out. It might have been noticed that the leopard hunter kept modestly in the rear.

'Just over there by those bushes, I believe,' he said airily.

Mr Brown strode into the bushes and pulled out – the leopard skin rug. There was certainly a new bullet hole in its head. The gallant sportsman began to splutter inarticulately.

'*What?*' began Mr Brown.

William, wearing his most sphinx-like expression, stepped forward.

'I thought it smelt a bit kind of stuffy, an' so I brought it out here las' night to be in the fresh air a bit, like what it is in spring cleanin's an' that.'

The gallant sportsman was still gibbering.

'B-but I *heard* it – I—'

William turned his inscrutable countenance to him.

'I' 'fraid p'raps it was me you heard,' he said. 'I can't sleep, so I got up an' jus' played about the garden a bit – jus' to make me sleep better – fresh air an' exercise like what they say makes you sleep – I was

58

playin' mos'ly round the summer-house—'

Mr Falkner looked sharply at William, but William's face was a blank.

'Er – excuse me a minute,' murmured Mr Falkner, and quietly went indoors.

The gardener came past.

'Did you hear anything about a leopard escaping from the circus at Offord?' said Mr Brown to him.

'There ain't no circus at Offord,' replied the gardener gloomily as he passed on. 'There ain't no circus anywheres round here.'

Mr Brown turned to William.

'Who told you about this leopard?' he said sternly.

'Ginger,' said William unblinkingly.

'Who told him?'

'He's not quite sure,' said William, in the voice of one repeating a lesson. 'He's forgot. He thinks p'raps it was someone in the village.'

'Well, you'd better go and tell Mr Falkner that you're sorry you made a mistake.'

William went slowly indoors. But Mr Falkner had gone. He had found a train just going up to Town, and he had accompanied it. He had left a note to say that he had been called suddenly to Town and would they kindly send his things after him.

'Dear me! What a pity!' said Mr Brown, looking as if he had suddenly discovered the elixir of perpetual youth. 'You can't apologise after all, William. Well, never mind.' He slipped a half-crown into William's hand and went off, his face wreathed in smiles.

It was two hours later. The Outlaws sat on the floor in their beloved old barn. In the midst of them were large paper bags of bullseyes, liquorice lumps, barley sugar and chocolate cigars. The half-crown had been well expended. The Outlaws were munching happily.

'What sort've a noise did you make?' Ginger was saying as he puffed out imaginary smoke from his chocolate cigar.

William emitted a blood-curdling growl.

'An' what did he say?'

'Oh-h-h-h-h-h! Oh-h-h-h! My holy aunt!'

It was an excellent imitation of the leopard hunter's quavering moan.

'An' what did he do?'

William rose.

'You come round to our summer-house an' I'll show you. Ginger be me growlin' an' I'll be him carryin' on. Come along.'

They collected the bags and strode off happily with their leader.

CHAPTER 4

WILLIAM LEADS A BETTER LIFE

IF you go far enough back it was Mr Strong, William's form master, who was responsible for the whole thing. Mr Strong set, for homework, more French than it was convenient for William to learn. It happened that someone had presented William with an electric motor, and the things one can do with an electric motor are endless.

Who would waste the precious hours of a summer evening over French verbs with an electric motor simply crying out to be experimented on? Certainly not William.

It wasn't as if there was any *sense* in French verbs. They had been deliberately invented by someone with a grudge against the race of boys – someone probably who'd slipped on a concealed slide or got in the way of a snowball or foolishly come within the danger zone of a catapult. Anyway, whoever it was had devised a mean form of revenge by inventing French verbs and, somehow or other, persuading schoolmasters to adopt them as one of their choicest tortures.

'Well, I never *will* wanter use 'em,' said William to his mother when she brought forward the time-honoured argument. 'I don't wanter talk to *any* French folks, an' if they wanter talk to me they can learn English. English's's easy's easy to talk. It's *silly* havin' other langwidges. I don' see why all the other countries shun't learn English 'stead of us learnin' other langwidges with no *sense* in 'em. English's *sense*.'

This speech convinced him yet more firmly of the foolishness of wasting his precious hours of leisure on such futile study, so he devoted all his time and energy to the electric motor. There was some *sense* in the electric motor. William spent a very happy evening.

In the morning, however, things somehow seemed different. He lay in bed and considered the matter. There was no doubt that Mr Strong could make himself extremely disagreeable over French verbs.

William remembered that he had threatened to make himself more disagreeable than usual if William did not know them 'next time'. This was 'next time' and William did not know them. William had not even attempted to learn them. The threats of Mr Strong had seemed feeble, purposeless, contemptible things last night when the electric motor threw its glamour over the whole world. This morning they didn't. They seemed suddenly much more real than the electric motor.

But surely it was possible to circumvent them. William was not the boy to give in weakly to any fate. He heard his mother's door opening, and, assuming an expression of intense suffering, called weakly, 'Mother.' Mrs Brown entered the room fully dressed.

'Aren't you up yet, William?' she said. 'Be quick or you'll be late for school.'

William intensified yet further his expression of suffering.

'I don' think I feel quite well enough to go to school this morning, mother, dear,' he said faintly.

Mrs Brown looked distressed. He had employed the ruse countless times before, but it never failed of its effect upon Mrs Brown. The only drawback was that Mr Brown, who was still about the house, was of a less trustful and compassionate nature.

Mrs Brown smoothed his pillow. 'Poor little boy,' she said tenderly, 'where is the pain?'

'All over,' said William, playing for safety.

'Dear! dear!' said Mrs Brown, much perturbed, as she left the room. 'I'll just go and fetch the thermometer.'

William disliked the thermometer. It was a soulless, unsympathetic thing. Sometimes, of course, a hot-water bottle, judiciously placed, would enlist its help, but that was not always easy to arrange.

To William's dismay his father entered the room with the thermometer.

'Well, William,' he said cheerfully, 'I hear you're too ill to go to school. That's a great pity, isn't it. I'm sure it's a great grief to you?'

William turned up his eyes. 'Yes, father,' he said dutifully and suspiciously.

'Now where exactly is the pain and what sort of pain is it?'

William knew from experience that descriptions of non-existent pains are full of pitfalls. By a masterstroke he avoided them.

'It hurts me to talk,' he said.

'What sort of pain does it hurt you with?' said his father brutally.

William made some inarticulate noises, then closed his eyes with a moan of agony.

'I'll just step round and fetch the doctor,' said Mr Brown, still quite cheerful.

The doctor lived next door. William considered this a great mistake. He disliked the close proximity of doctors. They were equally annoying in real and imaginary diseases.

William made little brave reassuring noises to inform his father that he'd rather the doctor wasn't troubled and it was all right, and please no one was to bother about him, and he'd just stay in bed and probably be all right by the afternoon. But his father had already gone.

William lay in bed and considered his position.

Well, he was going to stick to it, anyway. He'd just make noises to the doctor, and they couldn't say he hadn't got a pain where he said he had if they didn't know where he said he had one. His mother came in and took his temperature. Fate was against him. There was no hot-water bottle handy. But he squeezed it as hard as he could in a vague hope that that would have some effect on it.

'It's normal, dear,' said his mother, relieved. 'I'm so glad.'

He made a sinister noise to imply that the malady was too deep-seated to be shown by an ordinary thermometer.

He could hear the doctor and his father coming up the stairs. They were laughing and talking. William, forgetting the imaginary nature of his complaint, felt a wave of indignation and self-pity.

The doctor came in breezily. 'Well, young man,' he said, 'what's the trouble?'

William made his noise. By much practice he was becoming an expert at the noise. It implied an intense desire to explain his symptoms, thwarted by physical incapability, and it thrilled with suffering bravely endured.

'Can't speak – is that it?' said the doctor.

'Yes, that's it,' said William, forgetting his role for the minute.

'Well – open your mouth, and let's have a look at your throat,' said the doctor.

William opened his mouth and revealed his throat. The doctor inspected the recesses of that healthy and powerful organ.

'I see,' he said at last. 'Yes – very bad. But I can operate here and now, fortunately. I'm afraid I can't give an anaesthetic in this case, and I'm afraid it will be rather painful – but I'm sure he's a brave boy.'

William went pale and looked around desperately, French verbs were preferable to this.

'I'll wait just three minutes,' said the doctor kindly. 'Occasionally in cases like this the patient recovers his voice quite suddenly.' He took out his watch. William's father was watching the scene with an air of enjoyment that William found maddening. 'I'll give him just three minutes,' went on the doctor, 'and if the patient hasn't recovered the power of speech by then, I'll operate—'

The patient decided hastily to recover the power of speech.

'I can speak now,' he said with an air of surprise. 'Isn't it funny? I can talk quite ordinary now. It came on quite sudden.'

'No pain anywhere?' said the doctor.

'No,' said the patient quickly.

The patient's father stepped forward.

'Then you'd better get up as quickly as you can,' he said. 'You'll be late for school, but doubtless they'll know how to deal with that.'

They did know how to deal with that. They knew, too, how to deal with William's complete ignorance on the subject of French verbs. Excuses (and William had many – some of them richly ingenious) were of no avail. He went home to lunch embittered and disillusioned with life.

'You'd think knowin' how to work a motor engine'd be more *useful* than savin' French verbs,' he said. 'S'pose I turned out an engineer – well, wot use'd French verbs be to me 'n I'd *have* to know how to work a motor engine. An' I was so ill this mornin' that the doctor wanted to do an operate on me, but I said I *can't* miss school an' get all behind the others, an' I came, awful ill, an' all they did was to carry on something terrible 'cause I was jus' a minute or two late an' jus' ha'n't had time to do those old French verbs that aren't no use to anyone—'

Ginger, Henry and Douglas sympathised with him for some time, then began to discuss the history lesson. The history master, feeling for the moment as bored with Edward the Sixth as were most of his class, had given them a graphic account of the life of St Francis of Assisi. He had spent the Easter holidays at Assisi. William, who had been engaged in executing creditable caricatures of Mr Strong and the doctor, had paid little attention, but Ginger remembered it all. It had been such a welcome change from William the Conqueror. William began to follow the discussion.

'Yes, but why'd he do it?' he said.

'Well, he jus' got kind of fed up with things an' he had visions an' things an' he took some things of his father's to sell to get money to start it—'

'*Crumbs!*' interpolated William. 'Wasn't his father mad?'

'Yes, but that din't matter. He was a saint, was Saint Francis, so he could sell his father's things if he liked, an' he 'n his frien's took the money an' got funny long sort of clothes an' went an' lived away in a little house by themselves, an' he uster preach to animals an' to people an' call everythin' "brother" an' "sister", and they cooked all their own stuff to eat an'—'

'Jolly fine it sounds,' said William enviously, 'an' did their people let 'em?'

'They couldn't stop 'em,' said Ginger. 'An' Francis, he was the head one, an' the others all called themselves Franciscans, an' they built churches an' things.'

They had reached the gate of William's house now and William turned in slowly.

'G'bye till this afternoon,' called the others cheerfully.

Lunch increased still further William's grievances. No one inquired after his health, though he tried to look pale and ill, and refused a second helping of rice pudding with a meaning, 'No, thank you, not today. I would if I felt all right, thank you very much.' Even that elicited no anxious inquiries. No one, thought William, as he finished up the rice pudding in secret in the larder afterwards, no one else in the world, surely, had such a callous family. It would just serve them right to lose him altogether. It would just serve them right if he went off like St Francis and never came back.

He met Henry and Ginger and Douglas again as usual on the way to school.

'Beastly ole 'rithmetic,' said Henry despondently.

'Yes, an' then beastly ole jography,' sighed Douglas.

'Well,' said William, 'let's not go. I've been thinkin' a lot about that Saint man. I'd a lot sooner be a saint an' build things an' cook things an' preach to things than keep goin' to school an' learnin' the same ole things day after day an' day after day – all things like French verbs without any *sense* in them. I'd much sooner be a saint, wun't you?'

The other Outlaws looked doubtful, yet as though attracted by the idea.

'They wun't let us,' said Henry.

'They can't stop us bein' saints,' said William piously, 'an' doin' good an' preachin' – not if we have visions, an' I feel's if I could have visions quite easy.'

The Outlaws had slackened their pace.

'What'd we have to do first?' said Ginger.

'Sell some of our father's things to get money,' said William firmly. ''S all right,' he went on, anticipating possible objections, 'he did, so I s'pose anyone can if they're settin' out to be saints – of course it would be different if we was jus' stealin', but bein' saints makes it diff'rent. Stands to reason saints can't steal.'

'Well, what'd we do *then*?' said Douglas.

'Then we find a place an' get the right sort of clothes to wear—'

'Seems sort of a waste of money,' said Henry sternly, 'spendin' it on *clothes*. What sort of clothes were they?'

'He showed us a picture,' said Ginger, 'don' you remember? Sort of long things goin' right down to his feet.'

'Dressing-gowns'd do,' said Douglas excitedly.

'No, you're thinkin' of detectives,' said Henry firmly; 'detectives wear dressing-gowns.'

'No,' said William judicially. 'I don' see why dressing-gowns shun't do. Then we can save the money an' spend it on things to eat.'

'Where'll we live?'

'We oughter build a place, but till we've built it we can live in the old barn.'

'Where'll we get the animals to preach to?'

'Well, there's a farm just across the way from the barn, you know. We can start on Jumble an' then go on to the farm ones when we've had some practice.'

'An' what'll we be called? We can't be the Outlaws now we're saints, I s'pose?'

'What were they called?'

'Franciscans . . . After Francis – he was the head one.'

'Well, if there's goin' to be any head one,' said William in a tone that precluded any argument on the subject, 'if there's going to be any head one, I'm going to be him.'

None of them denied to William the position of leader. It was his by right. He had always led, and he was a leader they were proud to follow.

'Well, they just put "cans" on to the end of his name,' said Henry. 'Franciscans. So we'll be Williamcans—'

'Sounds kind of funny,' said Ginger dubiously.

'I think it sounds jolly fine,' said William proudly. 'I vote we start tomorrow, 'cause it's rather late to start today, an' anyway, it's Saturday tomorrow, so we can get well started for Monday, 'cause they're sure to make a fuss about our not turnin' up at school on Monday. You all come to the old barn d'rectly after breakfast tomorrow an' bring your dressing-gowns an' somethin of your father's to sell—'

The first meeting of the Williamcans was held directly after breakfast the next morning. They had all left notes dictated by William on their bedroom mantelpieces announcing that they were now saints and had left home for ever.

They deposited their dressing-gowns on the floor of the old barn and then inspected the possessions that they had looted from their unsuspecting fathers. William had appropriated a pair of slippers, not because he thought their absence would be undetected (far from it) or because he thought they would realise vast wealth (again far from it), but it happened that they were kept in the fender-box of the morning-room, and William had found himself alone there for a few minutes that morning, and slippers can be concealed quite easily beneath one's coat. He could have more easily appropriated something of his mother's, but William liked to do things properly. Saint Francis had sold something of his father's, so Saint William would do the same. Douglas took from his pocket an inkstand, purloined from his father's desk; Ginger had two ties and Henry a pair of gloves.

They looked at their spoils with proud satisfaction.

'We oughter get a good deal of money for *these*,' said William. 'How much did *he* get, d'you know?'

'No, he never said,' said Ginger.

'We'd better not put on our saint robes yet – not till we've been down to the village to sell the things. Then we'll put 'em on an' start preachin' an' things.'

'Din' we oughter wear round-hoop-sort-of-things on our heads?' said Henry. 'They do in pictures. What d'you call 'em? – Halos.'

'You don' get *them* till you're dead,' said Ginger with an air of wisdom.

'Well, I don't see what good they are to anyone *dead*,' said Henry, rather aggrieved.

'No, we've gotter do things *right*,' said William sternly. 'If the real saints waited till they was dead, we will, too. Anyway, let's go an' sell the things first. An' remember call everything else "brother" or "sister".'

'*Everything?*'

'Yes – *he* did – the other man did.'

'You've gotter call me *Saint* William now, Ginger.'

'All right, you call me Saint Ginger.'

'All right, I'm goin' to – Saint Ginger—'

'Saint William.'

'All right.'

'Well, where you goin' to sell the slippers?'

'*Brother* slippers,' corrected William. 'Well, I'm

73

goin' to sell brother slippers at Mr Marsh's 'f he'll buy 'em.'

'An I'll take brother ties along, too,' said Ginger. 'An' Henry take brother gloves, an' Douglas brother inkstand.'

'*Sister* inkstand,' said Douglas. 'William—'

'Saint William,' corrected William, patiently.

'Well, Saint William said we could call things brother *or* sister, an' my inkstand's goin' to be sister.'

'*Swank!*' said St Ginger severely, 'always wanting to be diff'rent from other people!'

Mr Marsh kept a second-hand shop at the end of the village. In his window reposed side by side a motley collection of battered and despised household goods.

He had a less optimistic opinion of the value of brothers slippers and ties and gloves and sister inkstand than the saints.

He refused to allow them more than sixpence each.

'*Mean!*' exploded St William indignantly as soon as they had emerged from Mr Marsh's dingy little sanctum to the village street and the light of day. 'I call him sim'ly *mean*. That's what *I* call him.'

'I s'pose now we're saints,' said St Ginger piously, 'that we've gotter forgive folks what wrong us like that.'

'I'm not goin' to be *that* sort of a saint,' said St William firmly.

Back at the barn they donned their dressing-gowns, St Henry still grumbling at not being able to wear the 'little hoop' on his head.

'Now what d'we do *first*?' said St Ginger energetically, as he fastened the belt of his dressing-gown.

'Well, anyway, why can't we cut little bits of our hair at the top like they have in pictures?' said St Henry disconsolately, 'that'd be better than *nothin*'.'

This idea rather appealed to the saints. St Douglas discovered a penknife and began to operate at once on St Henry, but the latter saint's yells of agony soon brought the proceedings to a premature end.

'Well, *you* s'gested it,' said St Douglas, rather hurt, 'an' I was doin' it as gently as I could.'

'*Gently!*' groaned Henry, still nursing his saintly head. 'You were tearing it out by the roots.'

'Well, come *on*!' said St Ginger impatiently, 'let's begin now. What did you say we were goin' to do first?'

'Preachin' to animals is the first thing,' said William in his most business-like manner. 'I've got Brother Jumble here. Ginger — I mean St Ginger, you hold Brother Jumble while I preach to him 'cause he's not used to it, an' he might try to run away, an' St Henry an' St Douglas go out an' preach to birds. The St Francis man did a lot of preachin' to birds. They came an' sat on his arms. See if you can gettem to do that.

Well now, let's start. Ginger – I mean St Ginger – you catch hold of Brother Jumble.'

Henry and Douglas departed. Douglas's dressing-gown, made by a thrifty mother with a view to Douglas's further growth, was slightly too big and tripped him over every few steps. Henry's was made of bath towelling and was rather conspicuous in design. They made their way slowly across a field and into a neighbouring wood.

St Ginger encircled the reluctant Jumble with his arms, and St William stood up to preach.

'Dearly beloved Jumble—' he began.

'Brother Jumble,' corrected St Ginger, with triumph. He liked to catch the founder of the order tripping.

Jumble, under the delusion that something was expected of him, sat up and begged.

'Dearly beloved Brother Jumble,' repeated William. He stopped and cleared his throat in the manner of all speakers who are not sure what to say next.

Jumble, impatient of the other saint's encircling arms, tried another trick, that of standing on his head. Standing on his head was the title given to the performance by Jumble's owner. In reality it consisted of rubbing the top of his head on the ground. None of his legs left the ground, but William always called it

'Jumble standing on his head', and was inordinately proud of it.

ST WILLIAM STOOD UP TO PREACH TO THE RELUCTANT
JUMBLE. 'DEARLY BELOVED JUMBLE,' HE BEGAN.

'Look at him,' he said, 'isn't that jolly clever? An' no one told him to. Jus' did it without anyone tellin' him to. I bet there's not many dogs like him. I bet he's the cleverest dog there is in England. I wun't mind sayin' he's the cleverest dog there is in the world. I wun't—'

'I thought you was preachin' to him, not talkin' about him,' said St Ginger, sternly. Ginger, who was not allowed to possess a dog, tired occasionally of hearing William sing the praises of his.

'Oh, yes,' said St William with less enthusiasm. 'I'll start all over again. Dearly beloved Brother Jumble – I say, what did that St Francis *say* to the animals?'

'Dunno,' said St Ginger vaguely, 'I s'pect he jus' told 'em to – well, to do good an' that sort of thing.'

'Dearly beloved Brother Jumble,' said William again, 'you mus' – do good an – an' stop chasin' cats. Why,' he said proudly, 'there's not a cat in this village that doesn't run when it sees Jumble comin'. I bet he's the best dog for chasin' cats anywhere round *this* part of England. I bet—'

Jumble, seizing his moment for escape, tore himself from St Ginger's unwary arms, and leapt up ecstatically at William.

'Good old Jumble,' said the saint affectionately. 'Good old boy!'

At this point the other two saints returned.

'Well, did you find any birds?' said St William.

78

'There was heaps of birds,' said St Douglas in an exasperated tone of voice, 'but the minute I started preachin' they all flew off. They din' seem to know how to *act* with saints. They din' seem to know they'd got to sit on our arms an' things. Made us feel *mad* – anyway, we gotter thrush's egg and Henry – I mean St Henry – jus' wanted one of those—'

'Well,' said St William rather sternly, 'I don' think it's the right thing for saints to do – to go preachin' to birds an' then takin' their eggs – I mean their brother eggs.'

'There was *lots* more,' said Henry. 'They *like* you jus' takin' one. It makes it less trouble for 'em hatchin' 'em out.'

'Well, anyway,' said William, 'let's get on with this animal business. P'raps the tame ones'll be better. Let's go across to Jenks' farm an' try on them.'

They crept rather cautiously into the farmyard. The feud between Farmer Jenks and the Outlaws was one of long standing. He would probably not realise that the Williamcans were a saintly organisation whose every action was inspired by a love of mankind. He would probably imagine that they were still the old unregenerate Outlaws.

'I'll do brother cows,' said St William, 'an' St Ginger do brother pigs, and St Douglas do brother goats, an' St Henry do sister hens.'

They approached their various audiences. Ginger leant over the pigsty. Then he turned to William, who was already striking an attitude before his congregation of cows, and said: 'I say, what've I gotter *say* to 'em?'

WILLIAM WAS ALREADY STRIKING AN ATTITUDE BEFORE
HIS CONGREGATION OF COWS.

At that moment brother goat, being approached too nearly by St Douglas, butted the saintly stomach, and St Douglas sat down suddenly and heavily. Brother goat, evidently enjoying this form of entertainment, returned to the charge. St Douglas fled to the accompaniment of an uproarious farmyard commotion.

Farmer Jenks appeared, and, seeing his old enemies, the Outlaws, actually within his precincts, he uttered a yell of fury and darted down upon them. The saints fled swiftly, St Douglas holding up his too flowing robe as he went. Brother goat had given St Douglas a good start and he reached the farm first.

'Well,' said St William, panting, 'I've *finished* with preachin' to animals. They must have changed a good bit since *his* time. That's all *I* can say.'

'Well, what'll we do *now*?' said St Ginger.

'I should almost think it's time for dinner,' said William. 'Must be after two, I should think.'

No one knew the time. Henry possessed a watch which had been given to him by a great-uncle. Though it may possibly have had some value as an antique, it had not gone for over twenty years. Henry, however, always wore it, and generally remembered to move its hands to a correct position whenever he passed a clock. This took a great deal of time and trouble, but Henry was proud of his watch and liked it to be as nearly right as possible. He consulted it now. He had put it right by his family's hall clock as he came out after breakfast, so its fingers stood at half-past nine. He returned it to his pocket hastily before the others could see the position of the fingers.

'Yes,' he said, with the air of an oracle, 'it's about dinner-time.' Though they all knew that Henry's watch had never gone, yet it had a certain prestige.

'Well, we've gotter *buy* our dinner,' said William. 'S'pose two of us goes down to the village, an' buys it

FARMER JENKS UTTERED A YELL OF FURY AND BORE
DOWN UPON THE OUTLAWS. DOUGLAS FLED SWIFTLY.

now with the two shillings we got for sellin' our fathers' things. We've gotter buy all our meals now like what *they* did.'

'Well, how d'we get the money when we've finished this? We can't go *on* sellin' our fathers' things. They'd get so mad.'

'We beg from folks after that,' said Ginger, who was the only one who had paid much attention to the story of the life of St Francis.

'Well, I bet they won't give us much if *I* know 'em,' said William bitterly. 'I bet both folks *an*' animals must've been nicer in those times.'

It was decided that Douglas and Henry should go down to the village to purchase provisions for the meal. It was decided also that they should go in their dressing-gowns.

'*They* always did,' said Ginger firmly, 'and folks may's well get used to us goin' about like that.'

'Oh, yes!' said Douglas bitterly. ''S easy to talk like that when you're not goin' down to the shop.'

Mr Moss, the proprietor of the village sweet-shop, held his sides with laughter when he saw them.

'Well, I never!' he said. 'Well, I never! What boys you are for a joke, to be sure!'

'It's not a joke,' said Henry. 'We're Williamcans.'

Douglas had caught sight of the clock on the desk behind the counter.

'I say!' he said. 'It's only eleven o'clock.'

Henry took out his watch.

'Oh, yes,' he said, as if he had made a mistake when he looked at it before.

For their midday meal the two saints purchased a large bag of chocolate creams, another of bull's-eyes, and, to form the more solid part of the meal, four cream buns.

Ginger and William and Jumble were sitting comfortably in the old barn when the two emissaries returned.

'*We've* had a nice time!' exploded St Henry. 'All the boys in the place runnin' after us an' shoutin' at us.'

'You should've just stood still an' *preached* to 'em,' said the founder of the order calmly.

'*Preached* to 'em!' repeated Henry. 'They wun't have listened. They was shoutin' an' throwin' things an' running at us.'

'What'd you do?'

'Run,' said the gallant saint simply. 'An' Douglas has tore his robe, an' I've fallen in the mud in mine.'

'Well, they've gotter last you all the rest of your life,' said St William, 'so you oughter take more care of 'em,' and added with more interest, 'what've you got for dinner?'

They displayed their purchases and their choice was warmly and unanimously approved by the saints.

'Wish we'd thought of something to drink,' said Henry.

But William, with a smile of pride, brought out from his pocket a bottle of dark liquid.

'I *thought* of that,' he said, holding it out with a flourish, 'have a drink of brother lik'rice water.'

Not to be outdone, Douglas took up one of the bags.

'An' have a sister cream bun,' he said loudly.

When they had eaten and drunk to repletion they rested for a short time from their labours. William had meant to fill in time by preaching to Jumble, but decided instead to put Jumble through his tricks.

'I s'pose they *know* now at home that we've gone for good,' said Henry with a sigh.

Ginger looked out of the little window anxiously.

'Yes. I only hope to goodness they won't come an' try to fetch us back,' he said.

But he need not have troubled. Each family thought that the missing member was having lunch with one of the others, and felt no anxiety, only a great relief. And none of the notes upon the mantelpieces had been found.

'What'll we do *now*?' said William, rousing himself at last.

'*They* built a church,' said Ginger.

'Crumbs!' said William, taken aback. 'Well, we can't do that, can we?'

'Oh, I dunno,' said Ginger vaguely, 'jus' keep on putting stones on each other. It was quite a little church.'

'Well, it'd take us more'n quite a little time.'

'Yes, but we've gotter do *something* 'stead of goin' to school, an' we may's well do that.'

''S almost as bad as goin' to school,' said William gloomily. 'An' where'd they get the stones?'

'They jus' found 'em lying about.'

'Well, come on,' said William, rising with a resigned air and gathering the folds of his dressing-gown about him, 'let's see 'f we can find any lyin' about.'

They wandered down the road. They still wore their dressing-gowns, but they wore them with a sheepish air and went cautiously and furtively. Already their affection for their saintly garb was waning. Fortunately, the road was deserted. They looked up and down, then St Ginger gave a yell of triumph and pointed up the road. The road was being mended, and there lay by the roadside, among other materials, a little heap of wooden bricks. Moreover, the bricks were unguarded and unattended.

It was the British workman's dinner hour, and the British workman was spending it in the nearest pub.

'Crumbs!' said the Williamcans in delight.

They fell upon the wooden bricks and bore them off in triumph. Soon they had a pile of them just outside the barn where they had resolved to build the church – almost enough, the head of the order decided, to begin on. But as they paid their last visit for bricks they met a little crowd of other children, who burst into loud jeering cries.

'Look at 'em . . . Dear little girlies . . , wearin' nice long pinnies . . . Oh, my! Oh, *don*' they look sweet? Hello, little darlin's!'

William flung aside his saintly robe and closed with the leader. The other saints closed with the others. Quite an interesting fight ensued. The saints, smaller in number and size than the other side, most decidedly got the best of it, though not without many casualties. The other side took to its heels.

St William, without much enthusiasm, picked his saintly robe up from the mud and began to put it on.

'Don' see much *sense* in wearin' these things,' he said.

'You ought to have *preached* to 'em, not fought 'em,' said Ginger severely.

'Well, I bet *he* wun't've preached to 'em if they'd started makin' fun of him. He'd've fought 'em all right.'

'No, he wun't,' said Ginger firmly, 'he din't b'lieve in fightin'.'

William's respect for his prototype, already on the wane, waned still farther. But he did not lightly relinquish anything he had once undertaken.

'Well, anyway,' he said, 'let's get a move on buildin' that church.'

They returned to the field and their little pile of bricks.

But the British workman had also returned from his dinner hour at the nearest pub, and had discovered the disappearance of the larger part of his material. With lurid oaths he had tracked them down and came upon the saints just as they had laboriously laid the first row of bricks for the first wall. He burst upon them with fury.

They did not stay to argue. They fled. Henry cast aside his splendid robe of multi-coloured bath towelling into a ditch to accelerate his flight. The British workman tired first. He went back after throwing a brick at their retreating forms and informing them lustily that he knew their fathers an' he'd go an' tell them, danged if he wouldn't, and they'd find themselves in jail – saucy little 'ounds – danged if they wouldn't.

The Williamcans waited till all was clear before they emerged from their hiding places and gathered together dejectedly in the barn. William and Ginger had sustained black eyes and bleeding noses as the result of the fight with the village children. Douglas had fallen during the flight from the British workman and caught Henry on his ankle, and he limped painfully. Their faces had acquired an extraordinary amount of dirt.

They sat down and surveyed each other.

'Seems to me,' said William, 'it's a *wearin*' kind of life.'

It was cold. It had begun to rain.

'Brother rain,' remarked Ginger brightly.

'Yes, an' I should think it's about sister tea-time,' said William dejectedly; 'an' what we goin' to buy it – her – with? How're we goin' to get money?'

'I've got sixpence at home,' said Henry. 'I mean I've gotter brother sixpence at home.'

But William had lost his usual optimism.

'Well, that won't keep all of us for the rest of our lives, will it?' he said; 'an' I don't feel like startin' beggin' after the time I've had today. I haven't got much *trust* in folks.'

'Henry – I mean, St Henry – oughter give his brother sixpence to the poor,' said Ginger piously. '*They* uster give all their money to the poor.'

'*Give* it?' said William incredulously. 'An' get nothin' back for it?'

'No – jus' give it,' said Ginger.

William thought deeply for a minute.

'Well,' he said at last, voicing the opinion of the whole order, 'I'm jus' about sick of bein' a saint. I'd sooner be a pirate or a Red Indian any day.'

The rest looked relieved.

'Yes, I've had *enough*,' said William, 'and let's stop callin' each other saints an' brothers an' sisters an' wearin' dressing-gowns. There's no *sense* in it. An' I'm almost dyin' of cold an' hunger an' I'm goin' home.'

They set off homeward through the rain, cold and wet and bruised and very hungry. The saintly repast of cream buns and chocolate creams and bull's-eyes, though enjoyable at the time, had proved singularly unsustaining.

But their troubles were not over.

As they went through the village they stopped in front of Mr Marsh's shop window. There in the very middle were William's father's slippers, Douglas' father's inkstand, Ginger's father's tie and Henry's father's gloves — all marked at 1/-. The hearts of the Williamcans stood still. Their fathers would probably not yet have returned from Town. The thought of their seeing their prized possessions reposing in Mr Marsh's window marked 1/- was a horrid one. It had not seemed to matter this morning. This morning they were leaving their homes for ever. It did seem to matter this evening. This evening they were returning to their homes.

They entered the shop and demanded them. Mr Marsh was adamant. In the end Henry fetched his sixpence, William a treasured penknife, Ginger a compass, and Douglas a broken steam engine, and their paternal possessions were handed back.

They went home dejectedly through the rain. The British workman might or might not fulfil his threat of calling on their parents. The saintly career which had looked so roseate in the distance had turned out, as William aptly described it, 'wearin'.' Life was full of disillusions.

William discovered with relief that his father had not yet come home. He returned the slippers, some-what damp, to the fender box. He put his muddy dressing-gown beneath the bed. He found his note unopened and unread, still upon the mantelpiece. He tore it up. He tidied himself superficially. He went downstairs.

'Had a nice day, dear?' said his mother.

He disdained to answer the question.

'There's just an hour before tea,' she went on; 'hadn't you better be doing your homework, dear?'

He considered. One might as well drink of tragedy the very dregs while one was about it. It would be a rotten ending to a rotten day. Besides, there was no doubt about it – Mr Strong was going to make himself very disagreeable indeed, if he didn't know those

French verbs for Monday. He might as well – If he'd
had any idea how rotten it was being a saint he jolly
well wouldn't have wasted a whole Saturday over it.
He took down a French grammar and sat down
moodily before it without troubling to put it right way
up.

CHAPTER 5

WILLIAM AND THE LOST TOURIST

WILLIAM, Ginger, Douglas and Henry were on their way home from school. Owing to the absence of one of the masters they had been given an extra hour to learn their homework. William had not used it to the best advantage. He had spent the first part of it making rats out of ink-sodden blotting-paper till he was summoned to the front of the room where his activities should be under the eye of Authority.

There, under compulsion, he opened his Shakespeare and idly committed to memory the lines chosen for his edification by his English master:

'Friends, Romans, countrymen, lend me your ears
I come to bury Caesar, not to praise him.
The evil that men do lives after them,
The good is oft interred with their bones,'

he murmured monotonously to himself, rubbing his eyes with his ink-stained fingers till the ink gradually overspread his freckled countenance. There was nothing unusual in that. As his mother plaintively remarked, William could never touch ink without 'getting all over with it'. She would have felt almost uneasy had William ever returned home from school without his customary coating of ink or mud.

William wandered home with Ginger and Douglas and Henry, chanting blithely: 'Friends, Romans, countrymen, lend me your ears.'

'Who was this Shakespeare, anyway?' said William.

'He was a pote,' said Douglas unctuously, 'an' he – well, he just lived an' died.'

'Din' he *do* anythin'?' said William.

'He wrote po'try.'

'That's not *doin'* anythin',' said William contemptuously. 'I can write po'try – I mean din' he *fight* or somethin'?'

'It says in the beginning of the book he *acted*,' said Henry rather vaguely.

'Huh!' said William. 'That's nothin'. *I* can act. I don' think much of *him*.'

'There's stachoos up to him in places,' said Henry, still with his air of comprehensive knowledge.

'Well, if *that's* all he did,' said William with disgust, 'they might jus' as well put stachoos up to *me*. I can write po'try an' act if *that's* all he did.'

William's heroes were all men of action. He was not a patron of the Arts.

They were passing Mrs Maloney's cottage. Mrs Maloney lived alone with a dog and a cat and a canary. She was very old and very cantankerous.

She hated everyone, but her hatred of boys was the absorbing passion of her life. And of all boys in the world the boys she most hated were the Outlaws. It was probably that alone which kept her alive. She visibly failed in health on the days on which she had no encounter with the Outlaws. On the days when she had joined battle with them she looked less infirm. On the date when she successfully routed them she looked almost hale and hearty.

The Outlaws were afraid of Mrs Maloney and Mrs Maloney's dog and Mrs Maloney's cat. They firmly believed her to be a witch. It was that fear which made it a point of honour with them never to pass the cottage without some act of daring aggression. To the Outlaws danger was the very breath of life.

There was a hole in the side of her garden hedge that bordered the field by the side of the road, and on their way home the Outlaws took it in turn to enter the field, crawl through the hole, and walk (or generally run) down Mrs Maloney's garden path to her gate and out into the road. They did no harm to the garden. But the sight of the hateful creatures in her garden threw the old lady into a frenzy. Considering her age and infirmities, she could move with remarkable speed, and not infrequently one or other of the Outlaws fell into her clutches.

That was a thrill full of ecstasy and terror for the Outlaws – a thing to dream of and talk of with bated breath and – dare again. Her cat and dog were loyal lieutenants who shared her hatred of the whole race of boys. The dog had bitten Henry and the cat had scratched Ginger only the week before.

Today it was William's turn to creep through the hole. Mrs Maloney was standing near the door. She was generally there ready for the fray when the Outlaws came home from school. Today Fate was not on their side. Ginger, Henry and Douglas were at the gate ready to open it for William's flying figure, but on this occasion William's figure did not fly. It was stuck in the hole.

When it emerged it was to face a furious Mrs Maloney, who grabbed his ears with claw-like hands, and thrusting her witch's face close to his, shook his head till it seemed to him that every one of his teeth was permanently loosened from its setting. He tore himself away at last and fled down to the gate that his friends were holding open for him. But that was not the end. William's cap had been shaken off, and with horror they saw Mrs Maloney pick it up, carry it up to her door and fling it down furiously and contemptuously upon the bench outside.

The Outlaws held a hasty meeting. It was unthinkable to go home in defeat, leaving their leader's cap in the hands of the enemy. They would never hold up their heads again. They discussed plans, standing in the middle of the road, watched suspiciously by the enemy from her back-door, where she still kept guard over her trophy.

'We've gotter get it back,' said Ginger sternly. 'It's William's cap, so I votes William goes in an' gets it back.'

'Yes, *you'd* feel like going back,' said William bitterly, 'if she'd shook everything loose in *your* head. All the bones an' muscles an' brains an' things that oughter be stickin' together's all loose all over the place. *You* don' know what it feels like.'

William being literally shaken from his position of leadership and being able to discuss nothing but the hypothetical condition of the inside of his head, Ginger evolved a masterly plan.

He found a long stick, and while William, Douglas and Henry drew down the enemy to the gate by short and daring excursions into the garden as if in attempts at rescue, Ginger leant over the hedge by the side of the cottage and fished up William's cap with his stick. The Outlaws then marched off yelling triumphantly, carrying William's cap proudly upon the end of the stick, while its late captor gibbered at them over the gate in inarticulate rage.

It was a half-holiday, and after, at his mother's earnest request, removing as much ink from his face and hands as could be removed by that hurried process known to William as 'washing', he sat down to lunch with a clear conscience.

'Half-holiday,' he murmured, 'an' I've done my homework – at least,' he qualified his assertion, 'I've done some of it – "The good has often entered into bones".'

'What *are* you talking about, William?' said his mother. 'And your face isn't clean yet.'

'Well, I've done all I can to it,' said William virtuously, 'I've *washed* it.' He threw a glance at his reflection in the glass. 'You oughter be able to tell by my hair that I've *washed* it.'

William's hair stood up round his face in damp, vertical spikes.

'Go and brush it, William,' said Mrs Brown wearily.

'Well, you know,' said William as though delivering a final deeply considered judgment, 'I've sometimes thought it's best to let your hair grow the way it grows *nat'rally*. Some hair grows flat nat'rally. Then you oughter brush it flat. But mine doesn't. It nat'rally grows up like this, an' I've sometimes thought it's better to leave it to grow its own way. It's more *nat'ral*. If—'

'Go and *brush* it, William,' said Mrs Brown.

William went slowly upstairs. He came down, his hair sleek and plentifully damped, murmuring: 'Fre'en's, Rome and countrymen, lend me some ears, I come to – well, anyway, the evil and the good men do lives into 'em.'

'Now, William, stop talking nonsense and eat your lunch,' said Mrs Brown patiently.

'That's jus' what I think,' said William, 'an' yet he's got stachoos put up to him an' no end of a fuss.'

After a hearty meal William set out joyously to join his companions. They had made no plans for the afternoon. They usually left things to Fate, and Fate seldom failed to provide them with an exciting programme.

They had arranged to meet at the corner of the road that led to Ginger's house. William was early at the trysting place. There was nothing to be seen at the corner but a car, and in the car were a weeping young woman and a sleeping old man. William stood and gaped. The weeping young woman was astonishingly beautiful, and William, in spite of his professed scorn of the feminine sex, was very susceptible to beauty.

William blinked and coughed.

The young woman turned sapphire-blue swimming eyes to him and gulped.

'Say, kid,' she said with an American twang and intonation that completed the enslavement of William, 'say, kid, what's the name of this lil' old town?'

William was too much confused to reply for a moment. During that moment fresh tears welled up into the blue eyes.

'I feel jus' like *nothing*,' sobbed the lady. 'I've lost the way an' I've lost the map an' I don't know where I am an Pop's gone to sleep an' – I – I don't know where I've got to.'

'Where did you want to get to?' asked William.

'Stratford,' said the lady. 'Stratford-on-Avon, that Shakespeare guy's place. If we don't do it today we'll never do it. We've not got one single other day left an' it'll *kill* me not to do it. Everyone I know's done it an' to go back home an' say I've not seen Stratford – well, I'd never hold up my head again – *never* – and I've lost the way and the map and Pop's gone to sleep and—'

She ended in a sob that reduced William's already melting heart to complete liquefaction.

'It's all right,' he said consolingly.

He didn't mean anything in particular. It was only a vague expression of sympathy and comfort. But the lady looked at him, her eyes suddenly alight with hope.

'You mean—' she gasped, 'you mean that this is Stratford? Oh, how *dandy!* Do you really mean that?'

Stronger and older characters than William would have decided to mean that when fixed by those pleading hopeful blue eyes.

'Yes,' said William after a moment's silence, which represented a short, victorious struggle with a never very recalcitrant conscience, 'this is Stratford all right.'

The lady leapt in her seat. Gone were all traces of tears.

'Say, kid, I jus' *adore* you. Now I've got to see it *all* jus' as quick as I can. Never mind Pop. He can go on sleeping. He hates looking at things, anyway. He goes to sleep on purpose.'

She opened the door and jumped down.

'Now the first thing I wanta see is Anne Hathaway's cottage. Can you direct me to that, little boy? Or – say are you doing anything particular this afternoon?'

'No,' said the unscrupulous William, deciding that Ginger, Henry and Douglas could get on very well without him.

'Well, now, would you be a reel cherub, and personally conduct me?'

'Yes, I would,' said William eagerly. He did not repent his rash statement as to the precise locality of Stratford-on-Avon. He almost believed it. If this vision wished it to be Stratford it *was* Stratford.

They set off down the road together.

'Is it far?' said the fair American eagerly.

William began to consider. He realised that he had embarked upon an adventure that would require careful handling, but William was not the boy to retire from any adventure before he was compelled.

He looked up and down the road.

'Whose cottage did you say?' he said at last.

'Anne Hathaway's.'

'Oh, no, it's not far now,' said William, hoping for the best.

The lady became confidential. She told him that her name was Miss Burford – Sadie Burford – and she jus' *loved* this lil' ole country, but Stratford was the thing she'd *longed* most *passionately* to see, and this was the happiest day of her life and wasn't it just the cutest little place and she'd be grateful to him all her life, she would sure.

William enjoyed it. He enjoyed walking with her, he enjoyed watching her astounding beauty, he enjoyed her twang. He was already practising it silently in his mind.

They turned the bend in the road and there in front of them was Mrs Maloney's cottage.

Miss Burford gave a little scream of ecstasy.

'*Thatched!*' she said. 'This must be Anne Hathaway's cottage.'

'Yes, this is it,' agreed William, torn between relief at having discovered an Anne Hathaway's cottage and consternation at the prospect of a second *rencontre* with Mrs Maloney in one day. He could see Mrs Maloney looking out of the window. William, as an artist, occasionally overreached himself. He made the mistake of not leaving well alone. Now, wishing to give a further touch of verisimilitude to the whole situation, he said carelessly—

'An' there's Anne Hathaway lookin' out of the window.'

'Does an Anne Hathaway *still* live here?' said Miss Burford excitedly.

'Well, I thought that was what you said,' said William bewildered.

'But I meant the one that lived hundreds of years ago.'

William was still more bewildered.

'She'll be dead by now,' he said, after a slight pause. But he wished the radiant vision to have everything she wanted. If she wanted an Anne whatever it was, she should have it.

'There's another living there now,' he went on.

'How *dandy*!' said Miss Burford. 'A descendant, I suppose?'

'Oh, yes,' agreed William. 'Yes – that's what she is.'

'Well – I've got to hurry. Will you knock, or shall I? Perhaps you know her?'

'Oh, y-yes, I k-know her all right,' stammered William, edging away as he spoke, his eyes fixed fearfully upon the cottage door. 'You – you don't wanter go *right* in, do you?'

'I sure do,' asserted Miss Burford.

'I – I wun't if I was you,' said William earnestly. 'I wun't go. She's *awful* bad-tempered, Mrs Maloney is – I mean Anne what you said is.'

'But I must go in – People *do*, I know.'

'Better not,' said William desperately, 'she's – she's deaf, too.'

'But I can shout.'

'That's no use. She can't hear shouting. And she's mad, too – she's sort of forgotten her name – she – she sort of thinks she's someone else – so it's no use goin' in, what with her bein' deaf an' mad. It's not reely safe. An' it's best from outside. It's not anything like as nice inside as it is outside.'

'But I've known people who've gone inside,' persisted Miss Burford. 'I've known them personally. It must be possible. It can't be very dangerous.'

She advanced boldly and knocked at the door. William stood in the background palely composed, but ready to flee if necessary. The door opened a few inches and Mrs Maloney's wrinkled face appeared round it. At the sight of William it became distorted with rage.

'Ah-h-h!' she growled. 'Ye little pest, ye—'

William, whose valour was wholesomely inter-mingled with discretion, was on the point of turning to flee and leaving this strange situation to disentangle itself as best it could, when he saw Miss Burford slip something into Mrs Maloney's hand, at which Mrs Maloney's wrath simmered down into a sullen distrust.

'Could I,' said Miss Burford, with disarming sweetness, 'could I just look at your historical cottage, Miss Hathaway?'

''Ysterical yourself,' snapped the owner; 'an' me name's Mrs Maloney, I'd have ye to know.'

Miss Burford turned to William with a sad smile.

'Poor woman!' she whispered.

Then she entered the kitchen. Mrs Maloney stood holding her ten-shilling note with both hands and watching her guest suspiciously. William's sole thought was to keep as near the door as possible in view of possible developments. Miss Burford looked round at the old-fashioned cottage, the old dresser and the flagged floor with a sigh of rapture.

'How lovely!' she breathed. 'How perfect!'

Mrs Maloney's suspicions deepened.

Then Miss Burford looked rather puzzled. 'I've seen photographs of it. I've sure got a wretched memory, but I had an idea there were more things in it, somehow. I've only a vague kind of idea of it, but I certainly thought there were more things in it.'

In his capacity of stage-manager, William spoke up with desperate boldness.

MRS MALONEY'S WRINKLED FACE APPEARED. AT THE
SIGHT OF WILLIAM IT BECAME DISTORTED WITH RAGE.

'There was,' he said, 'there was a lot more things, but they had to take 'em away when she – when she got like this.'

'Eh?' said Mrs Maloney sharply. 'What's he saying?'

'Nothing, nothing,' said Miss Burford pacifically.

But the suspicious rage upon the old lady's face was

WILLIAM WAS ON THE POINT OF TURNING TO FLEE.

not without effect. Miss Burford herself began to edge hastily towards the door. Mrs Maloney, purple-faced, uttered a threatening sound expressive of fury, and Miss Burford, throwing dignity to the winds, followed William's already fleeing figure.

'How awful!' she panted, when they had reached the safe refuge of the road. 'Poor woman! She's sure plumb crazy! But,' with a sigh of content, 'I've seen it. That's all I wanted to do. I can say I've seen it now.' She took from her pocket a little note-book, opened it and ticked off 'Stratford' and 'Anne Hathaway's Cottage'. 'There! Now I don't care how soon Pop takes me home.

'I've not brought my guide-book,' went on Miss Burford to William, 'but I reckon there's other things I oughta see in Stratford.' She looked across a field and caught sight of the stream that made its sluggish way through William's native village. 'The Avon,' she said, with an ecstatic sigh. 'Isn't it just dandy? But now, say, kid, isn't there anything else I oughta see belongin' to Shakespeare? I suppose – I suppose, now,' wistfully, 'there aren't any other of his folks about the place – kind of descendants, you know?'

The adventure seemed to be drawing to a close, and William did not want it to draw to a close. The beautiful sapphire eyes fixed on him wistfully had a strange effect on him. Before he knew what he was saying, he had said, modestly:

'There's me. I'm one of his folks.'

He was secretly aghast when he heard himself say that. But he merely continued to gaze at her with his most ingenuous expression.

'Well, now!' she cried in rapture. 'Isn't that jus' *luck*! You're one of his descendants? But – not in the direct line, I reckon.'

If William was going to be a descendant at all he was most certainly going to do the thing properly.

'Oh, yes,' he said, 'I'm d'rect all right.'

'Then you're re-lated to the old lady?' she said excitedly.

Again this took William out of his depth. He replied to it only by an uncertain smile.

'*Fancy!*' said Miss Burford. '*Fancy* that! I reckon you've got letters and records and relics of your house?'

'Oh, yes – no end of them,' said William. 'All over the place.'

Miss Burford thrilled visibly.

'I guess I was plumb lucky to strike *you* first go off,' she said. She looked at William almost with reverence. 'I can see a most dis-tinct likeness,' she said at last. 'I reckon, kid, you've been simply *brought up* on him, haven't you? I expect you jus' about know his works by heart.'

'Oh, yes,' said William, and quoted dreamily:

'Fr'en's, Rome and countrymen, lend me some ears
I come to bury Cassar in his grave.
The evil what he did is in his bones,
The good has entered – entered—'

He had a vague suspicion that he had gone wrong somewhere, and began again: 'Fr'en's, Rome, and countrymen—' But Miss Burford was delighted.

'Fancy!' she said at last. 'Fancy! I once read "The Tempest" – he wrote that, didn't he? Or am I thinking of "The Rivals"? – but I couldn't ever remember a line. What's your name?'

'William.'

'Of course,' she breathed, 'after him. Of course.'

At that minute Ginger and Henry and Douglas appeared. They stood in a row gazing with interest at William's new friend. William felt that their presence needed accounting for.

'Fr'en's of mine,' he introduced them laconically.

Miss Burford turned to them.

'I'm just congratulating William,' she said, 'on his famous ancestor.'

William was never one to grudge honours to his friends.

'They're all famous descendants, too,' he said graciously. 'Ginger – er—' William's acquaintance with classical poets was limited, but he did his best,

110

'Scott's, an' Douglas' – Douglas', Wordsworth's, an'
Henry – er – Henry's' – he left the realm of poets in
disgust for one with which he was more familiar –
'Henry's, Nelson's.'

Miss Sadie Burford had come over to England with
the firmly fixed impression that it was a country in
which anything might happen, and her expectations
were being gloriously fulfilled.

'Well, isn't that just – *dandy*!' she burst out with
enthusiasm. 'I'm just thrilled. Now we're all going to
William's home, where he's going to show me some of
those wonderful relics.'

William was nonplussed. The situation was growing
beyond him. He was rather pale as he walked along the
road with her. Ginger, Douglas and Henry hadn't the
remotest idea what was happening, but they gladly
joined the party, so as to be in any excitement that might
be going. Excitement was never far away from William.

Miss Burford was the only happy member of the
party. She chattered joyously about the Avon and
Anne Hathaway's cottage and 'The Tempest' and the
strong family likeness between William and the Bard
of Avon. In a fertile attempt to postpone the fatal
moment of exposure, William resolutely led the party
past the turning that led to his home. But Ginger, ever
obtuse, called out lustily: 'I say, 'f you're goin' to
William's home this is the way.'

William glared at him ferociously, then turned to Miss Burford with a sickly smile. He was beginning to wish he'd left her alone. She was pretty, but not pretty enough, he decided sternly, to make up for all this mess she was getting him into.

'I – I thought we'd go round home by the longer way,' he said, 'so – so,' then with a burst of inspiration, 'so as to get a better view of the Avon.'

'What's the Avon?' said Henry innocently, and yelled with unnecessary loudness when William kicked him.

William walked on one side of Miss Burford, Ginger on the other, Henry and Douglas behind. William's depression increased. To add to his troubles Ginger was supplanting him in the vision's favour. Ginger was prattling engagingly to the vision about the details of his daily life, and the vision was smiling at him affectionately. It was all very well for Ginger to prattle engagingly, thought William gloomily. She wasn't going to walk into Ginger's home and demand to see somebody's relics, whatever 'relics' were. He couldn't put off the fateful moment any longer.

At last the party came within sight of William's house.

'Here's William's house,' said Ginger gaily, leading the way into the gate.

'S-stop a minute,' said William hoarsely, 'I – I mus' jus' go in and ask—'

He hastened into the house, and stood a moment in the hall trying to evolve some plan. But for once he was at a loss. He could only stem the fatal tide. It would be easier to do something if he knew what 'relics' meant.

He returned, looking paler and fiercer than ever.

'I – I'm afraid,' he began, 'I mean, I've jus' found out that they've hid away those rel— what you said.'

'Relics?'

'Yes, that. Well, they've hid 'em away, case of burglary.'

This was an inspiration, but it failed of the desired effect. Miss Burford's countenance fell, but she did not retreat.

'What a pity! Well, I'm jus' disappointed. But I quite understand. I reckon I'd do the same myself. But I must jus' go in and have a look jus' so that I can tell 'em about it way back home.'

Determinedly she went up the the front door and rang. William stood behind her betraying his consternation only by the blank expressionlessness of his face. His untidy hair was by this time standing vertically, almost hiding his cap in spite of his midday smoothing.

Mrs Brown herself came to the door.

'*Good* afternoon,' said Miss Burford as she entered

the hall, followed by the boys, 'you'll pardon me, I'm sure, for intruding like this, but I simply *had* to see the house where the family lives now, though I understand that all the relics are put away for safety.'

Mrs Brown gazed at her in open-mouthed amazement.

'I see fine the likeness to the great man in your little boy,' declared Miss Burford, enthusiastically. 'I suppose you haven't kept the name – as a surname, I mean. What is your name?'

'B-B-Brown,' stammered William's mother, who was wondering whether or not to ring up the police at once.

'But Shakespeare as well, I'm sure,' went on Miss Burford, placing a hand on William's tousled head, and smiling down at his expressionless face. 'As a Christian name, I mean. It's William *Shakespeare* Brown, I'm sure. I expect you're quite used to people forcing their way into your house, aren't you? It's so wonderful. I'm so glad I actually *came* because you don't get *half* the information from the books. I've read "The Tempest", but that's about all. I've had a real *grand* time, and it's so good of you to let me come here – standing in the very house where his direct descendants live.'

Mrs Brown sat down weakly in a chair because her knees were too unsteady to support her any more.

'I must just fly now,' went on Miss Burford, 'or Pop will wake up and wonder what's the matter, and we oughta be getting back to London at once. Goodbye, and it's been a real honour to me to stand here in this house talking to you. I shall tell them all about it way back home.'

She went off, gaily calling back farewells and thanks as she went.

William, after one glance at the bewildered face of his mother, hastily followed her, murmuring something incoherent about 'seein' her off'. He saw the moment of explanations looming near, but wished to postpone it as far back as possible. He heard his mother calling him back, but hurried on with the fair sightseer, leaving Mrs Brown to demand explanations from the other Outlaws, whose professed ignorance she regarded with deep distrust.

When William and Miss Burford reached the car 'Pop' was just waking up.

'What – where – why?' he said sleepily. 'Where are we?'

'At Stratford, Pop, darling,' said his daughter brightly.

'Seen it?' asked her parent laconically. 'Got it ticked off?'

'*Sure*,' said Miss Sadie happily. 'I've had a real grand time.'

'Wal, come on, then,' he said, 'and let's git back to London for dinner. I'm jes' one ragin' vac-u-um.'

She got up beside him, smiling brightly.

'I guess I won't miss the way back,' she said. 'We came pretty straight. Say, kid —' she slipped something into William's hand — 'buy yourself some candy.'

They were gone.

William stood in the middle of the road, watching the cloud of dust till it had vanished. Then he stared almost incredulously at the ten-shilling note he held.

He had decided on his course of action when he reached home.

Mrs Brown had recovered slightly, but she was still curious and suspicious.

'I felt she might become violent any minute and murder us all,' she said. 'William, who was she, and why on earth did you bring her here?'

'I dunno who she was 'cept that she said she was called Miss Burford, an' I din' bring her. She jus' said she wanted to come.'

'But why?'

'You heard her talkin'. She jus' kep' goin' on like that. She jus' said she wanted to come to our house. That's all I c'n tell you. You heard her talking. She jus' told me that her name was Miss—'

'But where did you *find* her?'

116

'In a motor-car. Cryin'. She told me she was called Miss Burford.'

'Do stop saying that. What else did she say? What made her come with you?'

'I've told you. She said her name was Miss— All right, I won't say it. But I keep telling you what happened. She said that an' we walked about a bit an' she said she wanted to come to our house. I din' want her to. I din' ask her to. I din' think you'd like it. But she asked to come an' I couldn't stop her. I did all I could. I took her a longer way round. I simply don't know anything about her 'cept that she said her name was Miss Burford, an',' virtuously, 'I think I'd better go an' do my homework, cause I want to get on an' get good marks, an' – an' not waste your money, an' all that.'

The startling nature of this last announcement deprived Mrs Brown of the power of speech. William retreated to the morning-room and sat down at the table with a book. After a few minutes he opened the door cautiously. He could hear his mother talking to his sister.

'It was the *saddest* thing,' she was saying. 'I've no idea how William got hold of her or where she is now. She was quite young, but *absolutely mad – raving*. I wanted to ask William more about it, but he's doing his homework and I don't like to disturb him.'

William closed the door again silently, opened the morning-room window, lightly vaulted into the garden and sauntered down to the gate. There he found Ginger, Douglas and Henry. He took his ten-shilling note out of his pocket and held it up.

Ginger, Douglas and Henry turned head-over-heels in the road with delight.

William climbed to the top rung of the gate and looked down at them.

'Fr'en's, Rome and countrymen,' he began; then proudly and self-consciously through his nose, 'Say, kids, you're sure plumb crazy!'

When Miss Burford returned home, she gave a little lecture on her English travels.

She told of her visit to Anne Hathaway's cottage, whose present occupant was very old and suffering from senile decay.

She told how in the same town she met four boys, one a descendant of Shakespeare, another a descendant of Scott, another a descendant of the poet Wordsworth, and the fourth a descendant of Nelson. It was wonderful, wasn't it? Her lecture was a great success.

That Christmas one Christmas card was sent to William that never reached him. It was sent from America, and it was addressed to 'Master William Shakespeare Brown, Stratford-on-Avon, England'.

CHAPTER 6

THE MIDNIGHT ADVENTURE OF MISS MONTAGU

WILLIAM was relieved to hear that his family was not going away for August. William disliked holidays spent away from home. He was not one of those people whose nerves require a frequent change of scene. William could never tire of his beloved familiar woods and fields and ponds, his Outlaw friends, his dog, and a whole long summer's day before him to do in exactly as he liked.

Holidays away from home involved tidy clothes, hands and face and hair in a perpetual and uncomfortable state of washedness and brushedness, monotonous outings with his family (whose ideas of pleasure were always a source of amazement and horror to William), politeness to people whom he never wished to see again, and unceasing admonitions from every member of his family not to 'disgrace' them. Any following of his natural inclinations in any direction at all appeared to 'disgrace' them.

But at home, besides the ordinary delights of a carefree holiday, strange things often happened in

August. The Vicar (whose quite justifiable dislike of William was returned with interest) was generally away, and a 'locum' reigned in his stead. There was always a sporting chance that the 'locum' might be better tempered than the Vicar, and the Vicarage garden held endless possibilities of delight as jungle or prairie or goldfield, as well as the thrill of a real live enemy in the shape of the Vicarage gardener, who shared his master's well-founded dislike of the Outlaws.

This August, however, the 'locum' was disappointing. He proved to be an elderly, peevish gentleman, who shuddered at the very sound of the human boy's voice. To be quite fair to him, less elderly, less peevish men had shuddered at the sound of William's voice. One glance at him told William all he wished to know about him, and he promptly relinquished any dreams of authorised hunting or gold-digging in the Vicarage garden that he may have cherished. After all, unauthorised hunting and gold-digging were really far more exciting — crawling in through the hole in the hedge, creeping along through the shrubs with Red Indian precaution and silence, and occasionally flying like another Adam from Eden before the rheumaticky avenging angel that was the Vicarage gardener.

On the whole, though friendship with the Vicarage had its advantages, William considered that enmity with the Vicarage was a far, far better and more exciting thing. It was not for nothing that William and his friends called themselves the Outlaws.

But just after William had discovered that the 'locum' possessed none of the attributes that would have endeared him to the Outlaws, he made another discovery. He discovered that Mrs Frame, who lived next door, was going away, and had let her house for August. All William could discover was that the lettee was of the female sex. That told him little. His experience had taught him that while women can be much nicer than men, they can, on the other hand, be much more objectionable. On the whole, he would rather have had a man. You know more where you are with men . . .

Henry and Douglas had been reluctantly dragged to the seaside in the wake of families on pleasure bent. Only Ginger was at home. And Ginger, as untidy and tousled and unwashed as William himself, was, in William's eyes, the ideal companion.

They had raced and rambled and scrambled and wrestled and climbed trees and trespassed to their heart's content. Their internal mechanism, though fortified through the morning by a heavy diet of unripe wild crab apples, unripe hazel nuts, green blackberries and grass (which they chewed meditatively between their more violent pursuits) told them that the luncheon hour was approaching. Still munching merrily and humming discordantly, they approached William's house. They crept furtively round the back of it behind the shrubberies.

William did not know what he looked like, but he took for granted that his appearance was such as to provoke exclamations of horror and disgust from his family. He was right. His wiry hair stood up as usual in a thick jungle in the midst of which, at a crooked angle, nestled his cap. They had spent part of the morning damming a stream in the meadow with mud (which they also used as ammunition against each other during any divergence of opinion), and William's face and collar bore plentiful traces of that material. He had rubbed one eye with a mud-covered hand, and that eye was muddier than all the rest, which is saying a good deal. His collar and tie were at the angle they usually attained after a morning of William's normal activities.

William was just going into the potting-shed where he and Ginger were keeping a tin of beetles, when Ginger, who was peering through a hole in the fence, said in a sharp whisper: 'I say – I say – she's *come*!'

William joined him, putting his eye to the hole.

He saw in Mrs Frame's garden a tall woman who was not Mrs Frame. She sat in a chair reading. William could not see much of her face because it was hidden by the book, so he hoisted himself up and sat on the fence looking down at her. She looked up. He saw a face that did not reassure him – middle-aged and distinctly fierce. She saw – what we have described. It is only fair to her to say that what she saw did not reassure her either. But William, to do him justice, always made an attempt to establish friendly relationships.

'Hello,' he said. 'I live here. Next door.'

She looked at him as though she could not believe her eyes, as though he were surely part of a nightmare and must vanish if she looked at him long enough. But no, he stayed there. He was real. This dreadful apparition was real and said it lived next door. Horror and disgust settled upon her face.

'You impertinent little boy!' she said. 'Go away! Get down!'

William considered this command in silence for a minute. He was a stern lover of justice.

'I'm not *in* your garden,' he said judicially, 'an' I s'pose we join at this fence. You've got half an' we've got half. Well, I'm sittin' on *our* half. I wun't mind you sittin' on your half an' I don't see why—'

'*Get* – DOWN!'

William got down.

'Did you hear that?' he said to Ginger. 'Did you hear her carryin' on? Won't let me even sit on jus' our

123

bit of the fence. Thinks it's all hers. 'F I knew a policeman I'd jus' go and *ask* him about it. I bet you could get put in prison for doin' that, for not lettin' people sit on their own bits of a fence. Look at cats – cats sit on fences. Is she goin' to stop all the cats in the world sittin' on fences? You'd think from the way she went on that no one was *allowed* to sit on fences. Well, I'd jus' like to know what fences is *for* if folks can't sit on 'em——'

At this point William's mother saw him from the morning-room window.

'*William!*' she screamed in horror. 'Come in at *once* and wash your hands and face and brush your hair.'

William gave a sigh expressive of philosophic resignation, yelled, 'G'd-bye' to Ginger, who, at the maternal scream, had already begun to make his guilty way out of William's garden, and went indoors.

'I see Mrs Frame's tenant is here,' said Mrs Brown at lunch. 'She's a Miss Montagu. I must call.'

'I wun't if I was you,' said William.

'Whyever not?' said his mother.

'Well, if she treats you like what she treats me——' He ended with a dark look and attacked his rice pudding with vigour.

That evening came a letter from the new tenant complaining that the noise by William and Ginger in the garden had completely (underlined) spoilt her afternoon's rest which was most (underlined) important to her health. The next morning came a letter saying that William's singing in his bedroom in the early (underlined) morning was not only audible to her, but had given her a headache (underlined) from which it would probably be many days before she recovered. In the evening came another note to demand that William should not be allowed to look over the fence at her, as the sudden appearance of the boy's head had a most disastrous (underlined) effect upon her nerves. She added that if these persecutions (underlined) continued she would be obliged to consult her legal adviser.

William spent the next day with Ginger roaming far afield in search of adventure. But a note arrived in the evening to say that the boy's whistling as he passed her house on the main road was so penetrating (underlined) that she had been obliged to shut all (underlined) the windows on the front of the house, and her health had suffered considerably (underlined), as fresh air was essential (underlined) to it.

William's father divided his wrath impartially between the absent Miss Montagu and the present William. The present William came off the worst.

The auction sale was William's idea. He had attended an auction sale with his uncle the week before, and his uncle had purchased a 'lot' which included two small pictures of so hideous execution and design that he had generously presented them to William. William, who had been thrilled and surprised by the proceedings of an auction sale, decided to dispose of his two pictures by auction, and invited a select band of potential bidders to his garden.

'We won't make a *noise*,' said William to his mother when she remonstrated. 'We won't *disturb* her. We'll do it all in whispers.'

Mrs Brown went indoors hoping for the best. Mrs Brown spent most of her time hoping for the best. From her William had inherited some of his glorious optimism.

The potential bidders arrived. They were not representative of William's friends. Most of William's friends were away for August. These were merely a heterogeneous collection of such of his schoolfellows as he could muster. Most of them would in normal times have been beneath his notice on the score of extreme youth.

They sat down on the grass in William's back garden and stared around them suspiciously and critically. William stood behind the upturned wheelbarrow on which were the two pictures and held a gardening fork to represent the hammer. Ginger stood next to him. William held up one of the pictures. It was about ten inches square and represented a female with incredibly long hair and incredibly flowing robes, chained to a stake on a lonely seashore. She was simpering coyly at the spectators out of her ornate frame. It was called 'The Martyr'.

'Ladies an' gentlemen,' began William, 'first of all, we're goin' to sell this picture.'

'Whaffor?' said a very small person of the female sex, who was sitting on the grass in front. William turned on her a glance that should have annihilated her utterly.

'What do you mean — whaffor?' he said contemptuously. 'Why shun't we sell a picture?'

'Why should you?' said the small female, quite unannihilated.

William felt nonplussed. No one at the auction sale he had attended with his uncle had behaved like this. He didn't quite know how to deal with it. He decided to take the line of the high hand.

'We shall sell,' he said loftily, ''xactly what we like. We shall sell — camels 'f we want to.'

Camels was an inspiration. He felt that camels was rather good. He prepared to go on with the sale.

'Ladies an' gentlemen—' he began again, but the small female, who had been deeply considering his last remark, burst forth again.

'Camels!' she said. 'Whaffor d'you want to sell camels?'

'First of all,' went on William, 'we're goin' to sell this picture. First of all, ladies an' gentlemen, take a good look at this picture.'

'Who wants to *buy* camels?' said the small female passionately. 'What's the good of *sellin'* 'em?'

'Jus' look at this picture,' went on William. 'It's prob'ly a picture you'll never see again – you'll never again have a chance of buying a beautiful picture like this cheap.'

'Anyway,' said the small female, looking round the garden with the air of one delivering a crushing argument, 'where *are* your camels? Why don't you bring out your camels and start *sellin'* 'em, 'stead of *talkin'* about 'em?'

'Kin'ly stop int'ruptin',' said William, glaring at her sternly, 'we've not come here to listen to *you*. We've come here to sell these things – Ladies an' gentlemen, this picture is one of the most beautiful pictures in the world. If you'll jus' look at it for a few minutes.'

A very small boy in the front suddenly burst into tears.

'Boo-hoo!' he sobbed. 'Wanter buy a camel!'

The small female encircled him with tiny motherly arms and turned an indignant glance upon William.

'*Now* look what you've done, you nasty, cruel boy,' she said. 'You've made him cry. Well, where *are* your camels you keep talking about?'

The goaded William turned on her.

'I don't keep talking about 'em,' he said. 'I never said I had any camels.'

The small female opened eyes and mouth in horror.

'*Oh!*' she gasped. 'You *did*. Oh, you story-teller!'

The small boy's wails increased in volume.

'Want a camel,' he yelled as the tears ran down his cheeks.

'You jus' don' know how to *act* at auction sales,' stormed William indignantly. 'I'm tryin' to sell pictures an' here you keep carryin' on about camels.'

At this point the proceedings were interrupted by the arrival of Mrs Brown.

She looked pale and harassed and carried a note in her hand.

'Oh, William,' she said, 'how *could* you? She's written again. She says that the noise is ear-splitting and that her nerves can't stand it. She says —' she turned the note over helplessly — 'she says a lot of things all underlined and, oh, William, you did promise to be quiet.'

'I *was* bein' quiet,' said William, 'then they all started talkin' about camels, an' I can't stop 'em makin' a noise.'

William and Ginger sat disconsolately on the still upturned wheelbarrow. The spectators of the auction sale had indignantly departed, the small boy still wailing pitifully, and William and Ginger conversed in whispers.

'We'll have to have another some time,' whispered William. 'That one din' go right somehow. We'll have to have another an' jus' not *lettem* get talking about camels an' things.'

'What'll we do *now*?' said Ginger, looking down with distaste upon the two pictures that shared the wheelbarrow with them.

'Somethin' *quiet*,' groaned William. 'Let's play ball.'

William fetched a ball and threw it to Ginger. Ginger caught it and threw it to William.

William missed it and it went over the fence into Miss Montagu's garden.

William fetched another ball, and threw it to Ginger.

Ginger missed it and it went over the fence into Miss Montagu's garden.

Ginger went home and got his ball. He threw it to William. They threw it to each other and caught it for ten or eleven times.

Then it went over the fence into Miss Montagu's garden.

William fetched his bow and arrows. The fence by Miss Montagu's garden was the only place to fix the target. Every other side of the garden consisted of flower beds.

They shot busily at the target for ten minutes.

At the end of the ten minutes all their arrows were in Miss Montagu's garden.

'Well,' whispered Ginger gloomily, 'what we goin' to do *now*?'

William with all his faults never lacked courage.

He hoisted himself upon the fence cautiously to survey the enemy's ground. He was somewhat taken aback to meet the stern gaze of the enemy in person. But even so he was not routed. He met her gaze unflinchingly.

'There's a few of our balls an' things,' he said boldly, 'come over into your garden. Can I come and gettem, please?'

'No, you may *not*, you naughty little boy,' said the enemy furiously. 'I have collected them and I will keep them. Get *down*.'

William deliberately drew his features into a horrible contortion, and then descended from his perch. He had been slightly gratified and cheered by the shudder of horror that passed over the face of his enemy at his grimace. It is almost impossible to describe the gargoylelike masks into which William could twist his countenance.

'Well, what we goin' to do *now*?' whispered Ginger forlornly.

William looked around.

At their feet stood his beloved mongrel, Jumble. Jumble had joined in all his master's late pastimes of dam-building and mud-slinging. The plight of Jumble's coat was indescribable.

'Let's wash Jumble,' said William, making a grab at the unfortunate animal before the fatal word 'wash' could send him off like an arrow from a bow. He took off Jumble's collar and hung it carelessly over the fence.

Half-an-hour later one fairly dry dog and two fairly damp boys emerged from the wash-shed and made their way over to the fence.

There they stood and looked around in dismay.

'Where is it?' said William.

'You put it jus' there,' said Ginger.

They searched the ground at the foot of the fence. It was nowhere to be seen. William again hoisted himself on to the fence and looked down. Again he found himself gazing into the face of his enemy. His enemy held Jumble's collar in her hand.

''Scuse me,' said William severely, 'that's mine. I mean it's Jumble's.'

'I found it in my garden,' snapped his enemy.

'It must have fell down, then,' said William.

'I shall confiscate *everything* of yours I find in my garden,' said the enemy sternly.

She walked indoors. William sat motionless upon his fence. Through the window he could see her enter her dining-room and place Jumble's collar in a cupboard.

He descended from the fence. Upon his freckled frowning face was a set look of purpose.

It was midnight. William, wearing an overcoat and a black mask, climbed cautiously over the fence and crept up Miss Montagu's garden to Miss Montagu's dining-room window. In one pocket of his overcoat was his penknife, in the other a handsome pistol which had cost originally one shilling and sixpence, and which figured in most of the Outlaws' adventures.

When he reached the dining-room window he took his penknife out of his pocket and began to attack the catch. His black mask kept slipping over his eyes, so he took it off and put it in his pocket. Miss Montagu's dining-room window was exactly like his own dining-room window, and William, in his character of robber chief, had often slipped back the catch of that with his penknife. It was in any case a catch which an infant burglar could have manipulated in his sleep. William opened the window and entered Miss Montagu's dining-room. Here he donned his black mask. William, though sternly bent on what he looked upon as an errand of justice, was none the less thoroughly enjoying himself in his role. He opened the cupboard, and his eye beneath the black mask gleamed. There they were – his two balls, Ginger's ball, all his arrows, Jumble's collar. With a little snort of triumph he put them all into his overcoat pocket.

Then a sound at the door made him turn, and his heart seemed to leap up to the top of his head and then down to the bottom of his boots. Miss Montagu stood in the doorway clutching a pink dressing-gown about her. William looked round wildly for escape. There was none. The only alternative to flight was courage. He had recourse to that. He whipped his one-and-sixpenny pistol out of his pocket.

'Hands up,' he croaked in a deep bass voice. 'Hands up or I fire.'

It was a very dark night. All Miss Montagu could see was a vague form behind what was most certainly some sort of a revolver. She put up her hands.

'I – I'm unarmed,' she said with chattering teeth. 'I'm a p-p-poor defenceless woman – think of your wife – think of your s-s-sister – think of your m-m-mother – d-don't, I beg of you, d-do anything rash.'

'Sit down,' ordered William in his raucous bass.

She sat down.

'D-do be c-careful,' she pleaded. 'You know sometimes j-just an involunt-voluntary movement makes them g-go off. I haven't anything really v-valuable, I assure you. I – oh, d-*do* be c-*careful*,' she screamed as

William made a movement with his pistol.

William was backing past her slowly to the open window. At last he reached it. To his trembling victim on the chair who still held up her hands rather in the attitude of a lap dog in the act of begging, it seemed as if he vanished suddenly and completely into the night.

She made her way unsteadily to the window and peered out into the darkness. There was no sign of him.

The danger was over. It was obviously time for her to faint or have hysterics. But there is something unsatisfactory in fainting or having hysterics without an audience. She rang the bell violently. She screamed 'Fire! Murder!' at the top of her voice. Her domestics in various stages of undress gathered round her. Then, most effectively and dramatically and carefully, she fainted on to the hearth-rug.

Meanwhile William, in his bedroom in black mask and pyjamas, was dancing a war dance round three balls, a heap of arrows, and a dog collar.

William was down in good time the next morning, but he found his next-door neighbour already in the dining-room. She was hatless, and looked disturbed but important.

'Did you hear nothing?' she was saying excitedly to Mrs Brown – who was smiling quite pleasantly in her relief that the visit had not the usual purpose of complaining of William. 'My house has been ran-sacked – *ransacked* from top to bottom. And when I disturbed him – well, I believe there were two or three of them, yes I'm quite sure there were at least two of them – great *big* men, my dear Mrs Brown, both wearing masks – they covered me with revolvers.'

She became dramatic, and William looked on with great interest.

He saw Miss Montagu cover Mrs Brown with an imaginary revolver. Mrs Brown edged behind the sofa.

'They threatened me with instant death if I moved hand or foot,' continued Miss Montagu. She advanced threateningly upon Mrs Brown, the imaginary revolver in her hand. Mrs Brown sat down, shut her eyes, and gave a little scream. 'It was a most terrible experience, I assure you. I've been fainting on and off ever since.'

She sat down in Mrs Brown's easy chair, evidently with every intention of fainting on and off again. Ellen, the housemaid, was just bringing in the coffee. Mrs Brown flew to meet her, poured out a strong cup and flew back to Miss Montagu, who was wondering whether after all hysterics wouldn't be more effective. Ellen, startled out of her professional calm, said: 'What's 'appened?' and William watched the scene with his most inscrutable expression. Mrs Brown, in her panic, spilt half the hot coffee over Miss Montagu,

WILLIAM LOOKED ON WITH GREAT INTEREST. MISS
MONTAGU, HOLDING AN IMAGINARY REVOLVER,
ADVANCED THREATENINGLY ON MRS BROWN, AND MRS
BROWN EDGED BEHIND THE SOFA.

and Miss Montagu decided not to have hysterics after all, in case Mrs Brown, who was obviously losing her head, should use the rest of the hot coffee in an attempt to bring her round.

Then William's father entered. He greeted Miss Montagu curtly. Mr Brown, though a well-meaning man, wasn't at his best before breakfast.

'Well,' he said with one eye sternly fixed on William and the other apprehensively fixed on his visitor, 'what's he been doing now?'

'Oh, John, dear,' said Mrs Brown, 'it's burglars. Miss Montagu's had burglars in the night.'

'*Three* of them,' said Miss Montagu, with a sob. The thought of all she had endured, together with the shock of the hot coffee that Mrs Brown had spilt over her, was almost more than she could bear. '*Three* great *giants* of men. They've *ransacked* the place – they've stolen all my jewellery. They – they covered me with revolvers and threatened to take my life. They—'

'Have you told the police?' said Mr Brown, his eye wandering wistfully to the dish cover beneath which reposed his eggs and bacon.

'Yes, they're coming round to interview me. I'm completely unstrung by it. I can't tell you the state I've been in. If I've fainted once I've fainted a dozen times. Oh, there's the Vicar's "locum" passing the gate – *do* fetch him in, Mr Brown. I do so need spiritual solace after all I've been through.'

Mr Brown, wearing a hang-dog air, went out to intercept the Vicar's 'locum'. The Vicar's 'locum', wearing a still more hang-dog air, followed him up the drive and into the room.

'It's Miss Montagu,' explained Mr Brown shortly; 'she's had burglars. She's – she's rather upset.'

'I'm *unstrung*,' said Miss Montagu, wringing her hands and visibly cheered by her increasing audience. 'A gang of masked men. I resisted them and they shot. They missed me, but such was the shock to my nerves that I fainted, and when I returned to consciousness they were gone, but the place was *ransacked*—'

'Here's a policeman,' said Mr Brown cheerfully, 'just going into your house. Hadn't you better go and interview him?'

'Oh, fetch him in here, dear Mr Brown. I feel too much upset to *move*.'

Muttering something inaudible beneath his breath and with a long agonised look at the coffee pot and bacon dish, Mr Brown went out to intercept the policeman.

The policeman entered jauntily, taking his notebook out of his pocket. The Vicar's 'locum' seized the opportunity to slink away.

'It's *burglars*,' hissed Miss Montagu, with such

violence that the policeman started and dropped his note-book. 'My house was entered last night and I was attacked by a gang of men – *masked*.'

The policeman licked his pencil and turned his eye upon Miss Montagu.

'Was you roused by the noise, Miss?'

'Yes,' said Miss Montagu eagerly, 'I went down to confront them, and there I found five or six—'

'Five *or* six?' asked the policeman magisterially.

'Six,' said Miss Montagu after a moment's hesitation.

'Six,' repeated the policeman, licking his pencil again and beginning to write in his note-book. 'Six.' He wrote it down with great deliberation, and then said a third time: 'Six.'

'I confronted them,' went on Miss Montagu, 'but they gagged me and bound me to a chair.'

Mr Brown, unable to control any longer the pangs of hunger, had sat down at the table, and with a fine disregard of everyone else in the room, was attacking a large helping of bacon and eggs.

'A *chair*, did you say, Miss?' said the policeman brightening, as though they had arrived at last at the most important part of the evidence.

'Yes, a chair, of course,' said Miss Montagu impatiently. 'They gagged me and bound me to it and then I fainted. When I recovered consciousness

I was alone. The house was *ransacked*. My jewellery was gone—'

'Ransacked—' murmured the policeman, writing hard and moistening his pencil every other second. It seemed to be the sort of pencil that only acts when used in constant conjunction with human saliva. 'Ransacked – jewellery—'

He closed his book and assumed his pontifical air.

'You've left heverything,' he said, 'I 'ope, as they left it.'

Miss Montagu considered this question for a minute in silence. Then she spoke in the tone of voice of one who has been soaring in the clouds and suddenly fallen to earth with a bump.

'Oh, no,' she said in a flat tone of voice. 'Oh, no – I – I tidied up after them.'

Mr Brown, who had reached the marmalade stage and was feelish uppish, said: 'A great mistake,' and was at once crushed by a glance from the eye of the law.

'What exactly is missing, Miss?' then said the law pompously.

Miss Montagu spoke in the same voice. 'I – I can't be *quite* sure,' she said.

The policeman put his note-book into his pocket and squared himself as if for a fight.

'I'd better come and visit the scene of the crime with

you now, at once, Miss, and collect what evidence I can,' he said.

'I'll come with you,' said Mrs Brown compassionately to Miss Montagu. 'I'm sure you aren't fit to go alone.'

'Thank you so much,' said Miss Montagu. 'I feel that I might faint again any minute.'

Led by the policeman and supported by Mrs Brown, she made her way slowly to her own domain.

William's father snorted contemptuously and poured out another cup of coffee.

Over William's inscrutable countenance there flickered just for one moment a smile . . .

Miss Montagu was resting in her deck-chair in the garden. She had had a tiring day. She had had a constant stream of visitors who came ostensibly to inquire after her health, but really to elicit the whole thrilling story of the burglary. She felt exhausted, but she had the satisfaction of knowing that nothing was being talked about in the village but her burglary.

Suddenly she looked up. That wretched boy was sitting, actually *sitting*, on her fence, after all she'd said to him. In his arms he held a nondescript dog that looked as if it had numbered among its ancestors a sheep and a cat and a monkey. She was just going to order him to descend at once and go in to write to his father again when something attracted her attention.

The dog was wearing a collar. And the boy was looking at her in a meaning sort of way — a very meaning sort of way. Then, still looking at her, he took from one pocket a handful of arrows and threw them carelessly down into his garden. Then from the other pocket he took three balls and began carelessly to play with them. The words she had meant to say did not come. Instead she said faintly:

'W-where did you get those?'

The boy's look became still more meaning.

'From your house,' he said, still carelessly playing with his ball, 'last night. Don' you remember? I was wearin' a mask an' you was wearin' a pink dressing-gown an' you said you was a poor defenceless woman. And you told me to think of my wife an' not do anything rash. Don' you remember?'

Then, apparently losing all further interest in the subject, he returned to playing with his ball.

There was a long, long silence — the longest silence Miss Montagu ever remembered in all her life. She blinked and went rather pale. Then, after what seemed to her several hours, she spoke. She said in a small, faraway voice:

'They — they'll never believe you.'

'Oh,' said William casually. 'I'm not goin' to tell 'em if — I mean, there's really no reason why I should tell 'em.'

'HOW CAN YOU TELL SUCH AN UNTRUTH ABOUT LAST
NIGHT?' DEMANDED MISS MONTAGU.

WILLIAM STOPPED WHISTLING AND LOOKED AT HER.

There was another long silence – longer even than the first. But during it Miss Montagu's brain worked quite quickly. She understood what William's 'if' had meant. She looked up at that horrid, freckled, untidy-headed boy who was whistling so unconcernedly upon her fence and said sternly:

'How *can* you tell such an untruth about last night?'

William stopped whistling for a minute and looked at her.

'I hope you won't tell such a silly untruth to *anyone* else,' she said severely. 'If you don't — I mean,' with a slight display of embarrassment, 'I mean — I mean I was going to tell you that my nerves have quite recovered now and that no noise from your garden will disturb me. Also if your arrows or things come over here you may come over to fetch them.'

Then, with great dignity, she got up and swept into the house.

William watched her retreat with apparent unconcern.

CHAPTER 7

THE MYSTERIOUS STRANGER

IT was William's Uncle Frederick who was responsible for the whole thing.

He gave William a book called 'Hunted by the Reds'. A spell of wet weather was also partly responsible.

The Outlaws met in the old barn while the rain came down in torrents on and through the roof, and, having nothing else to do, read the story aloud in turns. Though the reading was frequently interrupted by criticism of each member's reading by the rest (resulting occasionally in physical conflict), and by long, heart-searching discussions as to the conventional pronunciation of such words as 'catastrophe', the interest of the story was proof against all interruption. It gripped. It did more than grip. It thrilled.

At first the Outlaws had taken for granted that the Reds must mean Red Indians. But they did not. They meant the Reds of Russia, modern Reds, the dreaded Bolshies.

The villain of the story was one Dmitrich (which

the Outlaws pronounced 'Dimtritch'), chief of the Reds. He murdered everyone he met on principle. He flung bombs about as carelessly as other men fling used matches. Finally, he captured a princess of the Whites and kept her a prisoner in his castle, trying to extort from her by cruel threats the secrets of the Whites. In the last chapter she was rescued from the villain by her faithful lover, Paulovitch.

The descriptions of Dmitritch were intriguing. He was cross-eyed and had a crooked nose. He was a most satisfactory villain in every way. Most of his remarks were prefaced by oaths represented on the printed page by blanks and dashes. This rather annoyed Ginger.

'Why can't they print wot he ackshully says?' he asked indignantly. 'It'd be much more int'restin'.'

'They daren't,' said Douglas in an awed whisper, 'they daren't print the ackshull words. They're too bad for print.'

'What sort of words, though?' persisted Ginger. 'That's all I want to know. It's not fair putting blanks. I bet they don't know themselves.'

'They do,' said William with an air of an oracle. ''Course they know. It's bad words — words like "Damn" an' "Hell" an' – an' – an' "Hell" an' "Damn". Bad words like that – "Hell" an' "Damn".'

'Well, that's only two,' said Ginger, still

dissatisfied. 'There's one – two – three – four blanks in what he says here. He says – one, two, three, four blanks an' then "Ho, would you, then? Curse you for a fool," an' then two more blanks. Well, that mus' be more than jus' "Hell" an' "Damn". There's six blanks in what he says there.'

William was slow to own himself in the wrong.

'Well, those are the only two bad words there are. I know they are. He'd say 'em over an' over again, of course. Like this: "Damn Hell, Damn Hell. Ho, there, what would you? Curse you for a fool. Hell, Damn." Like that. Over an' over again. "Damn Hell, Hell Damn".' William seemed to derive a certain pleasure from the repetition.

'I don't think you ought to keep on saying 'em like that, William,' said Douglas piously.

'Well, I like that,' said William indignantly. 'I don't want to say 'em, but I have to, to explain about 'em prop'ly. Ginger was saying there mus' be more'n two bad words an' I was only explainin' to him that there is only two bad words, but you use 'em over an' over again.'

'I think there is more'n two bad words,' said Henry slowly and thoughtfully. 'What about "By Jove!"'

'That's not bad,' said William.

'Well, what about "Darn!"' said Ginger.

William seemed to regard 'Darn' judicially.

'Yes, that's bad,' he said at last, as though 'Darn' had just passed some severe test. 'Darn's bad all right. Well, he'd just put that in somewhere, too.'

'Anyway, he might have been a norful-looking man,' said Ginger, 'whether he said two bad words or three or only blanks. He must have been a norful-looking man. Just fancy – cross-eyed an' a crooked nose. An' jus' think of all the orful things he did – murderin' people an' chuckin' bombs about an' – an' savin' those bad words all over the place an' carrying off the princess. I know what I'd've done to him if I'd met him.'

'What?' said William.

'I'd've killed him,' said Ginger boldly. 'I'd've gone up to him an' stuck a knife into him.'

'Would you?' jeered William. 'I guess he'd be too quick for you. He'd see you comin' an' throw a bomb or somethin' at you. He'd jus' say, "Darn damn hell" to you an'—'

'William,' protested Douglas patiently, 'you've gotter *stop* sayin' those words.'

'Well, he said them, din' he?' said William aggressively. 'If I'm sayin' what he'd've said I've gotter say the sort of words he did.'

'You needn't say 'em. You can say "Blank," can't you?'

'All right,' said William obligingly, 'I don' mind

doin' that. Well, then, he'd simply look at you with his cross-eyes an' say, "Blank, blank, blank, blank. Curse you for a fool. Blank, blank," and shoot you or bomb you, or cut your head off before you've got a chance to move. You talkin' about killin' him – a clever man like him— *You!*'

Ginger was annoyed.

'You talk,' he said indignantly, ' 's if I'd say I'd go up to him with a knife in my hand so's he'd know I was going to do it. I wouldn't, either.'

'Where'd you put it, then?'

'In my pocket.'

'Huh! You can't get any size of a knife that'd kill him *into* your pocket.'

'Maybe I wun't kill him with a knife at all,' said Ginger, shifting his ground. 'I daresday I wun't, after all. I'd pretend to take him a walk, an' when I got him into the middle of a bridge I'd push him into the water.'

'An' he'd swim out,' said William, with contempt.

'All right,' said Ginger huffily, 'kill him yourself.'

'I'd poison him,' said William. 'I'd get some deathly poison an' put it in his tea.'

'How d'you know he drinks tea?' said Ginger contemptuously. 'I should think he's the sort of man who drinks beer more'n tea.'

'Oh, do shut up about him,' said Henry. 'I've jus'

about had enough of him, anyway. I say, it's stopped rainin' an' it's dinner time. Let's go home.'

It was on their way home that they met him — unmistakably cross-eyed and broken-nosed.

They stopped still in amazement to stare at him.

'Dimtritch!' they gasped together.

He looked at them furtively as he passed.

'That's him — that's — that's simply him,' gasped Ginger. 'Abs'lutely straight out of the book!'

'Out of the book!' repeated William scornfully. 'Huh! That book's not a book. I mean it's true. It mus' be. I guess someone jus' wrote it to put people on their guard against him 'cause—'

''Cause they daren't do it 'cept in a book, 'cause they're afraid of him, an' his bombs,' supplied Ginger eagerly.

'I was goin' to say that,' said William coldly. 'You keep on int'ruptin'.'

'I b'lieve I can see a bomb in his pocket,' said Henry. 'Look, it's all bulging out — at that side. It looks to me 'xactly like a bomb.'

'You ever seen a bomb?' said William.

'I may've done,' said Henry. 'I may quite possibly have done. Anyway, it looked to me like a bomb. That's all I say. I can only say how it looks to me. I don't know how bombs look to other folks.'

The figure was already disappearing round the

bend in the road. The Outlaws hurried after it.

'Hope his bomb doesn't go off suddenly,' said Henry, who was keeping in the rear. 'Looks to me rather's if it would.'

'Well, it'd kill him first, wun't it?' said William.

'I don' know. He might turn round an' throw it back at us sudden.'

'He doesn't know we're here.'

'Oh, doesn't he! He knows everything. D'you remember when he led that other man – what d'you call him, Paulovitch – on an' on, thinkin' that he was followin', an' that Dimtritch din' know he was there, an' suddenly Dimtritch turned an' stabbed him an' left him for dead. D'you remember?'

The Outlaws perceptibly slackened pace.

'He's goin' in at Mr Jones's gate.'

'He's goin' to kill Mr Jones, p'raps.'

'Don' be silly. Mr Jones's gone away.'

'He mus' be the man who's taken Mr Jones's house while he's away.'

'What's he come to live here for, anyway?'

'Some plot, you bet – somebody he wants to bomb, or murder, or revenge, somehow.'

'I think he's got a princess imprisoned there in Mr Jones's house,' said Douglas, 'an' I think we ought to rescue her.'

'How?' said William.

'Well, we've gotter think of some plan for that,' said Douglas.

The discussion was resumed on the way to school the next afternoon.

'What we've gotter do,' said William, 'is to find out what he's doing here.'

'We don' even know what he's calling himself,' said Henry. 'He's sure to be calling himself something different from Dimtritch now.'

'How're we going to find that out?' asked Ginger.

'Once,' said Henry thoughtfully, 'I heard about a man who wanted to find out the name of a man who lived in a house and he went to the door and asked if Mr Brown lived there an' they said "No", and told him who did live there.'

'It's jus' half past two,' said William severely, 'an' we're goin' to be jolly late for school if we don't run jolly quick.'

So the Outlaws ran jolly quick.

It happened that they all came out of school at different times.

Henry's chemistry division was let out very early because something had gone wrong with the gas supply for the bunsen burners, and they popped in a most fascinating manner instead of lighting properly. The class would have preferred to stay and pop them, but old 'Stinks' sent them home.

'Of course he would,' said Henry bitterly, 'when there's anything int'resting to do, but on an ord'nary dull day when they light all right we've got to stay on till the end. That's *like* 'em.'

By ''em' he meant the mysterious and exasperating race of grown-ups who always seemed bent on ridding life of its glamour and romance. Fancy being able to pop a bunsen burner like that time after time indefinitely and not wanting to do it – more than that, wanting to stop other people doing it.

But Henry's dejection soon vanished, and he walked along briskly. Instead of going straight along the road he went in at Mr Jones's front gate, and with quickly beating heart went up to the front door and knocked. There was no answer. He knocked again. There was still no answer. He raised the knocker and beat a fierce rat-tat-tat upon the door.

'If nothing happens now I'll go away,' he said, almost hoping that nothing would happen.

But something did happen. The door opened very slightly and an old woman's face appeared round it. Henry was thrilled. She was wizened and lined and bent and sinister – just the sort of old woman one would guess would guard Dmitritch's house.

'Does Mr Brown live here?' he said boldly.

The old woman looked at him suspiciously.

'Eh?' she said.

'Does Mr Brown live here?' said Henry.

'Eh?' she said again.

Some of Henry's assurance departed.

'Does Mr Brown live here?' he said again rather nervously.

The old woman went away without a word. But she left the door open. Soon she returned with an ear-trumpet. She put this into her ear and, fixing a red, angry eye upon Henry, again said 'Eh?'

Henry was taken aback but undaunted. He knew how to deal with an ear-trumpet. His great-aunt had one.

'Does Mr Brown live here?' he yelled into it.

'No 'e doesn't,' she said, and slammed the door in his face.

Henry stared at the slammed door. He had just been going to ask who did live there when it was slammed in his face. He put up his hand and knocked again loudly.

Then suddenly overcome by panic at his daring he turned and fled down the drive. He hadn't succeeded, but, anyway, he'd tried. He'd have quite a lot to tell the others. He'd gone to the sinister door and seen the sinister old woman and caught a glimpse of the sinister dark interior with a sinister-looking hall table just visible in the sinister gloom. He'd be able to make quite a good tale of it.

The Mysterious Stranger

Ginger went home at the ordinary time – the close of afternoon school. He came home alone because both William and Douglas had been kept in by the French master and Henry had come home earlier. He made no effort to go straight home. With set, stern face he went to Mr Jones's house. The idea had come to him while putting on his coat and hat.

He walked boldly up to the front door and knocked. He had knocked loudly and imperiously, and the old woman answered his knock after only a very short interval. She opened the door a few inches and glared out. Now the old lady was very shortsighted, and the Outlaws were, as the saying is, much of a size. She could see no difference in them. Here was, in her eyes, the same boy who had been there a few minutes ago.

'What do you want *now*?' she snapped.

'Does Mr Brown live here?' said Ginger very pleasantly.

'Eh?' said the old crone.

'Does Mr Brown live here?' said Ginger, with an ingratiating smile.

'Eh?' said the old crone again. Ginger's voice was failing with nervousness.

'Does—' he began hoarsely.

The old crone went away and returned with the ear-trumpet.

'Does Mr Brown live here?' Ginger whispered into it faintly.

The old woman bared her teeth with a snarl of fury.

'How many times d'you want me to tell you, you saucy little 'ound?' she said. ''E *don't* live here *an*' I've told you so once, you—'

But Ginger, terrified by the sound of her high-pitched, angry voice, and the sight of her toothless bared gums, turned to flee in headlong panic back to the safety of the main road. He did not stop till he reached the turning into the road where his home was. Then he stopped, looked back fearfully, and uttered the one word 'Crumbs!'

Douglas was kept in half an hour by the French master and William an hour. William was kept in half an hour longer than Douglas because his ignorance of French verbs was half-an-hour deeper than Douglas's ignorance of French verbs. Douglas made occasional spasmodic efforts to learn French verbs and William didn't.

Between William and the French masters was waged a perpetual feud. William often explained to both the senior and junior French masters that he didn't see what good French was to him, as he'd decided never to go to France, an' if any French people wanted to talk to him in England they could learn English. He didn't see why he should learn the languages of people he wasn't ever going to talk to. When he spoke thus to the junior French master, the junior French master reasoned with him. When he spoke thus to the senior French master, the senior French master smacked his head. Of the two methods of dealing with him, William understood and preferred the latter. It took less time and you knew where you were. He possessed a father and an elder brother, and was quite used to having his head smacked. It was an argument that appealed to him.

Anyway, this explains why Douglas set off alone half an hour after afternoon school had ended, leaving William still staring moodily at a French grammar, and absently making darts out of blotting-paper.

It was no sudden whim on Douglas's part to go to Mr Jones's house. Henry's words had suggested the idea to him as soon as they were uttered, and he had decided then to call at Mr Jones's house on his way home. He walked quite jauntily up the door and knocked. No one came. He knocked six times. Finally, someone breathing very hard opened the door and a wizened old face appeared round it. The breathing changed to a snort as her eyes fell on Douglas. That boy again! Blast him! That boy again!

'Does Mr Brown live here?' said Douglas.

She couldn't hear what he said. She hesitated a

minute, then went to get her ear-trumpet. It might be an important message, or anything.

'Does Mr Brown live here?' shrieked Douglas into the ear-trumpet.

He was surprised at what happened. The wizened old creature seemed to spring at him with a snarl of rage. Douglas, in whom the instinct of self-preservation was strong, was in headllong flight down to the gate before the old hag could recover her breath from her snarl. Then she screamed after him in quavering fury.

'You come askin' me that again, you saucy little 'ound, an' I'll half kill you.'

Douglas did not stop running till he reached his own front door. Then he wiped his brow, said 'Crikey!' to himself, and turned his mind to the invention of plausible-sounding excuses to account for his lateness for tea.

William was at last released from his detention, less because he had mastered the intricacies of his French verbs than because the French master wanted his tea. William had not meant to call at Mr Jones's house. The idea never occurred to him till he had left Mr Jones's house far behind and had almost reached his own home.

As he went along the road with his characteristic slouch, he was thinking about the mysterious stranger with the crooked nose and cross-eyes, and quite suddenly Henry's words occurred to him. He wheeled round and began wearily to traverse the distance between his house and Mr Jones's.

The thought of the tea he was deliberately sacrificing made him feel rather bitterly towards the French master. He consoled himself by the hope that, like his own family, the French master's family did not allow tea to be kept 'hanging round' (the phrase is William's mother's) after five o'clock. He walked in at Mr Jones's gateway with a firm step and knocked loudly at the front door. No one answered it.

William was feeling hot and irritable. He lifted the knocker and rapped it with all his might seven or eight times. He was in no mood to be trifled with. At last a very old woman came to the door. William glared at her.

'Does Mr Brown live here?' he said coldly and distinctly.

William had a very confused impression of what happened next. As far as he remembered afterwards, the old woman set upon him without the slightest warning and knocked him down the front steps.

From there he picked himself up and, throwing valour to the winds, fled down to the gate. Shrill cries from the aged lady behind informed him that she'd learn him to come plaguin' folks all afternoon with his saucy tricks, the saucy little hound, him! William was thrilled to learn thus unmistakably that Mr Jones's hitherto innocent abode was now a nest of criminals who set upon honest people at sight and tried to break their necks.

His mother was out when he reached home and there was no sign of tea. He went into the drawing-room, where Ethel, his grown-up sister, was writing a letter.

'Where's tea?' he demanded morosely.

'Tea's over,' said Ethel, without looking up from her letter. 'You shouldn't be so late.'

'How could I help it?' said William indignantly. 'One of the masters wanted me to stay behind after school to do something for him, an' I din' think it polite to say I wouldn't.'

'Well, I can't help it,' said Ethel absently; 'you'll have to wait till supper now.'

''Strordinary,' said William distinctly, 'how some folks can see other folks starvin' an' – an' – knocked about—'

A hasty movement brought his bruised side in contact with a table. His feelings demanded some outlet.

'Blank!' he said, after a moment's deep thought. 'Blank, blank, *blank!*'

'I found out *somethin'* about that house,' said William, mysteriously and complacently, as soon as he met the others the next morning.

The others, who had been also looking mysterious and complacent and proud, seemed taken aback.

'So did I,' said Ginger and Douglas and Henry, speaking simultaneously. Then they all stared at each other in amazed silence. Henry broke the amazed silence.

'I called there on my way home,' he said, 'to ask if Mr Brown lived there an'—'

'So did I on my way home,' broke in Douglas.

'An' me, too,' said Ginger.

William looked at them bitterly.

'Yes, an' I called last,' he said, 'an' got half-killed with all you going messin' about first. If you'd left it to me—'

But his bitterness was soon lost in interest. They discussed their impressions excitedly. They agreed that she was probably Dmitritch's mother and if possible more wicked than Dmitritch. They agreed that the couple were probably imprisoning a White princess and planning to bomb the whole village in the interests of Communism.

Just as they had agreed upon this, the villain himself was seen to be coming down the road.

Aware that he was probably in the habit of killing his victims on sight, they hid behind the hedge, but, overcome by curiosity, threw caution to the winds and looked over the top of the hedge as he passed. The object of their scrutiny was somewhat disconcerted as he passed down an apparently deserted lane to see four boys' heads suddenly pop up over the top of the hedge and gaze at him with mingled earnestness and hostility, turning slowly to watch him the more closely as he pursued his way. As soon as he had passed they came out of their imperfect hiding.

'Let's follow him again,' said William.

Douglas, who was ever cautious, suggested that it might not be safe, but his caution was overborne by the others. After a slight delay, caused by a scuffle between Douglas and William, who had used the opprobrious word 'coward', the Outlaws set off with elaborate secrecy to stalk their prey. They crept along in single file by the side of the road in the shadow of the hedge, crouching down as they walked.

Their progress would have arrested attention anywhere and at any distance, but the Outlaws fondly imagined that proceeding in this way they made themselves practically invisible to the naked eye.

Dmitritch, fortunately, did not turn round. He walked fairly briskly and had soon left the village behind and was out in the open country, followed ever by four crouching figures in single file. When he disappeared into a wood, the four figures held a hasty consultation.

'What we goin' to do?' asked Ginger in a penetrating whisper.

'You said you'd kill him with a knife, din' you?' said William unkindly. 'Well, s'pose you go an' do it — go on an' kill him with a knife. You said you could.'

'I haven't got a knife with me,' said Ginger coldly, 'else I would.'

'Well, then you said you'd take him to the middle of a bridge an' push him in. Well, there's a bridge when he gets out of the wood. S'pose you do it now. We'll watch. You go an' take him to the middle of the bridge an' then push him in like what you said you would.'

'An' what about you?' said Ginger. 'Din' you say you'd poison him — put poison in his tea? Well go on. S'pose you go an' do it.'

'How can I put poison in his tea *now*?' said William irritably. '*Now* when he's out walkin'? Why don' you talk *sense*!'

'You can't, anyway,' said Ginger sternly. 'You don't know what *is* poison or where you *get* it or where his tea is or anythin'. You couldn't poison his tea if you tried.'

'I could poison his tea's much as you could push him off a bridge,' said William heatedly.

'How d'you know?' said Ginger. 'I've not tried pushin' him off a bridge yet.'

'An' I've not tried poisonin' him,' retorted William.

Henry interposed before the argument could develop further on these lines.

'Well, we're lettin' him go now,' he said; 'we oughter hurry up to catch him before he gets away, an' we oughter find out what he's come out to do.'

'I bet he's come out to – to make bombs or somethin',' said Douglas vaguely, 'but I don' think it's *safe*.'

'Oh, shut up about it being safe,' said William irritably. 'I think he's come out to meet other people in the plot. You know, com – communals an' people like that.'

'Well, let's go on,' said Henry, 'or we'll be losin' him.'

But, fortunately, Dmitritch had taken a rest on a fallen tree trunk and had only just resumed his walk when they entered the wood. They followed him through the wood in a silence broken only by Henry's whispered 'I believe I can see a bomb in his pocket,' and William's sibilant 'Sh!'

William was beginning to suspect that he was not that morning justifying his position as leader of the Outlaws. He hastily evolved a plan.

'I tell you what we've gotter do,' he said. 'We've gotter creep up behind him an' spring on him an' overpower him sudden, an' – an' – an' get all his secrets out of him.'

'How?' said the practical Douglas.

'By threats,' said William, 'by threats an' – an' –

threats. When we get quite near I'll say, "Spring," an'
all of you spring on him.'

They crept up abreast still crouching. The man in
front heard a slight sound and turned suddenly. He
saw the backs of four boys running violently away in
the opposite direction.

The sudden sight of the cross-eyes and crooked
nose had been too much for the Outlaws. The man,
slightly surprised, continued his walk. At the end of
the wood the Outlaws ceased their headlong flight and
clustered together, panting. They felt distinctly
sheepish. Each one was hoping someone else would
explain their actions first. William, as leader, under-
took the noble task of clearing their consciences.

'Well,' he gasped, 'we were jolly lucky to escape
alive. I guess he was jus' goin' to kill us.'

'I saw his hand goin' to his pocket where he keeps
his bombs,' said Henry breathlessly.

'Well,' said William, 'we've just gotter think of
some other way. We'll have a meetin' tonight an' think
out plans.'

Ginger went home with William to fetch a bow and
arrow which he and William jointly owned.

They crept as silently as they could up the hall.
Each of the Outlaws accepted as a matter of course this
dislike of the families of the other members. They
would have regarded with deep suspicion any

THE MYSTERIOUS MAN HEARD A SLIGHT SOUND AND
TURNED SUDDENLY.

evidences of a warmer feeling. It would have embarrassed them terribly.

To Ginger it was as natural for the grown-up

FOUR BOYS WERE RUNNING VIOLENTLY AWAY. THE
SIGHT HAD BEEN TOO MUCH FOR THE OUTLAWS.

members of William's, Douglas's or Henry's family to dislike him as it was for the flowers to bloom in the spring. Therefore, on his way up to William's bedroom, where the bow and arrows were kept, he tried instinctively to attract as little attention from William's family as possible. At the foot of the stairs they paused. The morning-room door was open. Mrs Brown evidently had a visitor.

'Have you heard anything of the man who's rented 'The Limes' from Mr Jones?' the visitor was saying.

'No,' said Mrs Brown with interest. 'Who is he?'

'It's a Mr Finchley – very ugly, but very distinguished, I believe. An author or something like that.'

'Is he keeping the Jones's maids on?'

'No. They've gone on holiday. He's got his old nurse, they say, to look after him. Deaf and very old, but a good worker. He's come here to be quiet. He's writing something or other. Well, I really must go, dear—'

Evidently they were coming to the door. William and Ginger flew with haste, but not without sound, up to William's bedroom. As the echoes died away they heard Mrs Brown's plaintive but resigned voice ejaculate the two words, 'Those boys!'

Upstairs in William's bedroom William turned to Ginger with a meaning look. 'Writing something,' he repeated. 'Old nurse! That's all *they* know – Huh!'

The Mysterious Stranger

The Outlaws met in the old barn. They discussed the affair in all its bearings. They went over again the previous history of Dmitritch as related in 'Hunted by the Reds'; they wondered where the noble Paulovitch was now, and what had happened to the fair princess.

'I bet he's somewhere round here,' said Ginger earnestly. 'I bet he'd never leave old Dimtritch to do his dastardly deeds without tryin' to stop him. I bet he wrote that book to let people know – people like us what had the sense to see it mus' be real, an' I bet he's somewhere round here doggin' old Dimtritch an' tryin' to catch him an'—'

'Gentlemen,' said a voice at the open door of the barn. 'You are right in everything. I am Paulovitch, and I am here trying to foil the old villain once more.'

The Outlaws gasped. A tall young man stood framed in the sunlight of the open door smiling at them. Certainly such might well be Paulovitch. But surprise had deprived the Outlaws of their usually so ready speech. The young man came into the barn and stood looking down at them.

'I was resting there by the hedge outside,' he said simply, 'and I heard everything you said. It is all quite true. I knew that I had found some trusty friends at last.'

'You – you're Paulovitch,' gasped William.

The young man bowed.

'That is my name,' he said.

'You – you wrote the book?' gasped William again.

'I wrote the book,' said the young man.

'An' did he imprison the princess like what you said?' said William.

'Yes,' said the young man.

'An' – an' you rescued her?' gasped Douglas.

'Alas, no!' said the young man. 'The attempt was unsuccessful. For the purposes of the book I pretended that I had rescued her. In reality he still holds her captive.'

'N-n-n-not at "The Limes"?' stammered Henry, quivering with excitement.

'Yes,' said the young man, 'at "The Limes". I'm going to try to rescue her tonight.'

The Outlaws thrilled visibly.

'C-c-can we help?' squeaked Henry almost hysterical with excitement.

'Yes,' said the young man. 'I think you can help quite a lot.'

Mr Finchley was sitting alone in his study. It was his old nurse's day out, and Mr Finchley was guarding the house. He never left the house unguarded. He was guarding it quite comfortably with a pipe and whisky and soda and a pile of foolscap paper.

Suddenly there came a violent knock at the door. Mr Finchley groaned and cursed softly to himself. Then he went to answer the door.

Four boys stood on the doorstep. Curious. And only the other day four boys had suddenly appeared, first looking at him over a hedge and later fleeing down the road behind him. Four boys seemed to be haunting him. Most curious!

'May we speak to you?' said one of them in a deep voice.

'Er – yes, I suppose so,' said Mr Finchley without much enthusiasm. 'Come in, come in!'

They trooped into the hall. Suddenly Mr Finchley felt rather touched. He found generally that his crooked nose and cross-eyes put children off. On the whole he was not sorry that this should be so, but he felt rather touched that these children had sought him out of their own accord.

'We want to show you something in Mr Jones's back garden, if you don't mind,' said William, the expression of his freckled face stern and forbidding.

Most curious children. However— 'All right,' he said. 'All right – come on.'

He closed the door very carefully and shuffled with them down the hall and out at the other door into the back garden.

As soon as they had gone down the little garden path to the right Henry murmured that he had dropped his handkerchief in the hall and ran back. In the hall he cautiously opened the front door, then

173

hastily returned to the others. He had seen Paulovitch crouching in the shadow of the laurels waiting for the opening of the door. It would not be long now before he had his princess again. Mr Finchley was beginning to feel irritable. He'd had a splendid idea for the next chapter and this would entirely put it out of his head. He began to feel distinctly annoyed.

'Well, well, well, well!' he said. 'What is it? What is it?'

'We just want to show you somethin' down at the bottom of the garden,' said William.

He spoke with excessive politeness and Mr Finchley was softened. Funny things, children, and, anyway, he might get some copy out of them. He always found a difficulty with any child characters he had to introduce into his books. It might be worth it. It certainly might be worth it. Not that these were normal children, he thought moodily – far from it. They were most – most strange children. Still, he was growing interested, in spite of himself. After all, anything might happen. It might be the beginning of a real adventure. He'd never had a real adventure. The greatest romance in his life had been the collecting of old English spoons. He had a valuable and almost unique collection of them. He'd brought them away with him for safety. He kept them in a safe in his study. He gloated over them every night. He loved them. Oh, bother these boys!

He wanted to get back to his spoons and his writing. That splendid idea he'd had for the next chapter had evaporated already. He knew it would. Oh, bother these boys –

'Now, come, come!' he said, trying to speak breezily, but firmly. 'I'm rather a busy man, you know. I can't waste all the afternoon.'

'We know you're a busy man,' said William meaningly, 'we know all about *that*!'

Curious the way he said it, thought Mr Finchley.

He felt suddenly apprehensive. There *was* something strange about them. He hoped – he hoped they weren't – dangerous or anything.

'It's this we want to show you,' said William.

They had arrived at an empty pigsty that stood at the farther end of Mr Jones's back garden.

Mr Finchley stared at it in amazement, his apprehension growing stronger each moment.

'Er – what?' he stammered.

'Jus' go in an' you'll find somethin' interestin',' said William.

Mr Finchley had not the slightest intention of going in. But he was taken unawares. One of the terrible boys suddenly opened the gate and another of the terrible boys suddenly pushed him in. Then they banged to the gate, bolted it and stood in a row glaring at him over the wall.

There was no doubt at all in Mr Finchley's mind now. He was in the presence of four youthful lunatics. Quite possible. There must be an institution for youthful lunatics in the neighbourhood from which these had escaped. He must be very careful. They were probably endowed with lunatic strength as they were certainly endowed with lunatic cunning.

He smiled at them uneasily over the pigsty door in an attempt to propitiate them. It would, of course, be fatal to anger them. They probably had weapons concealed about them even now.

'You're Dimtritch, aren't you?' said William sternly.

Mad. Hopelessly, ravingly mad. He must humour them, of course. 'Er – yes,' he said looking round for an unguarded spot in the pigsty wall.

'An' you know Paulovitch,' went on William.

'Y – yes,' said Mr Finchley. 'Very well. Very well, indeed.'

'An' you've taken the princess prisoner, haven't you?' said William sternly.

'Er – yes,' admitted Mr Finchley.

His eye picked out a nice unguarded spot in the wall and he made for it and scrambled up, only to be pushed down by a combined attack of the four young lunatics.

'Well, he's rescued the princess now,' said William

THE MAN SMILED AT THEM UNEASILY OVER THE PIGSTY
DOOR. 'YOU'RE DIMTRITCH, AREN'T YOU?' SAID WILLIAM.

triumphantly, '*rescued her – so* there!'

'Really?' said Mr Finchley, feigning great interest in
the communication. 'Really?'

'Yes,' said William. 'He's foiled you an' rescued her an' – an' you'd better be careful an'—'

'Exactly,' said Mr Finchley. He attacked another likely spot in the wall as he spoke, climbed over, successfully eluded his captors and sprinted up the garden path more nimbly than he had ever sprinted anywhere in his life before. The four youthful lunatics pursued him equally nimbly into the house.

'She's gone,' shouted William. 'He's taken her away all right.'

They followed him into the study. The safe door hung open, and the safe was empty.

'My spoons,' screamed Mr Finchley in dismay. 'Someone's taken my spoons!'

The young man was caught before he reached London. He was carrying the professor's spoons in a leather bag. At his trial he made quite a racy story of his coup. William and his friends were addressed as Dmitritch and Paulovitch for many weeks afterwards. They went about morose and bitter.

William said that that's what came of trying to help people, and Henry said it was enough to turn you into a communal yourself.

Very gradually the memory of the affair faded and the Outlaws again held up their manly heads. But if you want really to annoy William and the others you've only to mention Dmitritch or Paulovitch or the princess.

CHAPTER 8

THE SUNDAY-SCHOOL TREAT

WILLIAM was going to the village Sunday-school treat. He had been attending the village Sunday school under protest for the last year, and his enforced attendance had qualified him for an invitation to the annual treat.

The year before William had attended a superior Sunday school for the sons of gentlefolk held by one Miss Lomas at her home. Since her nervous break-down, however (which occurred shortly after William joined her class), he had, with the majority of her scholars, joined the village Sunday school. The smile with which the Vicar received the intimation that William was to return to the fold had been a mirthles one.

He had enjoyed William's short-lived removal to the more rarefied atmosphere of Miss Lomas's Sunday school for the sons of gentlefolk. William himself, though philosophical, was little better pleased. He endured Sunday school in the same spirit in which he endured clean collars and having his hair brushed.

He knew that he went there because his father said that he might as well go into an asylum straight off if he couldn't get a little peace from that boy on Sunday afternoons.

William looked forward to the treat with mixed feelings. On the one hand, his friends (known as the Outlaws) would be there. That would make for mirth and freedom. On the other hand, his grown-up sister Ethel would be there, and that would not make for mirth and freedom. Ethel always made it her duty to keep a stern eye upon her younger brother.

Ethel was to help with the tea, not because she had any official connection with the Sunday school, but because she was in the transitory state of falling back on the curate. Between her more exciting flirtations Ethel always fell back on the curate. He was a pale, dreamy youth with a long neck who proposed to Ethel several times during each of the falling back periods, but without much real hope. As a matter of fact, he had grave and quite justifiable doubts as to her suitability for the position of clergyman's wife. She was too pretty for one thing. Still, he proposed regularly and indulged in a certain half-pleasurable mournfulness each time she rejected him.

William allowed himself to be washed and brushed and put into his best suit, his mind fixed hopefully upon the treat to come. He had heard that there were

to be races and coconut shies and a roundabout. It was
not so much upon these lawful pleasures that his mind
was set as upon such lawless ones as were likely to
offer themselves to him in the company of his beloved
Outlaws.

There was Ethel, of course . . . He considered her
presence at a Sunday-school treat as little short of an
outrage. But he looked confidently to the curate to
occupy most of her time. William always kept a wary
eye upon his pretty sister's 'affaires'. He had on more
than one occasion found a knowledge of them useful.

He did not walk with Ethel to the field where the
treat was to be held. He always avoided walking with
Ethel. She objected to any interesting mode of pro-
gression such as leaping along with a stick or crawling
through the hole in the hedge or dragging one's feet
through the dead leaves.

So William, spick and span and shining with cleanliness and neatness, set off alone some time after Ethel.
He walked along the top of the fence by the side of the
ditch. It was a difficult balancing feat and more than
once proved too much for him. However, he picked
himself up from the muddy ditch and climbed up for
another attempt.

When the fence came to an end he walked along in
the ditch by the side of the hedge. Neither was that an
easy feat, as the bottom of the ditch was full of water

and he had to walk with one foot halfway up either bank. Occasionally he slipped. He very cleverly cut off a long corner by road, climbing through a hole in the hedge and walking across a ploughed field.

On reaching the treat field the first person he saw was Ethel talking to the curate by the gate. As her eyes fell upon him they dilated with horror. Ethel had left at home a small boy, clean and tidy and arrayed in his best. There met her gaze now a creature whose cap nestled crookedly among spiky dishevelled locks, whose roseate face was streaked with mud, whose collar was awry and begrimed with muddy finger-marks, whose nether limbs were encased in mud up to the knees, who slashed on all sides as he walked with a muddy stick salvaged from the ditch.

'What on *earth* have you been doing?' she said severely.

William's eyes opened innocently.

'Me?' he said, surprised and indignant. 'Do you mean *me*? Nothin'. Jus' comin' here. Same as anyone else. I've jus' come straight here. I've not done anythin'.'

Ethel turned angrily on her heel and walked away, followed by her enamoured curate.

William walked on whistling to himself and slashing gaily with his stick. Every boy knows that there are few sensations more delightful than the sensation of slashing with a stick. But occasionally a slash goes further than you mean it to. A stout gentleman, who had come to help with the races, gave a yell and seized William by the shoulders.

'Look here, my little man,' he said, trying without success to sound more pleasant than he felt. 'Look here, my little chap, don't go about hitting people's ankles like that. Let me have your stick, my little man. It's dangerous, you know, in these crowds.'

William, seeing that resistance would be useless, surrendered his stick and walked on, his hands in his pockets, whistling.

Miss Lomas, who had risen from the bed of her nervous breakdown for the first time in order to 'watch the dear little children enjoying themselves,' heard the sound of William's whistling and hastily retired again. Mere words cannot do justice to William's whistle. It suggested the violent squeaking of a slate pencil drawn forcibly across a slate.

He made his way across the field, his whistle opening a way for him through the crowds as by magic, and at the farther end of we field met the other Outlaws, Henry, Douglas and Ginger, with a whoop of joy. All had set out from home in a condition of spotless cleanliness, and all had in a remarkably short time managed to return to their normal and dishevelled condition.

An impromptu wrestling match (which was merely an expression of joy at reunion) was completing the transformation when the ringing of a bell summoned them to the middle of the field. There stood the fat gentleman surrounded by a crowd of boys. He saw William and gave him an apprehensive and sickly smile. He didn't like the look of William at all. There was a certain absence of meekness and conformity about William's expression that he felt boded no good.

Besides, there was the memory of that stick. He was already half regretting that he'd offered to help at all.

'Fall in for the first race, little boys,' he said. 'We'll have ten in the first heat.'

He put William among the first ten. He thought he'd like to get William over. He was the sort of man who goes to the dentist at once if he feels a twinge of toothache. He arranged the ten in a nice straight row. William crouched in correct position, hands on the ground, and looked about him.

'Ready!' said the stout gentleman. William suddenly noticed his next-door neighbour. It was Hubert Lane – a school-fellow and a mortal enemy. Between William and his friends and Hubert Lane and *his* friends raged a deadly feud.

'Steady!' said the fat gentleman.

Slowly and deliberately Hubert Lane put out his tongue at William.

'Go!' said the fat gentleman.

To his surprise the line did not move forward as he had expected. Instead the boy – that boy, the boy he disliked, the boy who looked so untidy and possessed that fiendish whistle and had hit him on the ankle – hurled himself suddenly upon his next-door neighbour and a general scrimmage ensued. All the other competitors joined the fray. Apparently half were on that boy's side and half on the other.

More and more boys joined in from among the bystanders till every boy present was engaged in the combat on one side or the other, and the racecourse was a bedlam of fighting, shouting, scrimmaging boys. The fat gentleman rang his bell frienziedly, and finally ran almost in tears to find someone in authority to quell the riot. He found the curate first.

The curate was standing with Ethel near the entrance gate. He was flattering himself that he was getting on with her better than he had ever got on before when the fat man came up.

'Please come at once,' panted the fat man. 'The boys are all fighting and I can't do anything with them!'

The curate looked at him coldly for a minute, then said, 'I'll come in a minute,' and turned back to Ethel.

'I beg your pardon,' he said. 'What were you saying just now when he interrupted?'

The fat man wrung his hands hopelessly and ran off to try and find someone else.

The fight was brought to an end by the victory of William's side, and the consequent flight of Hubert Lane's. William's side pursued the other through the gate and some way down the road, then returned black-eyed and dishevelled, arm-in-arm, chanting discordant pæons of victory.

Some of them demanded races, but the fat man had gone home, and after ringing his bell in turn for some time for the sheer love of the noise it made, they scattered among the other parts of the 'treat', combining again with a rush to blockade the entrance gate at any attempt on the part of the routed army to return to the festal ground.

The Vicar, who hated boys, had taken refuge in the tea tent and was pretending not to see or hear anything of what was going on.

The Outlaws went to the coconut shies. Fate was favouring William. Not only had he routed his enemy, but by a lucky shot he knocked down a coconut. He swaggered off whistling shrilly, his coconut under his arm, his admiring Outlaws around him.

They sat down in a secluded part of the ground, then after a few minutes rose and swaggered on again, leaving only the empty shell behind them. Near the toffee-stall they met the curate and Ethel.

The Sunday-School Treat

Ethel was smiling sweetly upon the curate, and the curate, delirious with happiness, and seeing her little brother through a roseate haze of sentiment, slipped a shilling into William's hand as he passed.

He regretted it instantly, because he did not like William, and he knew that generosity to William was no magic pass into Ethel's good graces, and a shilling is a shilling; but William took no chances and had hastily converted the shilling into a large and sticky-looking mixture of treacle toffee plentifully mingled with desiccated coconut at the nearest stall, before the curate had time to explain that he'd given him a shilling by mistake for a threepenny piece, and would he please give it back?

The Outlaws retired to the hedge with their booty, and again in a few minutes walked on, their faces freely ornamented with coconut and toffee, leaving a large empty paper bag behind them.

The roundabout was next to the coffee-stall, and the Outlaws, still sucking, climbed upon the horses and held on to the poles. The man in charge looked at them rather suspiciously as he started the machine.

His suspicions were justified. He had no sooner started it than, challenged by William, the Outlaws all began to climb their poles in an attempt to gain the roof. The man in charge, however, was equal to the occasion. He had boys of his own. He stopped the machine, ordered them down, boxed their ears, and sent them off. Still sucking, they wandered on. The grown-ups who were to help with the tea were now coming on to the ground.

Suddenly three of these bore down upon the Outlaws with cries of horror. They were Ginger's mother, Henry's mother, and Douglas's mother. Ginger, Henry and Douglas turned to flee, but too late. Each mother had her offspring firmly by the arm and was gazing down with honor into countenances upon which the battle and the coconut toffee had left their copious traces.

'Go home at once and wash,' they said.

William slunk away hastily in the opposite direction, feeling grateful that his mother had been prevented by a previous engagement from helping with the tea.

Once clear of danger (for he had been afraid that Ginger's mother or Henry's mother or Douglas's mother, with the grown-up's usual gift of officious interference in other people's business, might order him home to wash, too!), and seeing that Ethel was still at the other end of the field concerned only with the curate, he thrust his hands into his pockets, and, uttering again his nerve-racking whistle, strolled on through the grounds. He met no friends or enemies and nothing happened.

William began to feel rather dull. He was conscious, too, of a heavy sensation of sleepiness, caused probably by the combined effects of the battle, the roundabout, the heat, and a surfeit of coconut toffee.

In the hedge, at the end of the ground, was an inviting hole, and William, who never could resist inviting holes, crawled through into the next field and lay down on the grass by the roadside, and, surrendering himself to his sensation of drowsiness, went to sleep.

He awoke to hear people talking just near him. He looked around cautiously. Two men sat on the seat by the river.

'I've decided to kill Ethel,' one of them was saying.

William sat up with a start of horror and indignation. He had often imagined himself wreaking terrible and dramatic vengeances on his sister after some more than usually unwarranted piece of interference on her part, but he'd never gone so far as to kill her – even in his imagination.

Besides, he decided, it would be one thing for him to think of killing her, but quite another thing for a perfect stranger to think of it. William's indignation increased. It was little short of impertinence for a complete stranger to contemplate killing his sister. Cautiously he peered over the long grass that evidently concealed his recumbent form from the speakers.

The man who had just spoken was a good-looking young man, with brown, curly hair. His companion was middle-aged and bald.

'How are you going to do it?' said the older man.

'Push her into the river, I think,' said the young man.

William turned and crept cautiously through the hole and back into the treat ground. He felt that he must warn Ethel at once of this dastardly plot against her life. He hurried up to her, still agog with horrified excitement, where she stood talking to the curate. She was looking rather peevish. The curate always bored her after half an hour, and she was beginning to wish she hadn't come.

'I say,' gasped William, as he joined them.

'Do go and wash your face or do *something* to yourself,' said Ethel with disgust.

William ignored her and spoke to the curate.

'I've just heard two men plottin' to push Ethel into the river.'

'*What?*' said the curate. Two hours in Ethel's company had gone to the curate's head. In his own mind he had been rescuing her from far more dramatic dangers than this. This seemed quite credible, almost contemptible.

'Push her into the river, did you say?' he repeated.

'Yes,' said William, his imagination getting the better of him; 'they were planning to wait till she came out of the field an' then spring out an' push her into the river an' drown her.'

'What *cheek*!' said Ethel indignantly.

The curate put a hand on her arm.

'Leave this all to me,' he said hoarsely. 'Keep quite calm.'

Ethel shook off his hand.

'I *am* keeping calm,' she said irritably; 'keep calm yourself.'

'I'm quite calm,' he said reproachfully. 'I'm only thinking what is the best measure to adopt. My instinct is, of course, to attack them in person, but the law being what it is I think that it would perhaps be better policy to approach the policeman. Where did you say these men are, William?'

'On the seat by the river,' said William, 'an they were plottin' to get Ethel by herself an' tie her arms up so's she couldn't swim an' then throw her into the river.'

'But — why?' said the curate.

''Cause they don't like 'er, I s'pose,' said William. 'Well, I can understand *that*, but I don't see it's any reason for throwin' her into the river.'

'You oughtn't to say that,' said the curate reproach fully. 'You—'

But Ethel interrupted, stamping her foot.

'Isn't anyone going to *do* anything?' she said.

'Yes, I am,' said the curate with dignity. 'I'm going to consult the police.'

The policeman was standing just inside the entrance gate leaning against the fence and engaged in the occupation of looking bored. He was new to the job and inclined to be rather punctilious. He took out a new clean notebook and a new clean pencil and interviewed William in an official manner and with an official frown. William, who was beginning to feel that his story sounded a bit thin and needed embellishing, duly embellished it.

'They were talking about Ethel, my sister, an' they said they were goin' to kill her, an' one of them wanted to shoot her, but the other said no, it would make too much noise, an' the best thing would be to get her an' gag her an' tie her up an' throw her in the river, an' I came back to tell someone 'cause I know she's maddenin' sometimes, but I think killin' her's a bit thick, an'—'

'Be *quiet*,' said Ethel, stamping her foot again.

The policeman put his hand on William's neck and ordered him to lead him to the spot where he had overheard the men. The policeman was secretly worried because he couldn't think of the exact name of the offence. 'Murder' seemed rather a premature name for it. 'Attempted murder' wasn't much better, and he couldn't think of anything else.

Behind him walked Ethel and the curate, and behind them the participants in the Sunday-school treat. Seeing the policeman leading William off the field by the neck they imagined that a long overdue Nemesis had overtaken that young scoundrel at last, and followed gleefully.

'There they are!' said William, pointing to the two men, who were still on the seat.

The policeman marched forward with massive dignity and laid a hand on their shoulders.

'I arrest you,' he said dramatically, 'on a charge of—' the word suddenly occurred to him, and he brought it out impressively: 'Conspiracy.' In order that the word might not elude him again he took out his nice new notebook and wrote the word 'Conspiracy' on the first page.

'B – but—' gasped the young man.

'Anything you say,' said the policeman majestically, 'may be used as evidence against you.'

'I protest,' said the young man.

But the curate, brought face to face with the would-be murderer, could not restrain himself.

'You scoundrel!' he said. 'I learn that you have just been planning to throw this – this young lady,' pointing to Ethel, 'into the river.'

'YOU SCOUNDREL!' SAID THE CURATE. 'I LEARN THAT
YOU HAVE BEEN PLANNING TO THROW THIS YOUNG
LADY INTO THE RIVER.'

The young man's eyes rested upon Ethel. Amazement and admiration succeeded each other in his face.

'Certainly not,' he said. 'I've never seen this young lady before.'

'CERTAINLY NOT,' SAID THE YOUNG MAN. 'I'VE NEVER
SEEN THIS YOUNG LADY BEFORE.'

The policeman took out his notebook to enter this statement, then thought that he might as well make quite certain of it.

'Are you quite sure of that?' he said.

A smile – boyish and disarming – came into the nice young man's face.

'Well,' he said, 'I should hardly be likely to forget, should I?'

Ethel blushed and lowered thick curling lashes over her blue, blue eyes.

'Yes,' broke in William indignantly, 'but I was sittin' here an' I heard you talkin' about Ethel and you was sayin'—'

The middle-aged man broke in.

'I think I see a light,' he said. 'My friend here is a writer of serial stories and we have taken a cottage near for a short holiday. We were discussing one of his plots in which there seemed to be an over-abundance of characters, and in which another mysterious disappearance more or less would make no difference. We were deciding that Ethel might go. Perhaps this young lady's name is Ethel?'

'Yes,' said Ethel, with another glorious blush.

The policeman made a sound expressive of annoyance, took out an indiarubber and erased the word 'Conspiracy' from his nice new book, turned on his heel scornfully, and went moodily back to his post.

Silly mess-up! He'd never had any real luck since he joined the force just over a month ago – not even a burglary!

The participants in the Sunday-school treat, seeing that nothing was happening, trailed back to the ground, and someone sent an urgent message to the curate to come and give away the competition prizes, as the Vicar had a headache and had gone home. The curate gave a sardonic laugh as a tribute to the Vicar's headache, and a dark, threatening scowl at the man whom he still looked upon as Ethel's murderer. He half contemplated throwing him into the river, even now; then decided that it would be an anti-climax, and followed the policeman gloomily back to the ground.

'What's happening up there?' said the curly haired young man, his eyes still fixed ardently upon Ethel.

'A Sunday-school treat,' said Ethel.

'What are you doing at it?'

'I'm just helping,' said Ethel.

'Could I come and help, too?' said the young man.

Ethel gave him her shattering smile.

'I don't see why you shouldn't,' she said.

The middle-aged man sighed, and set off by himself down the road.

The young man went back with Ethel to the scene of the treat.

William stood and watched them. 'Huh!' he said

scornfully, when they had finally disappeared from his view.

Then he went down the road towards his own house. On the road he met Ginger, Douglas and Henry, looking clean and depressed.

'Hello!' they greeted him. '*You* been sent home to wash, too?'

William ignored the question.

'I've jus' been saving Ethel's life,' he said, 'and how much d'you think she's give me for it?'

'Dunno!' said the Outlaws.

'*Nothin*',' said William bitterly. 'Let's go and play Red Indians.'

CHAPTER 9

WILLIAM THE PHILANTHROPIST

WILLIAM tramped loudly down the stairs singing lustily: 'I want – to *bee* – happy, but I – can't *bee* – happy—'

'Neither can anyone else while you're making that foul row,' said Robert, his elder brother, coming out of the morning-room and slamming the door behind him.

'D'you think,' said William sternly, 'that no one c'sing in the house but you? D'you think—'

'Shut up,' interrupted Robert, furiously, going into the dining-room and slamming the door behind him.

William went into the garden, continuing his interrupted song:

' ''Till I've made you – happy too-hoo.'

His 'too-hoo' ranged from E flat to F sharp.

The dining-room window was thrown open and a book whizzed past William's ear, narrowly missing him.

Robert's infuriated voice followed the book.

'Will you shut up?' he said. 'You're driving me mad.'

'I'm not driving you mad, Robert,' said William, meekly. 'That's nothin' to do with me, Robert.'

Robert leaped over the window-sill and started in pursuit.

William was prepared for this, and fled down the drive, Robert returned to the dining-room. At the gate William hesitated, then raised his untuneful voice in a challenging: 'I want – to *bee* – happy—' He looked expectantly towards the house, but Robert had slammed both window and door and had taken up his novel. William, slightly disappointed, continued his raucous progress down the street.

Here he met the other Outlaws. They joined him and his song. Their ideas of key and actual notes varied. No one, even though he were familiar with the immortal ditty, would have recognised it as rendered by the Outlaws. It had become merely an inferno of untuneful sound.

They made their way to the old barn where they always held their meetings. Their exuberance died away somewhat when they entered the barn and found Violet Elizabeth awaiting them. Violet Elizabeth was the daughter of Mr Bott (of Bott's Digestive Sauce), who lived at the Hall.

Violet Elizabeth was six years old. She possessed bobbing curls, blue eyes, a lisp, and an imperious temper, and she had, without invitation, or even encouragement, attached herself to the Outlaws. The Outlaws had tried to shake her off by every means in their power, but she possessed weapons (chiefly weapons of tears, and pertinacity) against which they were defenceless. Violet Elizabeth, following them wherever they went, weeping tears of rage and screaming screams of rage whenever they attempted to send her away, had broken their nerve. They now accepted her presence as an inevitable evil. They let her into all their plans and counsels simply because they had tried every means (except physical violence) to keep her out and all had failed. She accepted their lack of cordiality as part of their charm, and was inordinately proud of her position. She greeted them cheerfully now from her seat on the floor.

'Hello!'

They ignored her and gathered round in a circle which Violet Elizabeth promptly joined. She was no whit abashed.

'Your fathe ith dirty,' she said scornfully to Ginger; and to William: 'D'you call that noith you wath making down the road *thinging*?'

William felt that the dignity of his position as leader of the Outlaws must be upheld. He looked at her sternly.

'If you don't shut up speakin' without bein' spoke to,' he said, 'we'll – we'll chuck you out.'

'If you do,' said Violet Elizabeth serenely, 'I'll thcream an' thcream an' thcream till I'm thick,' and added with pride, 'I can!'

'Well,' said William, hastily turning to the others, 'what we goin' to do?'

A thin drizzle was falling, and the countryside was unusually uninviting.

'Let's go on readin' the book,' said Douglas.

It was found that in anticipation of this demand Ginger had brought the book and William had brought a bottle of liquorice water. The act of reading was in the Outlaws' eyes inseparable from the act of imbibing liquid refreshment. They read aloud in turns, and those who were listening passed from hand to hand the bottle of liquorice water. It was an indispensable rite.

'Who'll read first?' said Ginger, taking the book out of his pocket.

'I will,' piped Violet Elizabeth, with an eager flutter of her bobbing curls.

'You *won't*,' said William sternly; 'you can't read straight, you can't. You can't say words. How old are you?'

'Thix,' said Violet Elizabeth proudly.

'Thix!' jeered William. 'Thix!' Violet Elizabeth only beamed proudly.

'You – you can't – read straight,' ended William,

slightly deflated by her complacency.

'I can,' said Violet Elizabeth. 'I'm at Book II, I am, in reading. I've finished Book I. I *muth* be a good reader if I'm in Book II.'

'Well, anyway,' said William, 'who asked you to come here?'

He felt that this was unanswerable, but Violet Elizabeth answered it.

'I athed mythelf,' she said with dignity.

'Oh, come on,' said Douglas impatiently, 'let's get on with the reading. You begin, Ginger.'

'Yes,' said Ginger bitterly, 'you'll get me readin' an' then you'll go an' drink up all the liqu'rice water.'

'No, we won't, Ginger,' William reassured him. 'I've got another in my pocket.'

He took it out and held it up.

'Promise you won't begin that till I've finished readin',' said Ginger.

'Promise,' said William.

'Thay 'croth my throat,' prompted Violet Elizabeth.

'You shut up,' said William rudely.

'Thut up yourthelf,' rejoined Violet Elizabeth with spirit.

The book was the story of Robin Hood, and it made a special appeal to the Outlaws.

'They was Outlaws same as us,' said William with satisfaction.

'I think that was a jolly good idea,' said Douglas, taking a deep draught and wiping his mouth with the back of his hand in conscious imitation of the gardener, whom he greatly admired. 'It was a jolly fine idea taking money from rich folks to give it to the poor. I think it was a *jolly* good idea,' he ended, handing the bottle to Henry, who was sitting next to him. Henry held it gloomily up to the light.

'You've taken a *jolly* long drink,' he said mournfully; 'you've drunk more'n *half of* it all in one swallow.'

'Well, I bet you can't do it,' said Douglas. 'I bet *you* can't drink all that straight off like that without stoppin' to breathe.'

'There's nothin' to be *proud* of,' rejoined Henry indignantly, 'in havin' a mouth like a rhinoceros.'

Douglas fell upon him to avenge the insult, but William separated them.

'There's no room in here,' he said; 'wait till it's finished rainin' an' then you can have a proper fight outside. An', anyway, you'll be spillin' the liqu'rice water. Give it to me, Henry.'

He took it and drained it to the last drop.

'*Well!*' said Ginger in the voice of one who is aghast at the depravity of the human race. '*Well* – he's drunk it all up before my turn.'

'Well, there's the other bottle,' said William.

'Yes, but I didn't think you'd go an' drink up all the first one straight off like that.'

'It had to be drunk up some time, hadn't it?' said William.

'*Well!*' repeated Ginger. 'Fancy sayin' that. Fancy drinkin' it all up an' then sayin' that – sayin' it had to be drunk up some time – before it came to my turn—'

''S Douglas' fault,' said Henry, who was still nursing his grievance. 'Douglas drinkin' up all that lot in one drink like – like a rhinoceros—'

'You're thinkin' of camels,' said William; 'it's camels what drink a lot. They've got lots of stomachs an' they can fill them all with water at once an' it takes them over the desert, an' when they get thirsty they jus' drink up one of their stomachs. You're thinkin' of camels.'

''Scuse *me*,' said Henry with dignity, 'I think I oughter know what I'm thinkin' of – an' I'm *not* thinkin' of camels. I—'

It was Violet Elizabeth who put an end to the incipient quarrel.

'I think it would be tho nith,' she said in her shrill little voice, 'if we did that – took thingth from rich people to give to poor people, thame ath they did.'

This suggestion was received in silence. The Outlaws looked at William, the leader. William screwed his freckled countenance into a thoughtful

frown and ran his hand through his wiry hair.
William's best friends could not have called him a
handsome boy. Nor did they. Violet Elizabeth's idea
appealed to William's adventure-and-romance-loving
soul. But it had one serious drawback. It had been
proposed by Violet Elizabeth, for whom William
professed a most profound contempt. His contempt
for the proposer (which was almost a point of honour
with him) struggled hard with his secret delight at the
proposal.

'I was jus' goin' to say that,' he said at last rather
sternly: 'That's jus' like a girl saying *jus*' what I was
goin' to say — not givin' anyone else time to say
anythin' — talkin' an' talkin' all the time. Well,' he
added, 'what'll we do and how'll we do it?'

'Let's get guns an' shoot all the rich people,' said
Ginger ferociously.

'Yes,' said William scornfully, 'an' then get put in
prison. No, we've either gotter find some — some
unfathable woods where we can attack the travellers an'
no one ever be able to find us, or else do it all in secret.'

'Well, there aren't any un — any woods like what
you said round here,' said the practical Douglas.

'How can we do it in secret, anyway?' said Henry
rather contemptuously.

'Like robbers do, of course,' said William. 'D'you
think robbers walk up to people with guns an' shoot

them straight off, 'cause if you do, let *me* tell *you* they *don't*. There wun't be any *sense* in it, would there, Ginger?'

'I dunno,' said Ginger gloomily. 'All I say is he might have left a *drop* at the bottom 'stead of drinkin' it *all* up like that.'

'Well, I think,' said William, 'that we oughter do it in turns — each one of us take something from a rich person an' give it to a poor. Not all at once, or else people'd get suspicious.'

'Wath thuthpiciouth?' inquired Violet Elizabeth.

William ignored her.

'Well, who'll do it first?' said William.

'Me firtht,' chanted Violet Elizabeth.

'I should say *not*,' said William severely. 'You're goin' to be last.'

'I'm not — I'm goin' to be firtht,' said Violet Elizabeth.

'Well, let *me* tell *you*, you're *not*,' said William.

Violet Elizabeth's eyes brimmed with tears. Her lip quivered.

'I am,' she said. 'My fatherth rich — I oughter be firtht becauth my fatherth rich.'

The truth of this was irrefutable. Mr Bott, of Bott's Digestive Sauce, was very rich indeed. He lived and breathed and had his being in an atmosphere of all-enveloping plutocracy.

'It's all our money,' said Henry lugubriously. 'We eat his sauce.'

'*We* don't,' said William severely; 'it's made of black-beetles. I once met someone who lived near the works an' they said that you can see carts an' carts full of black-beetles goin' in every mornin' and then carts an' carts of sauce goin' out every night. It's all made out of black-beetles.'

'I don't care if it ith,' said Violet Elizabeth. 'We never uthe it.'

'We once got a bottle,' said Douglas, 'an' it went bad.'

'I don't care if it did,' said Violet Elizabeth, 'an' if you don' let me be firtht, I'll thcream an' thcream an' thcream till I'm thick — I can!'

The Outlaws looked at her in apprehension. William called to his aid his dignity as leader of the Outlaws. He had had experience of Violet Elizabeth's screams.

'Well,' he said judicially, 'we'll give you an hour to get something, an' if you don't we'll put someone else first. We'll stay here an' wait for you, an' if you don't come with somethin' in an hour we'll give someone else a turn.'

'All right!' sang Violet Elizabeth, pirouetting round joyfully, her fair curls bobbing. 'I'm firtht! I'm firtht! I'm goin' to thteal! An' I don' care if it *ith* made out of black-beetleth!'

It was still raining. They finished the Robin Hood book while she was away. William took out the second bottle of liquorice water and Ginger's spirits rose. He had the first drink (one swallow only allowed) and claimed that it beat Douglas's swallow by several lengths. Douglas disputed this claim, and, the rain having stopped, they all went out to the field for the fight which was to decide the capacity of their respective swallows. The decision was never reached, for Violet Elizabeth arrived just as they were carrying on an indecisive wrestling match on the ground.

Violet Elizabeth danced gaily up to them. In her hand she held a string of pearls worth several thousand pounds.

'I found theetfa in a bocth in Mummyth drawer,' she shrilled excitedly. 'She's left the key in the hole, tho I juth turned it an' took them. Wathn't I clever?'

William took them and looked at them contemptously.

'Beads!' he said with scorn.

'They're nithe beadth, William,' said Violet Elizabeth, with pleading in her voice, 'they're *pearl* beadth.'

'But *beads* is no good,' said William patiently. 'We don' want to give beads to the poor what are starving for food an' drink.'

'Let's sell 'em,' said Ginger.

This suggestion was considered a good one, and the five of them went down to the village.

At the end of the village was a small and dingy secondhand shop in whose window reposed a dirty collection of old iron, photograph frames, bits of tawdry jewellery and old furniture. This collection was seldom disturbed.

William, as spokesman, entered the shop carrying the string of pearls, followed by the other Outlaws.

Mr Marsh, who owned the shop, was out, and his mother, deaf and almost blind and very old, sat behind the counter.

'We want to sell this, please,' said William, a businesslike scowl upon his freckled countenance.

'Eh?' said the old dame, her hand to her ear.

When he had repeated it four times she seemed to understand, and stretched out a skinny hand for the pearls.

She peered at the pearls through her ancient spectacles.

'What is it, lovey?' she said.

'Beads,' said William.

'Eh?' said the old dame again.

When he had repeated it four times she said:

'What sort of beads, dearie?'

'Pearl beads,' yelled William.

Yes. She remembered. They'd had some pearl

THE OLD DAME PEERED AT THE PEARLS THROUGH HER
ANCIENT SPECTACLES.
'WHAT SORT OF BEADS, DEARIE?' SHE ASKED.
'PEARL BEADS,' YELLED WILLIAM.

beads last week, and Jim had given the owner six-pence, marked them two shillings, and sold them within a week.

She handed William sixpence and the Outlaws filed out of the shop.

'Sixpence!' said William. ''S not much – isn't sixpence.'

'It'll do to start on,' said Ginger optimistically.

'It'll have to,' agreed William.

'Anyway, I thtealed 'em,' squeaked Violet Elizabeth, with pride, 'I thtealed 'em for the poor.'

'Now we've got to find the poor,' said Henry brightly.

They looked up and down the road. One solitary figure was shambling down it – James Finch, the village reprobate. He was a merry, unprincipled, good-for-nothing ne'er-do-well.

'*He* looks poor,' said Ginger pitifully. 'Look at him, poor ole man. He looks awfully poor.'

'He'th got holth in hith booth,' squeaked Violet Elizabeth, ''an' holth in hith clo'th, poor ole man.'

'Give him the money, William,' said Henry. 'Poor old man!'

William stepped forward with the sixpence and accosted the dilapidated figure.

'Are you hungry an' thirsty?' asked William.

'I'm thirsty,' said the old man, with a wink.

'Here you are then,' said William.

'Thank you,' said the old man.

He took the sixpence and went into the 'Blue Lion'.

The Outlaws watched him, their hearts warmed by the glow of virtue.

'Poor man,' said Violet Elizabeth. 'He *mutht* be thirthty. Heth gone for a nithe drink of lemonade.'

'Starvin' for drink,' put in Ginger sententiously.

'Isn't it nice to think what pleasure we've been able to give the poor old man?' said Henry.

'And all with jus' a few beads,' said Douglas.

'Whose turn is it to get something next?' said Ginger.

'Bags me,' said William.

Old Lady Markham, who lived at the Manor House in the next village, was on her way in her carriage to visit Mrs Bott. Beside her was Angela, her six-year-old granddaughter, who had been staying with her, and whose home was a few miles beyond the Bott mansion. The carriage was to drop Lady Markham at the Botts', then proceed to Angela's home to drop Angela, then return to the Bott mansion to pick up Lady Markham.

'Where you goin', Gramma?' said Angela.

'To visit a Mrs Bott, dear,' said Lady Markham.

She sighed as she spoke. The Botts were Lady Markham's pet aversion. She had long known of, and delighted to disappoint, Mrs Bott's frenzied attempts to 'know' her. She had managed for a very long time to escape an introduction to Mrs Bott, but last week she had been caught unawares and introduced at the Vicarage. She had, however, managed to infuse into her greeting a whole refrigerator full of ice.

But suddenly she found that she needed Mrs Bott. She was holding a charity *fête* in her grounds and found herself hampered on all sides by lack of funds.

'Ask Mrs Bott to be on the committee,' said her neighbours. 'She'll stock every stall in the place. She's made of money, and she loves throwing it about as long as it makes a splash.'

At first old Lady Markham had merely laughed scornfully. Finally she had capitulated. She was on her way to the Bott mansion now to ask Mrs Bott to be on the committee.

'I've had a lovely stay with you, Gramma, darling,' sighed Angela.

'So glad, dear,' said Lady Markham absently.

'I meant to buy you a good-bye present, Gramma, darling, but I hadn't time before we came away, so may we stop at the first shop we pass and me buy you something?'

'Oh, no dear,' said Lady Markham. 'You mustn't buy me anything.'

'Oh, I *must*! *Please!*' said Angela in distress.

'Very well,' said Lady Markham with a smile.

'Then we'll stop at the first shop we pass,' said Angela happily.

The first shop was Mr Marsh's.

Angela descended from the carriage and entered the shop importantly, holding a half-crown tightly in her hand.

'Good-afternoon,' she said. 'Please, have you anything for two-and-six?'

The old lady took up the pearl necklace, which was still lying on the counter. 'You can have these beads for two-and-six, missie,' she said.

'Oh, thank you,' said Angela; 'they *are* pretty.'

She danced back to the carriage.

'I've got some beads for you, Gramma,' she said. 'You *will* wear them, won't you?'

'Oh, darling,' said Lady Markham in dismay.

Angela's face fell.

'Oh, *Gramma*!' she said reproachfully. 'They're very *good* beads. They cost two-and-sixpence.'

'Very well, darling,' said Lady Markham with a sigh of resignation, 'put them on.'

Lady Markham was extremely short-sighted. All she knew was that her granddaughter had slipped a string of whitish beads round her neck. She covered them carefully with her scarf, then completely forgot them.

The carriage stopped at the Bott mansion. Lady Markham said good-bye to her granddaughter, slipped a ten-shilling note into her hand, and descended from the carriage.

The carriage proceeded to Angela's home and Lady Markham entered the Bott mansion.

Mrs Bott was so excited at the news that Lady Markham had called that she was afraid she was going to have hysterics and not be able to receive her. But she mastered her emotions and went to the drawing-room, where Lady Markham was waiting.

Mrs Bott was quivering with apprehension lest she should fail to live up to this high honour done her. She had striven long and earnestly to 'get in with' Society as typified by Lady Markham. She felt that the day of her dreams had come at last, with Lady Markham's card on the tray on the hall table she could now die happy.

She hoped that Botty would stay in the study (where he was engaged in studying a novel and a cigar) and not join them in the drawing-room. Botty was a hardworking man and a good husband, but there was no denying that he dropped his aitches. He generally picked them up as quickly as he could, but he dropped them with a bang and the picking up only drew attention to their fall.

Mrs Bott, small and plump, dressed in an expensive

dress, was sitting on an expensive chair hoping that Lady Markham guessed how much they'd had to pay for it at an antique dealer's. She moved her hands about frequently to show her rings, and she chattered excitedly, glowing with pride and pleasure.

'Oh, yes, Lady Markham, I'll be on the committee with the greatest pleasure. I'll certainly have a stall. What stall? Oh, any stall at all, Lady Markham – The provision stall if you like. I could stock it complete out of the garding, you know. The gardeners could see to the cutting of the things and one of the chauffeurs could bring the stuff over in one of the cars.'

It was nice to say 'one of the chauffeurs' and 'one of the cars.' The only drawback to the phrases was that they gave no inkling of how many cars there were. On the other hand, 'one of the three chauffeurs' and 'one of the seven cars' were rather cumbersome for ordinary conversation.

'Or the fancy stall,' went on Mrs Bott, brightly. 'I could stock it complete in Town – jewellery an' leather an' suchlike. Regardless, you know. Or I wouldn't mind takin' on one or two stalls. Stockin' 'em both. Regardless. It's such a pleasure to work in the cause of charity, I always think. I say to Botty—'

'Botty?' said her ladyship rather faintly.

'Yes, Botty. My hubby. I say to him, "Why is all this here boundless wealth given to us, I say, except to give others a leg up?" Believe me, Lady Markham, when I had a stall at the *fête* here – crowded it was – of course, our garding holds *hundreds* – I spent six hundred pounds on stuff for the stall. I did, indeed, and didn't take a penny out of the profits for expenses either. Believe me.'

Lady Markham sat upright in her pseudo-Jacobean chair and stared in front of her. Mrs Bott was rather disappointed. Nothing friendly or chatty about her visitor, she thought . . . Didn't seem a bit interested in things.

'Of course, the place is a responsibility. Forty acres. Believe me. Twenty indoor servants and ten outdoor ones. A responsibility. Not from the money point of view, of course – oh no. We don't have to think of that. Botty can do things regardless – but it's the *feeling* of responsibility. Why, last week I was quite queer and I put it down to that.'

'Queer?' said Lady Markham.

'Yes, liver,' said Mrs Bott.

'Oh, queer . . . You mean ill.'

'That's right,' said Mrs Bott. No, she wasn't easy to talk to, thought Mrs Bott with an inward sigh. Funny how stiff some of these Society people were. Really difficult to entertain. Nothing to say for themselves.

'Of course,' went on Mrs Bott, 'it was a relief and no mistake to get the furnishing of this place off our minds. You'd hardly believe me if I told you what Botty had to fork out for the furnishing of the place.'

She paused, but Lady Markham asked no question. Again Mrs Bott sighed to herself. Like mummies these people were. Took no interest in anything.

'Guess how much I've paid for that chair you're sitting on now.'

'I've no idea,' said Lady Markham, without even looking at the chair.

'A hundred quid. Down.'

'Did you?' said Lady Markham, without the slightest interest.

Perhaps, thought Mrs Bott, she took no interest because she didn't believe that it was a real antique. Perhaps she didn't believe that her diamonds were real. That was a horrid thought, when Botty had paid so much for them. Then for the first time she began to notice the visitor's jewellery. She had thrown open her scarf and revealed a string of pearls.

Very good pearls, thought Mrs Bott.

Very like her own upstairs. Very, very like her own pearls upstairs.

In her own string of pearls there was a pearl near the middle of a much darker colour than the others. There was a similar pearl here. In her own string of pearls upstairs (they were graduated in size) there was one which always seemed to Mrs Bott to be not quite the right size. There was just such a one here. A small diamond was missing from the clasp of her own string of pearls upstairs.

'Allow me to draw that curting,' said Mrs Bott. 'The sun's on your back.'

She slipped behind her visitor's back to the window and drew the curtain, her eyes fastened on her visitor's neck. Yes, the same diamond was missing. It was all Mrs Bott could do not to scream for help. It must be – it couldn't be – it couldn't be – it must be – She must at all costs go up to her room and see if her pearls were there. She collected her faculties as best she could.

'Er – I'm sure you'd like to meet my little girl, Lady Markham,' she said. 'Er – I'll – I'll go and try to find her.'

She ran upstairs panting, her fat little face purple. Heaven's alive! It couldn't be – it couldn't be – She opened her drawer and – there lay the open case where she kept her pearls – empty. It was – it couldn't be. But it *was* – With a firm hand she repressed another incipient attack of hysterics and went down to her husband in the study.

'B-B-B-B-Botty!' she gasped. 'She's stolen my pearls.'

Mr Bott stared at her in amazement. He, too, was short and stout and, as a rule, amiable looking.

''Oo – Who 'as – has, love?' inquired Mr Bott.

'That Lady Markham has,' sobbed his wife. 'She c-c-c-called and I was in the garden and she m-m-m-m-must have slipped upstairs and t-t-t-t-taken them. They're g-g-g-g-gone.'

''Ow – how do you know *she's* taken them, love?' said Mr Bott.

'She's w-w-w-w-*wearing* them, Botty,' sobbed Mrs Bott. 'She's g-g-g-g-got them on. I've s-s-s-seen them. The diamond's gone out of the c-c-c-c-clasp an' *all*!'

'Now don't 'ave – have – 'ysterics – hysterics, love,' said Mr Bott soothingly.

'B-but it *can't* be true, Botty, can it?' she pleaded, wiping her eyes. The sight of the real lace on her handkerchief and the thought of what it had cost soothed her somewhat. 'She *c-c-c-can't* have taken them.'

Mr Bott shook his head wisely. 'I'm afraid it's true, love,' he said sadly. 'I was readin' an article in last week's Sunday paper, and it said there that practically all these haristocrats – aristocrats – are dec –' (he hunted the elusive word a minute in silence, then gave it up –) 'decayed. Most of 'em thieves. Some of 'em – brilliant figures in Society an' secretly the 'eads – heads – of gangs of thieves. She must be one of them.'

'Oh, but, Botty, why should she w-w-w-w-*wear* them?'

'Nerve,' said Mr Bott solemnly. 'She thought you'd never notice them. Nerve. Now, look here, old lady, go in and talk to her agreeable-like, you know, seem quite 'appy – happy – and keep her there and I'll send for a policeman.'

'Oh, *Botty*!' screamed Mrs Bott. 'You mustn't.'

'Yes, I must,' said Mr Bott firmly. 'If you'd read that article you'd feel the same as what I do now. They ought to be exposed. That's what I feel. Decent citizens same as what I am – ham – am – ought to show 'em up. Now you go back to her, old lady, and leave all the rest to me.'

Mrs Bott went back.

Lady Markham tried to stifle a yawn. Really, these people were amazing. The woman goes out of the room in a most peculiar and abrupt manner, stays away nearly twenty minutes and then returns in a state that her ladyship can only diagnose as partially inebriated – red in the face and talking in a strange and disconnected fashion. Lady Markham began to wish that she had not come. After all, they could have managed without Mrs Bott's money. She'd had no idea these people were so peculiar.

Then suddenly the door opened and the village policeman appeared.

Now the village policeman was a youth who had lived on Lady Markham's estate all his life and looked up to her as lower in rank (and only *just* a little lower, even so) to the Queen alone. It was Lady Markham who had kept his grandmother out of the workhouse, had provided his mother with nurses and nourishment in her recent illness, and had been instrumental in getting him into his present position.

He looked round the room blankly. He'd been sent in to arrest a lady who was in the drawing-room and had stolen Mrs Bott's pearls. He looked round and round the room, gaping. It happened that Lady Markham had sent for him that morning, but the messenger had not been able to find him.

'Oh, Higgs,' said her ladyship kindly, 'you shouldn't have come here after me. It was nothing important – only the orchard's been robbed again. If you'll call at the Manor at half-past six I'll give you all details.' She turned to Mrs Bott. 'Excuse his coming here after me,' she said graciously. 'I sent for him about a small matter this morning and he probably thought it was urgent.'

Outside in the passage the unhappy Higgs faced a furious Mr Bott.

''Aven't – haven't – you *done* it?' stormed Mr Bott.

'No, sir,' gasped Higgs. 'There was no one there, sir. No one but Mrs Bott an' Lady Markham, sir.'

'But it is Lady Markham,' stormed Mr Bott, 'it is Lady Markham, I tell you. Didn't you 'ear – hear – me sayin' it was the lady with Mrs Bott. I've got *proof*!'

'Oh, no, sir,' protested young Higgs earnestly, 'I

couldn't do that sir. Honestly I couldn't do that, sir.'

For answer, Mr Bott opened the drawing-room door and pushed Higgs into the room.

'Well, Higgs?' said her ladyship.

The miserable Higgs put his hand to his collar as if to loosen it.

'D-d-did you say six or half-past six, your ladyship?' he stammered.

'Half-past six,' said her ladyship coldly.

Higgs returned to the impatient Mr Bott.

'Well?' said Mr Bott.

Higgs took out a handkerchief and wiped the perspiration from his brow.

'I can't, sir,' he gasped. 'Honest, I can't.'

'You can and you will,' said little Mr Bott. 'Come in with me.'

He entered, holding Higgs by the arm. Higgs looked wildly round for escape. Lady Markham looked from one to the other in amazement.

'Now, Higgs,' prompted Mr Bott; but at this point a diversion took place.

Violet Elizabeth entered, followed by the four Outlaws. The four Outlaws looked sheepish. This was Violet Elizabeth's stunt, not theirs. They had been in the wood for the last hour lying in wait for unwary travellers, but no travellers, wary or unwary, had passed. Their sole 'bag' had been a tin box deposited by a naturalist in what he thought was a safe hiding place while he went into the village for a drink.

Violet Elizabeth addressed herself to her father.

'Do you want a thnake to make into thauth?' she said. 'Becauth we'll thell you one for three shillingth.'

'What!' bellowed Mr Bott.

'William thayth,' lisped Violet Elizabeth placidly, 'that you make thauth out of black-beetleth.'

Mr Bott turned a red and ferocious eye upon William. 'Tho we thought that perhapth you'd like a thnake, too.'

'WHAT!' boomed Mr Bott.

He looked as if he were going to burst with fury. Mrs Bott wondered whether to have hysterics now or wait till later. She decided to wait till later. Lady Markham pinched herself to see whether she was awake, and found rather to her surprise, that she was.

'We thought,' continued Violet Elizabeth unabashed, 'that a thnake might do ath well. Ith a nithe thnake. Ith athleep now.'

She took off the lid of the box and peeped in. But the snake was apparently no longer asleep. With a strong untwisting of its coils it came out upon the carpet. It was of the grass-snake variety, but rather unusually large in size and unusually light in colour, and for that reason had been collected by its collector, the naturalist.

Mr Bott leapt upon the grand piano.

'Send for the gamekeepers!' he shouted. 'Tell them to bring their guns.'

Higgs stepped forward, took up the snake and dropped it out of the window.

Mrs Bott could restrain her hysterics no longer. She

VIOLET ELIZABETH TOOK OFF THE LID OF THE BOX, BUT
THE SNAKE WAS NO LONGER ASLEEP. IT CAME OUT UPON
THE CARPET.

burst into tears, leaning for comfort upon Lady Markham's breast and flinging her arms round her neck.

'Oh, you wicked woman!' she sobbed. 'Why did you steal my pearls?'

Of course there were explanations. There were explanations between Mrs Bott and Lady Markham,

MR BOTT LEAPT UPON THE GRAND PIANO. 'SEND FOR THE GAMEKEEPERS!' HE SHOUTED. 'TELL THEM TO BRING THEIR GUNS!'

between the Outlaws and Lady Markham, between Higgs and Mr Bott, between Violet Elizabeth and everyone, and (later and far less pleasant) between the Outlaws and their respective parents. But explanations are wearisome things and best left to the imagination. As William said: ''Straordinary how some people in this world like to make a fuss over every *single* little thing!'

CHAPTER 10

WILLIAM THE BOLD CRUSADER

IT was the curate, a well-meaning but misguided young man, who in a quite justifiable attempt to enliven the atmosphere of Sunday school, gave on the spur of the moment a stirring lesson on the history of the Crusades. The curate was very young, and only discovered when he had actually launched into the subject that his knowledge of it was less wide than he had imagined. So his account of the great movement was perhaps slightly bewildering to the uninitiated.

But what he lacked in knowledge he made up in enthusiasm. Even William, Douglas and Ginger (who with Henry, were known as the Outlaws, and who attended Sunday school under protest in order that their parents' Sabbath afternoon calm might be as undisturbed and the Sabbath afternoon calm of the Vicar and curate as disturbed as possible) caught the enthusiasm. They caught it late, it is true. They were only weaned from their interest in the race between Ginger's tortoise and Douglas's tortoise when the curate was well into his subject, and partly because of that, and partly because the curate's knowledge contained some startling gaps, the impression the Outlaws gleaned was more inspiring than accurate.

They certainly found the main fact inspiring enough. It seemed to put religion in an entirely new light. That meekness and humility and turning the other cheek generally enjoined by their religious teachers had never been really acceptable to the Outlaws. But thus spreading religion by an array of banners and swords and spears and coats of mail, this marching upon unbelievers with all the glorious panoply of war, was quite another matter.

Henry (who had not been to Sunday school) met them afterwards, and, to the best of their ability, they imparted to him what they had heard.

'Jus' all joined together and *fought* 'em an' made 'em join religion,' said William.

'Went about jus' fightin' anyone what worshipped idols,' added Douglas.

'An' people *lettem* 'cause they was doin' it for religion,' contributed Ginger with a certain wistful envy.

'Jus' *fightin'* everyone what didn't belong to religion,' put in William, to make the idea yet clearer.

'But what I can't understand,' said Ginger slowly, 'was how they *could* fight folks prop'ly goin' about with their legs crossed.'

'They didn't *fight* with their legs crossed,' explained

William earnestly, 'they only went cross-legged after they died.'

There was silence while this stupendous idea sank slowly into the listening Henry's brain. Then:

'Gosh!' he ejaculated, impressed.

'It's true,' said William, ''cause he told us it in Sunday school.'

Any small excitement at this time would have diverted the Outlaws' interest from the subject of the Crusaders, but no excitement of any sort took place. School life was unusually dull. Home life was unusually dull. Nothing happened. Life flowed on with a calm and almost unbearable monotony. Even the ordinary school feuds seemed to be temporarily in abeyance. There were no enemies to fight, no coups to plan, no insults to avenge. Lessons were duller than ever. Worst of all, their ordinary games of Red Indians, robbers, and pirates seemed to have palled. The Outlaws were bored. And all the time, like the lump of leaven in the parable, the idea of the Crusaders was silently at work in their minds.

It was William who first broached the subject as they sat rather moodily in the disused barn where they held all their meetings. They had made abortive attempts to play Red Indians, robber chiefs and pirates, and had given them up because obviously their hearts were not in them.

Suddenly William remarked tentatively: 'I suppose there isn't any folks worshippin' idols left nowadays, is there?'

Sudden interest gleamed in every face.

'I daresay there is if only you *knew*,' said Ginger darkly. 'They do it in secret, of course, 'cause they know they'd get hung if the Vicar found 'em.'

The Outlaws brightened visibly.

'Well, let's keep a look-out,' said Henry; 'let's look round in church on Sunday an' see who isn't there an' then go an' see what they're doin' instead.'

Full of new ardour, the Outlaws went home and spent a good deal of time collecting weapons. Ginger tried to make a coat of mail out of an old fire-guard, but after tearing his coat in two places gave it up. William polished up his one-and-sixpenny pistol and lent his airgun to Henry, whose only weapon was a poker which, though probably more efficacious as a weapon of offence than either the pistol or the airgun, certainly had an unprofessional appearance.

The congregation at church next Sunday was disconcerted by four separate small boys, each with his family near the front of the church, who spent the entire service (when they were not being forcibly tweaked into position by the nearest member of their families) turning round and fixing every member of the congregation severally with what appeared to be a baleful stare. As a matter of fact, it was only a stare of concentration while the Outlaws memorised those inhabitants of the village who attended church and were, therefore, outside the sphere of their prospective activities. The recipients of the stares (especially if they had any personal knowledge of the Outlaws) felt apprehensive. Had they known the truth they would have felt only relief.

'William,' said Mrs Brown on the way home, 'I felt simply *ashamed* of you. Turning round and staring at people all the time. I don't know *what* the Vicar thought.'

'Well, if he knew *why*,' said William enigmatically, 'he'd feel *glad*.'

'And I don't know what your father would have said if he'd been there,' went on Mrs Brown severely.

His father! That was an idea – his father seldom went to church. It might be a good plan to begin on his father. But on second thoughts William decided that it mightn't. It might annoy his father, and William had a wholesome awe of his father – not from any vague speculation as to what his father might do if annoyed, but from actual painful knowledge of what his father could do and had done when annoyed. He decided that after all it might be wiser to begin operations outside his family circle.

The Crusade, however, did not move very fast at

the beginning. The first step had been the collecting of their armour, and that had been in its own way enjoyable. The second step had been a marking down of the non-attenders at church, and that had held a certain interest, though the list had turned out to be an unexpectedly large one.

'We can't fight all those,' William had said, slightly depressed. 'They'd conquer us first battle.'

'Yes,' said Ginger hopefully, 'but we'd attack 'em one by one – singly, you know, before they've time to warn each other.'

But Ginger's optimism failed to communicate itself to the others, though Henry tried to lighten the atmosphere of gloom by saying:

'Well, we've got some jolly fine weapons, anyway.'

'Yes, but not enough to conquer half the village,' said William irritably. 'I think it's simply disgraceful, the amount of – of disbelievers there is.'

'It's *un*believers he called 'em, William,' said Henry with an annoying air of knowledge.

'Well, it's *dis*believers *I* call 'em,' said William crushingly, and then, turning his mind temporarily to fresh woods and pastures new. 'Let's go an' collect conkers, anyway.'

But the next day things brightened. It was Henry who brought the news.

'I say,' he said breathlessly as he joined them,

'General Moult's got an idol. I heard someone talkin' about it. It's an Injun idol an' he keeps it in his drawing-room.'

The Crusaders' spirits rose. '*Good!*' said William, the leader, in a business-like tone of voice. 'That'll do to begin on, then.'

They held a parade. William drilled them for a few minutes. The drilling was not an entire success, owing to the divergence of opinion as to the relative positions of right and left, and each order entailed several minutes' argument on the subject. But their equipment was a subject for justifiable pride. Ginger had returned to his attempts to make a coat of mail, and had this time partially succeeded. He had found an old meat safe and discovered that it was quite possible to encase the upper part of his person in it. It hampered his movements considerably, but he affirmed that it would probably save his life by keeping bullets and spears from his more vital parts. William had his pistol, Henry had William's airgun, Ginger had his coat of mail, and Douglas had a murderous-looking gardening fork.

'What about a banner?' said Henry suddenly.

A banner, they all agreed, was an absolute necessity, and a further meeting was arranged for the designing and fashioning of a banner. After some discussion they decided that the legend should be

'Down with Idols', and William was to bring the material for it. He arrived, proudly bearing a broom-handle, a large square of white cardboard, and a blue pencil.

Their first difficulty was the spelling of the word 'idols'. It was Henry who came to the rescue.

'It's I-D-Y-L-S,' he said. 'I know, 'cause my mother's gotter book called "Idyls of the King," and it's spelt that way on the back.'

'Gosh!' said William deeply shocked. 'Does the king worship 'em?'

Then slowly and laboriously he printed the words 'Down with Idyls' upon the white cardboard, nailed it upon the broom-handle, and decided that the time was ripe for action.

The Outlaws, for all their bravery, were not devoid of the virtue of caution. General Moult was very large in the body and short in the temper, and William, who drew up their plan of action, decided that the idol must be removed in its owner's absence and that on this occasion a pitched battle must, if possible, be avoided.

At two o'clock that afternoon General Moult might have been observed setting forth in the direction of the golf links. At quarter past two the Crusaders might have been observed setting off in the direction of General Moult's house. They carried their panoply of war as unobtrusively as possible. William held his banner downwards so that its legend might not be read by the passer-by. The others carried their weapons in a drooping, furtive manner. They did not wish to be overpowered by possible enemies before they had gained their object.

But once inside General Moult's garden, they formed themselves boldly in fighting array. William, with his banner, was in the van. Behind him walked Ginger in his meat safe and behind Ginger the other two. They marched up to the front door, meeting with no accident on the way, except that Ginger tripped over a stone and had to be helped up by his leader, as his coat of mail imprisoned his arms.

The front door stood conveniently open. They marched in. Still meeting with no opposition, they entered the drawing-room. There stood the idol on a pedestal by the wall. William seized it with a dramatic flourish and tucked it under his arm. Then they formed up again to march out. But by this time an enemy barred their way – an enormous woman in a print dress and a cooking apron. She held a rolling-pin in her hand. It was General Moult's cook.

'Ye young blackguards!' she roared with a thick brogue. 'I'll teach ye to come playin' your tricks in dacent people's houses, I will.'

She proceeded to impart the promised instruction. William and Douglas received boxes on the ear that sent them staggering out into the hall, and Henry received the full impact of the rolling-pin in the small of his coat. Ginger's coat of mail fulfilled its wearer's highest expectations by receiving the full brunt of the cook's palm, but disappointed him by dealing him a startling blow on the head.

It says much for the Crusaders' presence of mind that they withdrew with a certain degree of order. That is to say, William still carried his banner, Ginger his meat safe, Henry his airgun, and Douglas his gardening fork. The idol lay (fortunately unbroken) on the hearthrug to mark the scene of the brief and inglorious conflict. The cook picked it up and replaced it with an irate bang on its pedestal.

AN ENEMY BARRED THEIR WAY – A WOMAN IN A PRINT DRESS AND A COOKING APRON. SHE HELD A ROLLING-PIN.

'Bad cess to 'em!' she muttered fiercely.

The Outlaws ran too hard to find breath for speech till they had safely reached the road.

Then Ginger summed up the situation quite aptly with the remark:

WILLIAM SEIZED THE IDOL AND TUCKED IT UNDER HIS ARM. THEN THEY FORMED UP TO MARCH OUT AGAIN.

'No luck *there*!'

And Douglas said breathlessly: 'Crumbs! Wasn't she *wild*!'

And William, who was feeling slightly dizzy, added:

'Well, let's go home now. It mus' be about tea-time.'

If it had not been for the banner and the coat of mail, probably the whole matter would have ended there. But William was proud of his banner and Ginger was proud of his coat of mail, and they had much enjoyed the sensation of marching to battle thus bedecked, though they had to admit that the actual battle had proved a disappointment. So it was Ginger who found fresh fuel for their crusading zeal and William who (to mix our metaphors) seized eagerly upon it.

Ginger arrived at the meeting place the next day breathless with excitement.

'That Miss Frampton what lives at the end of the village,' he said, 'she's a — a spirituist.'

'What's a spirit — what you said?' demanded William sternly.

'She — she worships things called meejums,' said Douglas rather doubtfully.

'What's a meejum?' demanded William.

'It's a sort of ghost,' said Douglas.

'Gosh!' ejaculated Henry. 'Fancy worshippin' ghosts!'

'Well, let's go there,' said Ginger, already girding on his meat safe.

'All right,' said William, taking up his banner.

The other two were less eager. 'I can still feel her rolling-pin on my back,' said Henry.

'Well, we're not goin' to her this time,' said William encouragingly. 'We're goin' to someone quite different.'

'Yes, but how d'you know they'll be any better?' said Douglas gloomily.

This question was unanswerable, so William wisely did not attempt to answer it. But they were not really reluctant to follow William's leadership. They took up their weapons, and soon they were walking down the road in the direction of Miss Frampton's house. Once inside the garden gate they proudly displayed their warlike panoply, forming in order of battle, and marched up to the front door – William first with his banner, then Ginger with his meat safe, then the other two.

The front door was open, but the Crusaders had had a salutary lesson in entering open front doors uninvited. They halted.

'Better ring, p'raps!' whispered Douglas hoarsely.

'Yes,' said William. ''S all very well for you to say

241

that – right at the back. You can get away quick enough if anythin' goes wrong.'

'There's someone in the garden,' said Ginger. 'Let's go round there.'

So they marched round there.

A young man was in the garden. He came forward to meet them.

'Hel-*lo*!' he said in amazement.

'We've come to see Miss Frampton,' said William, scowling fiercely.

The young man read the legend on William's banner and burst into a hearty laugh.

'No, I don't agree with you,' he said. 'I don't agree with you at all. I'm in the middle of quite a promising one myself and I don't agree with you . . . By the way, may I introduce myself? I'm Miss Frampton's nephew.'

A very pretty girl came out of the French windows of the house on to the lawn.

'What's the matter, Bobbie?' she said laughing. 'Who are they?'

He pointed an accusing finger at William's banner.

'They're Puritans. They're kill-joys. Look at 'em! Down with idyls, indeed! Don't take any notice of them, Paula. Don't listen to—'

'We'll *make* you,' said William pugnaciously; 'we'll *fight* you!'

242

The young man at once squared his fists and adopted a fighting attitude.

'All right,' he said, 'come on. I'll take on the lot of you. Put down your guns and pitch-forks and— Come on.

'DON'T TAKE ANY NOTICE OF THEM, PAULA,' SAID THE
YOUNG MAN.
'WE'LL MAKE YOU,' SAID WILLIAM PUGNACIOUSLY; 'WE'LL
FIGHT YOU!'

They laid down their weapons and charged in a body. The young man seemed to make a gentle movement with his fists, and a second later William and Ginger picked themselves out of a bed of hardy annuals, and Douglas and Henry from the bottom of the bank, where they had rolled.

'Come on!' said the young man again.

They came on again and exactly the same thing happened.

'Don't hurt them, Bobbie,' said the girl, still laughing.

'I'm not hurting them,' he said. 'I'm only tickling them up a bit. Come on, now. Put some ginger into it this time.'

They came on. They put some ginger into it and they received some ginger in return.

William, as he crawled out of a holly bush, whither the impact of his ginger with the young man's ginger had impelled him, decided in his capacity as leader that the exhibition was too ignominious to be allowed to continue. He went to his banner and picked it up with the air of a guest preparing for departure.

'We came to see Miss Frampton, not you,' he said coldly to the young man.

'Well, won't you wait?' said the young man. 'She'll be here any minute now.'

'No, thank you,' said William, 'we'll call again,'

and added 'p'raps,' for he was, on the whole, a truthful
boy and didn't mean to call again. He didn't mean ever
to go anywhere where there was a possibility of
meeting this young man again.

The other Crusaders picked up their weapons and
accompanied him.

'You put up a jolly good fight,' called the girl after
them. 'He's a light-weight champion.'

The Crusaders, slightly battered, walked home.

'Well, it wouldn't have been right to hurt him in
front of her,' said Ginger, whose gift for putting a good
face on things amounted almost to genius.

'He din' seem to mind hurtin' us,' said Douglas
bitterly.

'He din' mean to hurt us,' said Henry judicially.
'He's just sort of made strong.'

They entered the barn and sat down.

'Well,' said Henry gloomily, 'it doesn't seem to be
comin' to much, does it? I can still feel where she hit me
on the back with the rolling-pin yesterday, an' now
I've got an awful bruise down my leg where he
knocked me on to the path. I don' wonder they got
cross-legged if they got as much knockin' about as
what we're gettin'. I feel I'm goin' to get cross-legged
an' cross-eyed an' cross-armed an' cross-everythinged
if it goes on much longer.'

William had not been listening. He had been sitting

on the ground by his beloved banner, gazing absently into vacancy, a frown upon his freckled face. And suddenly the frown faded from it and a light seemed to shine forth. It was the light of inspiration. His followers knew it well. Their spirits rose when they saw it.

'*I* know what we'll do,' said William. 'You see, *Chapel's* disbelievers, isn't it? Well, on Sunday—'

The Crusaders gathered round and listened in breathless excitement.

It was rather a fortunate Sunday for William, because his father had gone away for the weekend and was not coming back till Monday morning.

William displayed an unusual willingness and punctuality in setting off for Sunday school. Had anyone cared to watch his departure (which nobody did) they would have noticed that he went out in rather a furtive manner by the side gate, and that he carried with him a piece of white cardboard nailed to a broom-handle.

The Church Sunday school began at three o'clock, but the Chapel Sunday school began at quarter to three. It was generally supposed that this arrangement was an unprincipled attempt on the part of the chapel to draw into their fold such mothers as considered an extra quarter of an hour's peace on Sunday afternoon of more importance than many doctrines.

It was, however, the habit of the members of the Church Sunday school to assemble outside the school at about a quarter to three, in order, apparently, to work up their youthful spirits to that pitch of exuberance necessary to the full enjoyment of Sunday school. The curate never came to unlock the door till the third stroke of three. He did not like Sunday school, and rather counted on his pupils taking a quarter of an hour to get into their places before he need begin operations.

But this Sunday there was surging excitement outside the school. William and his supporters were making speeches, fiery speeches, inflammatory speeches, warlike speeches. William stood balanced precariously on the edge of the rain butt and Ginger stood on a window sill. William held up his banner and Ginger held up his meat safe.

The members of the Sunday school understood little of the confused rhetoric delivered by William and Ginger. But they understood one thing quite clearly. They understood that instead of the usual dreary repetition of collects and hymns, William was proposing a scrap of some sort under his leadership, and they hailed the idea with joy. When William ended his speech with the question: 'Will you all come with us now and fight em?' they answered 'Yes' as one boy, and cheered and turned somersaults to mark their complete agreement with his sentiments, whatever they might be.

And out they surged into the main road. William walked first with his glorious banner and by his side walked Ginger in his glorious meat safe. The others followed behind, a seething, dancing, scuffling, singing crowd of small boys all eager for the fight that William had promised them. One small boy had dashed home for a trumpet, which he blew loudly and incessantly all along the road. People watched the strange procession from the windows, open-mouthed with astonishment.

The Chapel Sunday school was generally supposed to be better organised than the Church Sunday school. Certainly its pupils sat round quietly while a large man with a beard drew from the story of Cain and Abel the moral that it is very wrong indeed to murder one's only brother. But suddenly a faint, far-away sound reached this peaceful scene and the listeners pricked up their ears. It was a strange sound – singing, shouting, the noise of a trumpet, the tramping of many feet were its component parts. It drew nearer. It roused a certain martial excitement in the breasts of the bored Chapelites. It drew nearer still. The large man faltered in his graphic description of Cain's brand. Then suddenly it happened . . .

The door burst open, and for just one second there

was a clear view of a freckled boy carrying a banner inscribed 'Down with Idyls', another boy in a meat safe, and a crowd of boys behind. Then all was confusion. They swarmed into the room with obviously hostile intent, and the Chapelites rose without hesitation and with gleeful abandon to close with them. The room suddenly became an inferno of fighting, shouting boys. The man with the beard did what he could. His lesson on Cain and Abel seemed to have been pitifully wasted. Someone sent to fetch the Vicar and the curate, and they came and also did what they could.

The curate joined the fray and thoroughly enjoyed himself. It was a much more exhilarating affair even to him than the lesson on the Athanasian Creed he had prepared. As I have remarked before, he was a very young man. The Vicar received a butt in the abdomen and retired to the little room at the back to wait till it was over. He thought, and rightly, that this sort of thing was more in the curate's line than his. The man with the beard tried to calm the tumult by playing peaceful hymns on the harmonium, but that only seemed to inflame the combatants.

It was a glorious fight – a red-letter fight in the annals of the village, a fight which the combatants would describe to their children and children's children. No one except the Outlaws knew what they were fighting about. It was just a fight – a primitive fight – the surprise invasion of alien territory by one army and the defence of their native heath by the other – the sort of fight that dates from pre-Homeric days – the sort of fight that rouses primitive emotion and satisfies dimly felt primitive needs.

It lasted an hour.

Mr Brown returned home on Monday morning shortly after breakfast.

He saw at once that something had gone wrong.

'Everything gone all right?' he said tactfully to his wife.

'Oh, *no*, John,' said Mrs Brown tearfully. '*Everything's* gone wrong.'

'For instance?' said Mr Brown, surreptitiously glancing through the morning paper.

'Well, I just heard from old Jenks, and he can't come and cut up those logs for us this morning, and we've none to be going on with and – oh, *much* worse than that—'

'Yes?' he prompted gently. 'William—'

'*Oh!*' she gasped. 'Have you heard?'

'I've heard nothing,' he said dryly. 'I'm merely suggesting the most unlikely source of trouble I could think of.'

'It's *awful*, John,' moaned Mrs Brown, 'the most *terrible* thing happened yesterday. I'm afraid William's got religious mania.'

She told him the story, and just the flicker of a smile passed over Mr Brown's countenance. He folded up his paper.

'Well,' he said, 'it sounds like the sort of religious mania that can be treated at home. Where is the Lion Heart?'

'The Lion H – You mean William?'

'I mean William.'

'I think he's upstairs.'

Mr Brown stepped into the hall.

'William!' he called.

'Yes, father,' answered William meekly, with the old, old attempt to propitiate outraged Authority by a tone of deferential humility.

But Mr Brown's voice was suavely polite.

'Can you spare me a minute?'

William's heart sank. Of his father suavely polite and his father furiously angry, he much preferred the latter. Of course, it hurt at the time, but it was soon over. He realised, however, that in the matter of parental manners, offenders can't be choosers.

He came slowly downstairs. His father led him out into the back garden where lay a pile of logs.

'Here are some idols for you to demolish, William,' he said pleasantly.

'They're not idols,' said William.

'No, but you can imagine they are. You can work

off your crusading energy on them without, I may add, the assistance or the company of your friends. You know the size we have them chopped into, don't you?'

William glared furiously at the logs. Had chopping the logs been forbidden, William's soul would have yearned to chop them. Had the chopping been an act of wanton destruction it would have appealed immeasurably to William's barbarian spirit. But the chopping was a task enjoined on him by Authority. So William loathed it.

'You mean chop 'em all up?' he said at last in horror.

'I see you're beginning to get the idea, William,' said his father encouragingly. 'Your brain works slowly but surely.'

'B-but,' said William, 'it'll take me all morning.'

'That is precisely the idea, William,' said Mr Brown. 'As it happens, I'm not going to the office today, so I can keep a friendly eye on you from the morning-room window and see how you're getting on.'

And it did take him all morning. And all morning Mr Brown sat comfortably reading in an easy-chair at the morning-room window.

That is why, when anyone mentions crusades or crusaders, a bitter, bitter look comes into William's face.

CHAPTER 11

THE WRONG PARTY

IT was arranged that William was to give a party. Neither William nor his parents particularly wanted to give a party, but it was demanded by the social code.

Certain boys had asked William to their parties, and William, responding reluctantly to pressure applied by Authority, had attended those parties; therefore, whether William wanted to or not, William must have a party to 'ask back' the boys whose parties he had attended. As a matter of fact, he was more ready to fulfil his social duty this year than he generally was.

Robert and Ethel, William's elder brother and sister, had given a party, and so William was eager to show himself as good as they and have a party too. Robert's and Ethel's party certainly had not been an unqualified success, chiefly owing to the fact that William had mistaken one of their guests for a burglar and kept him imprisoned in the greenhouse for part of the evening, but William considered that his mistake had been quite justifiable and that it was silly to have let a little thing like that spoil a party.

William left all the arrangements of his party in his mother's hands – except the invitations, upon which he kept an anxious and rather distrustful eye. He had a deep suspicion that his mother would sacrifice his pride on the altar of the social code by inviting some of his deadly enemies to his party just because their mothers had asked her to lunch or Ethel knew their elder sister, or some equally futile reason.

Mothers never seem to realise the serious and deadly nature of a school feud. They say such things as, 'Yes, dear, you may not like him, but I think you ought to try to love everyone,' or 'I think we *must* have him to tea, dear, because his mother sent in those nice flowers from her garden last week.'

The origin of the feud between William and his supporters and Hubert Lane and his supporters was, as they say in history books, hidden in the mists of antiquity. No one knew exactly when or how it had arisen. It seemed to have been there from time immemorial – a heaven-sent institution to enliven the monotony of school life by fights and ambushes and guerilla warfare. School life would be dull indeed without such occasional relaxations.

William kept an eye upon the invitation list for his party because he was afraid that a Hubert Lanite might somehow creep upon it unobserved – a Hubert Lanite whose parents, with mistaken zeal, would probably force him to attend the festivity – and then trouble would ensue.

But the feud was a feud of many years' standing, and Mrs Brown, who had suffered more than once in her well-intentioned attempts to act as peacemaker, was quite willing to humour William in this, and no Hubert Lanites were asked, though, to William's horror, Mrs Lane sent in a pot of her home-made chutney to Mrs Brown just a week before the party.

For a few hours, in which the fate of the world seemed to tremble in the balance, Mrs Brown hesitated, but on William's hinting darkly that if Hubert Lane came to the party he, William, would not attend it in any circumstances or in any capacity, she decided to ask Mrs Lane to tea instead and explain to her how much they were all hoping to see darling Hubert at William's party next year.

When the week before the party arrived, William allowed his mind to set itself at rest. All the invitations had been sent out and the answers received, and the list remained pure and unspotted from the Hubert Lanites.

William himself behaved with a certain amount of circumspection. When he met a Hubert Lanite he contented himself with a boxing match or merely the hurling of those primitive vituperations so dear to boyhood. (Such as, 'Oh, it's you, is it? Sorry – I thought jus' at first it was a monkey!') It was William's prospective guests who made the mistake. They could not keep themselves from taunting the Hubert Lanites with the fact that they had not been invited to William's party. They impressed the fact of William's party so deeply on the Hubert Lanites that William's party seemed to loom in their minds as the only important event of the year.

William began to have an uneasy suspicion that the Hubert Lanites were planning some coup. They talked together in little groups. They laughed – nasty, sniggering, secret laughs, as if in anticipation of some future joyful triumph. William looked forward to his party with a certain amount of apprehension. A boy who is giving a party is at a disadvantage in dealing with his foes. 'I hope it'll go off all right,' he muttered the night before.

'Well, it's got more chance than most people's,' said Robert bitterly. 'I suppose you won't mess up your own party as you mess up most things.'

'No, but somebody else might,' said William darkly.

Ginger arrived first, and it was Ginger who announced the fact that the Hubert Lanites were concealed among the bushes in William's garden engaged in the enjoyable occupation of jeering from the darkness at each exquisitely dressed guest as he or she stood in the light of the porch on the front steps waiting to be admitted.

Soft cries of, 'Oh, my!' 'Oh, cripes! Look at *him*. Someone's washed his face for him.' 'Oh, look at his hair. He's been an' put treacle on it.' 'Oh, isn't she bee-utiful!' 'Watch this one! Isn't he *lovely*! He's got new shoes with bows on.' 'There's old Douglas – Dun't he look hungry? He's wondering what they've got for supper. Not much, poor old Douglas – they've not got much. We've had a look through the window.'

The guests entered one by one, embarrassed and indignant. They were only restrained from hurling themselves into the bushes to mortal combat by memories of frequently repeated maternal injunctions as to their party clothes and party manners. William made loud complaints to his family and insisted on the necessity of his leading his party out into the night to do battle with the enemy, but Mrs Brown was firm.

'No, William, you're most *certainly* not to,' she said. 'I shan't think of it. I never heard such an idea. Going out fighting in the garden, indeed, at a party. Well I can't help it. They're very rude little boys, that's all I can say, but you must take no notice of them. Simply behave as if they weren't there. That's the only dignified thing to do.'

'But I don't *wanter* do anything dignified,' persisted William. 'I wanter *fight* 'em.'

'Most *certainly* not, William,' said Mrs Brown. 'If your father were here, of course—'

Her tone implied that Mr Brown would have made short work of the Hubert Lanites. But Mr Brown was a wise man, and when any of his offspring were giving parties went out to spend the evening with a friend.

William appealed to Robert, but Robert was unsympathetic.

'It's a pity,' he said, 'if someone messes up your party, but, when all's said and done, you messed up ours.'

'Yes, but I *thought* he was a burglar,' said William, with exasperation in his voice.

When Robert, however, showed himself at the front door for a minute he was greeted with loud murmurs of mock admiration and ribald derision from the darkness. Robert's dress suit was not of long standing, and he still felt self-conscious in it. He flung himself furiously in the direction of the murmur, tripped over something, and fell full length into a laurel bush. The murmur changed to a muffled pæan of joy and triumph.

Robert went indoors and slammed the door, and then went upstairs to change his shirt. He felt that he disliked his younger brother's friends more than he had ever disliked them in his life before.

The Wrong Party

Downstairs William and his friends were making a sincere effort to forget the presence of their enemies outside, but it happened that the drawing-room curtains had been taken down because the conjuror who was to perform afterwards in the morning-room, wanted them, and so William and his guests in the drawing-room felt themselves exposed to the unsympathetic and mocking gaze of countless Hubert Lanites lurking in the bushes.

Over the proceedings there was a strange air of constraint. In every youthful breast seethed only a bloodthirsty desire to sally forth into the night in search of vengeance. Failing this, they didn't want to do anything else. They were certainly not going to play silly games or dance silly dances or do anything that might give their watching enemies outside further handles against them.

They, were painfully conscious of unseen but all-seeing eyes outside noting their every movement for possible derisive reproduction on future occasions. The safest thing was to disappoint them by having no movements and speaking as little as possible. They refused to play games or dance at all.

'I can't get any *go* into it!' almost sobbed Mrs Brown to Ethel.

'Well, let's turn the conjuror on,' said Ethel, 'and see if that melts the ice.'

The conjuror was therefore dragged, much against his will, from the dining-room, where he was comfortably consuming a very satisfactory meal, to the morning-room, where his outfit awaited him, and the guests were summoned from the drawing-room. They came with joy and relief, glad to get anywhere where they felt that their every movement was not watched by hostile mocking eyes.

'I wish they'd begin to get rough,' whispered Mrs Brown pathetically to Ethel as they filed in.

'You said you hoped they wouldn't,' said Ethel.

'Yes, but I didn't know they'd be like this,' said Mrs Brown.

The guests had thrown anxious glances at the window curtains as they entered. To their partial relief they found them partially drawn. The heavy curtains did not quite meet and the window was open, so that there was a distinct, if small, space through which unseen enemies might watch the scene. The guests fixed their gaze on that space with mingled apprehension and ferocity.

Then gradually they forgot it.

He was a very good conjuror. He drew yards of coloured paper out of an empty tumbler. He turned a penny into a half-crown and – a less exciting transformation – a half-crown into a penny. He did wonderful things with a pack of cards. He gave a card to Ginger and then found it inside his own watch, having shrunk to an eighth of its size. Then he took a box and put a table-napkin into it. He put it on his magic table under his magic cloth. Then he whipped away the cloth and took up the box again.

'I believe it's changed to a rabbit,' said the conjuror with a smile.

But it hadn't.

It had changed to a dead cat.

There came a muffled snigger from the window.

Slowly the truth dawned on William and his guests. The Hubert Lanites had actually dared to tamper with the conjuror's outfit.

Wild beasts could not have restrained them then.

They rose in a body and surged out into the night.

The sally, of course, was a failure. The Hubert Lanites had wisely not awaited vengeance, but had beat a strategic retreat immediately on seeing the successful result of their coup. The rabbit was discovered a few minutes later by the frantic conjuror underneath the bureau, where Hubert Lane had provided it with a little pile of assorted greens, which it was sampling with appreciation.

It was decided by William's family that on the whole his party had not been a success. This belief was shared by the mothers of the guests. The mothers of the guests based their belief chiefly on the state of the guests' toilets when the guests returned to the bosom of their families.

'His dancing pumps simply *covered* with mud,' wailed one.

'His suit all messed up as if he'd been falling about among bushes,' said another.

The Outlaws went about for the next few days looking grimly determined. It was extraordinary how elusive and self-effacing the Hubert Lanites had become all of a sudden. Though the Outlaws searched the village from end to end with murder in their hearts they met not a single one.

The Hubert Lanites went into the village, when they did go into the village, in bands and took to flight on sight of the Outlaws. They had met the Outlaws in deadly combat before and had no false pride about admitting that discretion is the better part of valour.

It was William who first heard the rumour that Hubert Lane was going to give a party. The Outlaws abandoned the idea then of vengeance by pitched battle. They still wanted an eye for an eye and a tooth for a tooth, but they decided that it was meeter that the punishment should fit the crime.

The first thing to do, of course, was to discover the date of Hubert Lane's party. But this was less easy than at first it seemed. For Hubert Lane had not invited a single one of William's supporters and had furthermore sworn all his guests to secrecy. The Outlaws exercised all their ingenuity in various attempts to discover the all-important date. It was, of course, almost impossible to plan any sort of coup before they heard when the party was to take place and what was to happen at it.

They held several meetings at which the chief item on the agenda seemed to be mutual recrimination for the non-discovery of the date of Hubert's party.

Ginger lived nearest to Hubert Lane, so he came in for the lion's share of abuse.

'I simply can't *think* why you don' find out when he's havin' his ole party,' said William scathingly.

'An' I simply can't think why *you* don',' retorted Ginger with spirit.

'Well, aren't I doin' all I can,' said William with righteous indignation.

'What're you doin'?' said Ginger pugnaciously.

'I'm – er – well, I'm goin' about askin' folks,' said William.

'So'm I,' said Ginger.

But there came a day when Ginger entered the meeting place his face wreathed in proud smiles.

'I've found out,' he said simply.

'Tell us! How? When?' gasped the Outlaws excitedly.

'I was in the cake-shop,' explained Ginger

breathlessly, 'buyin' some humbugs – the big sort – the kind they make there, you know—'

'Got any left?' put in Douglas tentatively.

'Oh, never mind about the old humbugs,' said William. 'Get *on*!'

'I finished 'em all,' said Ginger apologetically to Douglas. 'They don' last long that sort, an' I only got two penn'oth.'

'Get ON!' repeated William.

Ginger got on.

'Well jus' when she'd finished weighin' 'em an' I was watchin' her jolly hard, I can tell you. They're jolly mean in that shop, you know. They don't stop till the scales get right down. They just get 'em movin' a bit an' then they take 'em off an' put 'em in the paper, an' often's not they wun't go *right* down. I think they oughter lettem go *right* down with a bang an' if they don' they oughter put some more on. Why, once when they was weighin' me somethin' it only jus' woggled a *teeny* bit an' they began takin' 'em off to put in the bag and I said—'

'What were they? Humbugs?' said Douglas with interest.

'What'd you say to 'em, Ginger?' said Henry.

'Get ON 'bout Hubert Lane's party,' said William, who was a boy of one idea.

'No, it was acid-drops,' said Ginger, 'an' I said –

Oo-oo!' as William laid him low and took his seat astride on his chest. 'All right. I keep tryin' to tell you an' all you keep int'ruptin'. Well, Mrs Lane came in an' ordered thirty chairs for December the 28th in the evenin' an' a lot of cakes an' stuff, so that mus' be the day of the party.'

William arose from Ginger's chest and raised his discordant young voice in a yell of triumph.

On the evening of December 28th four small boys might have been seen creeping through the Lane's garden in the darkness at half-past six. The party would be sure to begin about seven. Parties always began about seven. The Outlaws wished to be firmly entrenched in their position by seven.

William as usual had drawn up their plan of operations. A tree grew up the house and from its branches an open window on the first floor could easily be gained. This William knew was the box-room. Here, in the midst of the enemy's castle, the Outlaws had decided to entrench themselves till the party had begun. Their plan of operations included, among other things, a complete failure of electric light throughout the house.

Exactly how this was to be accomplished William was less certain than he pretended to be, but he had read up the chapter on electricity in his 'Boys' Book' and was hoping for the best.

Successfully, and with far less noise than anyone who knew them might have expected, the Outlaws climbed the tree in the darkness and took up their positions in the box-room. It was dusty and not very comfortable. William insisted on their hiding in case anyone should come into the room, and caused a certain amount of discontent among his followers by claiming as his perquisite the only comfortable hiding place – a roomy cupboard. Only the gravity of the situation and the certainty that a noise of any sort would probably bring the whole nest of Hubert Lanites about their ears prevented their putting the matter to the only test recognised by the Outlaws, that of physical strength. A diversion was caused by Douglas, who, with a little scream of joy (which was instantly 'Sh'd!' by the other Outlaws with a 'Sh!' much louder than the original scream) said that he could see a rat. Investigation, however, proved that it was an old bedroom slipper of Mr Lane's, and at the sound of a door opening on the landing the Outlaws hastily retired to their hiding-places – William to his comfortable cupboard, Ginger, Douglas and Henry to their cramped positions behind boxes and packing cases that were several sizes too small for them.

Someone went downstairs, and then came unmistakable sounds of the arrivals of guests – motors, greetings, the constant ringing of the front door bell.

The Wrong Party

The Outlaws strained their ears to distinguish actual individual Hubert Lanites, but all they could hear was the confused murmur as each guest arrived. Gradually this was followed by silence.

'They're all doin' somethin',' said Ginger.

'Dancin',' suggested Henry.

'There's no music, silly,' said William. 'I bet it's games.'

'You'd hear more noise if it was games,' said Douglas. 'I bet it's the conjuror.'

'Well, I bet it isn't. I bet they're not havin' a conjuror,' said William. Then, 'I'm goin' down to see what it is.'

This bold statement was received with a gasp of dismay.

'They — they'll *get* you!' said Ginger apprehensively.

'Well, I bet they won't,' said William, 'any more'n if I was an Injun. I can *creep* down jus' as quiet's if I was an Injun. If an Injun wanted to know what they was doin' he'd jus' *creep* down there an' back an' nobody'd hear him. Well, that's what I'm going to do.'

With deep misgivings, watching his departure with anxious eyes from their hiding-places, the Outlaws let him go.

William crept on to the landing. The landing was empty. Cautiously he peered over the banister. The stairs were empty. As far as he could see the hall was empty. Very cautiously he crept down the stairs. A door just inside the front door was open and from it came a buzz of conversation. William's curiosity was aroused. Evidently the party was there and something was going on. William wanted to know what was going on. He crept along the hall and peeped through the hinge of the half-open door. Then he stood motionless, paralysed with amazement. Where was Hubert Lane's party? This room was full of grown-ups.

Suddenly the door opened and someone came out.

'Yes, it's in here,' she said to William. 'Go straight in.'

Before William could resist or think of any excuse or explanation he found that he was being piloted into the room. The room was full of chairs in rows, and the chairs full of people.

'There's lots of room in the front row,' said somebody, and William found himself being led up to the lots of room in the front row. He was too astonished to do anything but sit on the chair to which they had led him. He looked around him wildly. In front of him was a table which contained a glass of water and behind which stood a learned-looking, spectacled man, holding a sheaf of papers in his hand. Behind William sat rows of grown-up people. Some he knew and some he didn't, but all looked earnest and intelligent. A very fat lady and a very fat gentleman had now taken the two seats next to him, hemming him in and cutting off his retreat. The fat lady leaned towards him with a fat smile.

'It's so nice to see a boy like you taking an interest in this subject,' she said kindly. 'You may find some of it a bit above your head, but I'm sure you'll enjoy it.'

Upstairs the other Outlaws awaited their leader in breathless suspense. And their leader did not return.

'They've *got* him,' said Douglas gloomily, 'I said they would.'

'Well,' said Ginger, 'then we've gotter go down an' rescue him, that's all.'

At the thought of this long-deferred pitched battle with the Hubert Lanites their spirits rose. They crept on to the landing. The landing was empty. They looked over the banisters. The stairs were empty. They crept down the stairs. The hall was empty. Then suddenly a woman came out of a door near the front door. They turned to flee, but it was too late.

'In here,' she said pleasantly. 'Are you with the other little boy? He's in the front row.'

Apprehensive, aghast, bewildered, they allowed themselves to be ushered into the room and up to the front row. They sat down on the other side of the fat lady and gentleman. The lecturer was just beginning to lecture.

Ginger leant across.

'William,' he said.

'*Sh!*' said everyone.

He 'Sh'd.'

'Ladies and gentlemen—' began the lecturer.

BEHIND THE TABLE STOOD A LEARNED-LOOKING MAN
HOLDING A SHEAF OF PAPERS IN HIS HAND.

The Wrong Party

It was an interesting lecture – interesting, that is, to a certain type of mind. It did not interest the Outlaws. It abounded in such strange words as 'ethics' and 'utilitarianism' and 'Spinoza' and 'Cartesians' and

'IT'S SO NICE TO SEE A BOY LIKE YOU TAKING AN INTEREST IN THIS SUBJECT,' SAID THE FAT OLD LADY KINDLY. 'I'M SURE YOU'LL ENJOY IT.'

'empiricism' and 'Nietzsche' and 'evolution'. It would not in the most favourable circumstances have interested the Outlaws and these were not the most favourable circumstances.

William's paralysis of bewilderment was gradually disappearing and the truth of the matter was gradually dawning on him. This was not Hubert Lane's party at all. This was a drawing-room meeting given by Mrs Lane, and it was for this that Ginger had heard her ordering chairs and refreshments.

Moreover, it had been easier to get in than it would be to get out. He doubted whether he could push past the fat lady and gentleman. He doubted whether he dare stir in this densely packed, breathlessly silent room. He was sure they'd turn him back at the door, even if he got as far as that.

But he decided to have a jolly good try. He remembered a device that had occasionally secured him a temporary retreat from a tight corner in school. He clapped his handkerchief to his nose as though that organ had suddenly begun to bleed, rose hastily, walked over the fat lady's toes, fell over the fat gentleman's umbrella, scrambled up and fled down the room. To his surprise and relief, no one barred his way or questioned the sanguinity of his nose.

The lecturer was slightly put out by the incident, but quickly recovered himself and continued his discourse. He was discoursing now on Kant. Ginger looked at William's empty seat. What William had done he could do. As the lecturer was raising his right hand to emphasise the fact that Kant often offends against his own principles, Ginger clapped his handkerchief to his nose and followed his leader's example, even to the lady's toes and the gentleman's umbrella. Hardly had the door closed on him when Douglas, his handkerchief to his nose, made his hasty and noisy exit.

Henry was left alone. He had not acted quickly enough. He felt certain that no one in the room would believe that his nose was bleeding if he put his handkerchief to that organ and followed his friends now. But – he brightened. There were other bodily afflictions. Puffing out one cheek to its fullest extent, clapping his hand to it and assuming what he fondly imagined to be an expression of extreme agony, he started from his seat and rushed from the room.

He did not stop till he had reached the garden. There among the bushes crouched William, Ginger and Douglas. They hailed him with joy.

'Look what I've got,' said William gleefully, 'found it on the hatstand.'

In the light from the hall he proudly displayed his trophy. It was Hubert Lane's school cap. Every schoolboy knows that the filching of his cap is the deadliest insult that can be offered him.

'Let's go home quick,' said Douglas.

'Jus' a minute,' said William.

A light came from an open window on the other side of the house. William crept round to this noiselessly, followed by the others.

From the lighted window came a boy's voice.

'I am looking forward to your party next Thursday, Hubert,' and Hubert's answer:

'Well, don't you tell anyone it's next Thursday anyway.'

The Outlaws went home. And as they went they lifted up their strong young voices and chanted:

'Thursday! It's going to be next Thursday! It's goin' to be next Thursday.'

But next Thursday is another story.

CHAPTER 12

WILLIAM STARTS THE HOLIDAYS

THE Christmas holidays had arrived and William and the other Outlaws whooped their way home from school at the unusual hour of 11 a.m., to the unaffected dismay of their families. They had listened to a stirring address from their form master (who felt as little regret at parting from the Outlaws as the Outlaws felt at parting from him), but they had been more intent upon the unauthorised distribution and mastication of a bag of nuts they had bought on the way to school than upon the high ideals which their form master was holding up for them, and so missed many words of counsel and inspiration which might (or might not) have made a difference to their whole lives.

Anyway, having finished the nuts (and deposited the shells in the satchel of their enemy, Hubert Lane), the Outlaws leapt out of the school buildings and whooped and scuffled and shouted their way home.

'We've broke up!' yelled William, as he entered the hall, and flung his satchel with a clatter upon the floor.

275

Mrs Brown came out of the morning-room, rather pale at this invasion of her usual morning quiet.

'I – I'd forgotten you were breaking up today, William,' she said. Her tone betrayed no ecstatic joy at the realisation of the fact.

William turned a somersault, and came into violent collision with a small table which held a vase of flowers.

'Sorry,' said William, still cheerfully, as he repaired the damage as best he could. (That is to say, he picked up the table, replaced the vase on it, picked up the flowers, put them in the vase – mostly wrong way up – and rubbed the spilt water into the carpet with his foot.)

'Oh, don't, William!' moaned his mother. 'I'll ring for Emma – your boots are so dirty.'

'Sorry,' said William again, slightly hurt, 'I was only tryin' to help.'

'Haven't – haven't you come home rather early?' said Mrs Brown.

'No,' said William heartily, 'we always come out this time breaking-up mornings. We've broke up.' He chanted on a note that made Mrs Brown draw her brows together, and raise her hands to her ears.

'William *darling*,' she said plaintively. Then, 'What are you going to do, dear – just till lunch-time, I mean?'

There was a note of resigned hopelessness in her

276

voice. Mrs Brown was a woman without any political ambition whatever, but if Mrs Brown had been put in charge of the Education Department of the Government for a month, she would have made several drastic changes without any hesitation. She would have made a law that no holidays should last longer than a week, and if they did, free treatment for nervous breakdown was to be provided for all mothers of families, and that on 'break-up days' school should continue until late in the evening. Mrs Brown considered it adding insult to injury to send children home at eleven o'clock in the morning on the last day of term.

'Er – what are you going to do till lunch, dear?' said Mrs Brown again.

William considered the possibilities of the universe.

'I might go into the garden an' practise with my bow and arrow,' he said.

'Oh, *no*, dear,' said Mrs Brown, closing her eyes, 'please don't do that! It does annoy your father so when the windows get broken.'

'*Oh!*' said William indignantly. 'I keep explainin' about that. I wasn't aimin' at that window. It was just that my hand slipped jus' when I was shootin' it off. I was aimin' at somethin' quite diff'rent.'

'Yes, dear,' said Mrs Brown, 'but your hand might slip again.'

'No, I don't think it will,' said William hopefully.

'I'll try an' keep it steady – and it doesn't always break windows, you know, even when it slips.'

'No,' said Mrs Brown. '*Not* the bow and arrows, William,' and added with consummate tact, 'You don't want to risk breaking things so near Christmas, you know, William.'

There was certainly some sense in that. It was an argument that appealed to William.

'Well,' he said thoughtfully, 'there's the airgun. It's quite different from the bow and arrows,' he put in hastily. 'I think p'raps I oughter keep on practisin' with the airgun, in case there's another war.'

'No, William,' said Mrs Brown. '*Not* the airgun.' Then tentatively and without much hope, 'You – you wouldn't like to do a little quiet school work, would you, William dear, so as to keep your hand in for next term?'

'No, thank you,' said William quite firmly.

'I think it would be rather a good idea,' said Mrs Brown, still clinging to the vision of peace that the proposal summoned up to her eyes.

William considered for a moment in gloomy silence the vision of unadulterated boredom that the proposal summoned up to his eyes. Then he brightened.

'I don't think so, mother,' he said at last. 'I don't think it fair on the other boys to go workin' in the holidays.'

While Mrs Brown was slowly recovering from this startling vision of William conscientiously refraining from holiday work for the sake of his class-mates, William had yet another idea.

'S'pose I try to mend that clock that's gone wrong – the one in the dining-room,' he said brightly.

Mrs Brown groaned again. William had hoped that she'd forgotten the last occasion he'd tried to mend a clock, but she hadn't.

William had certainly succeeded in reducing it into its component parts, but having done that had not been able to resist the temptation of trying to make a motor-boat of the component parts, and when finally they were taken to the clock-maker, it was discovered that three or four important component parts were missing.

William suspected a duck who had been on the pond when William had launched his motor-boat and the pond had taken the motor-boat to its bosom. William insisted that he had salvaged all the parts that the muddy bosom of the pond could be induced to yield, and that if there were any missing that duck must have eaten them.

William watched the duck with morbid interest for some days and imagined several times that it looked pale and unhappy. Anyway, the upshot of it all was that William's father had to buy a new clock, and that

William went without pocket-money for several months. But all this had been more than a year ago. William wished that the memories of grown-ups were not so inordinately long. He'd have liked to try his hand at a clock again.

'No, William,' said Mrs Brown, 'most certainly not.'

'Well, what shall I do?' said William, slightly aggrieved.

Mrs Brown had an idea.

'Well, William, it's so near Christmas time – wouldn't you like to be thinking out some little presents for people?'

'I've hardly any money,' said William, and added enigmatically, 'what with windows and things.'

'Well,' said Mrs Brown encouragingly, 'it isn't the money you spend on them that people value. It's the thought behind it. I'm sure that with a little thought you could make some very nice presents for your relations and friends.'

William considered the idea in silence for some minutes. Then he brightened. It seemed to appeal to him.

'All right,' he said. 'I'll go an' think upstairs, shall I?'

Mrs Brown drew a breath of relief.

'Yes, William,' she said, 'I think that will be very nice.'

The plan seemed to succeed beyond Mrs Brown's fondest dreams. She did not see or hear of William for the rest of the morning. It was almost as if he were still at school. He appeared at lunch, but was silent and thoughtful. A sense of peace stole over Mrs Brown.

After lunch, Ethel and Robert came to her in the morning-room.

'I say,' said Robert in a mystified voice, 'I thought William was breaking up today.'

'He is,' said Mrs, Brown, 'he has broken up. He came home about eleven o'clock.'

'He's very quiet,' said Ethel lugubriously.

Mrs Brown smiled a fond, maternal smile. 'Dear little boy,' she said. 'He's upstairs thinking out his Christmas presents to people.'

'Well,' said Robert, 'let's make the most of it, and talk over the party.'

Robert and Ethel were giving a party to their friends, and William was being let into it as little as possible. Mingled with an elder brother and sister's instinctive feeling that the admission of a small schoolboy brother into their plans would in some way cheapen the whole thing was an equally instinctive fear of William. Pies in which William had a finger had a curious way of turning into something quite unexpected. William could generally prove that it had nothing to do with him, but still – the result was the same.

So Robert's and Ethel's party was a 'secret', only to be discussed when William was safely out of the way. William, of course, knew that it was to take place and professed an utter indifference to it, while privately he spent a good deal of time and ingenuity trying to ferret out the details of it. So far they had managed to keep secret from him the fact that after supper there was going to be a short one-act play.

Ethel and Robert had lately joined the Dramatic Society and at present no function of any kind was complete to them without a one-act play. The shining lights of the Dramatic Society (including Ethel and Robert) were going to take part in the play. They kept this part of it particularly a secret from William, because William rather fancied himself both as actor and playwright, and they felt that if William knew that a play was going to take place under his roof it would be practically impossible to protect the play from the devastating effects of William's interest in it.

They discussed the dancing (which was to take place before supper) and the supper, and the play (which was to take place after supper), and Ethel's dress and Mrs Brown's dress, and the invitation list and the extra 'help' they would need for the evening, and whether Robert's dress-suit had better go to the tailors to be pressed or not.

Finally Mrs Brown became a little anxious and said

to Ethel: 'Ethel, dear, I wish you'd just run upstairs and have a look at William. He's so quiet. I hope he's not feeling ill or anything.'

Visible gloom settled on the faces of Robert and Ethel at the mention of William.

'Ill!' repeated Robert with deep feeling.

'Yes, you know, mother,' said Ethel, 'we'd hear enough row if he felt ill. But—'

She went obediently from the room and Mrs Brown and Robert continued the discussion. Just as they were deciding that Robert's suit had better go to be pressed they were interrupted by a cry of 'Mother!' from Ethel upstairs, and leapt to their feet: 'Oh, it's William,' moaned Mrs Brown; 'he *is* ill.'

'More likely he's set the house on fire,' said Robert gloomily.

They dashed upstairs. William, his face and hands and hair and clothes freely adorned with green paint, sat on his bedroom hearthrug, which had shared in the wholesale application of green paint. On the hearthrug was a once-white straw hat of Ethel's, upon which William had obviously devoted much labour and green paint. He had, moreover, filled it with earth, and planted in it a cyclamen from the greenhouse.

'Look,' said Ethel, almost – but not quite – speechless with fury. 'My – my best hat!'

'Why, it's quite an ole hat, Ethel,' said William,

'I've seen you wear it heaps. I thought you must have about done with it.'

'B-but, William,' gasped Mrs Brown, 'what on earth have you been doing?'

'Well, you said *think* out Christmas presents, an' *make* 'em an' don' spend money on 'em, so I thought

'LOOK!' CRIED ETHEL, ALMOST SPEECHLESS WITH FURY.
'MY – MY BEST HAT!'

I'd start on Ethel's, an' it took me ever so long to think of anything that I could make and that wouldn't cost money an' then I thought that I could paint one of Ethel's hats an' make it look like a kind of fancy plant pot with the paint from the shed, an' put a plant into it from the greenhouse. I thought it was rather a good idea,' he ended modestly.

'But my *hat*!' almost sobbed Ethel.

'It's a straw hat,' urged William, 'you don't want a *straw* hat in the winter.'

'But it was almost new. I want it for next summer.'

'Oh, next summer,' said William patiently. 'I guess this flower won't last as long as that. I guess you can use it again next summer.'

'And have you taken any of my things?' demanded Robert sternly.

'No, Robert,' said William meekly. 'I haven't, honestly. I was just *thinking* how I could make a nice cushion for mother out of two of your coloured handkerchiefs, stuffed with some ole things of mine, but I hadn't taken 'em, not yet.'

That was why, when William discovered about the play, he was told that he was not to see it either at rehearsals or on the evening of the party.

'Well,' said William, 'if you messed up one of my ole caps, d'you think I'd make that fuss? Not that I *mind* not seeing the ole play,' he added hastily. 'In fact,' putting himself well out of Robert's reach, 'it's rather a relief to me. I'm jolly sorry for the poor folks that have gotter watch poor Ethel and Robert tryin' to act.'

Then he leapt lightly over the window sill into the garden before Robert could get at him.

The day of the party arrived. William, shining with cleanliness, his hair brushed and greased to a resplendent sleekness, encased in his Eton suit, an expression of frowning intensity upon his freckled face, stood a little way from the rest of his family as the guests began to arrive. Some of the guests called out: 'Hello, William.' Others ignored him.

William tried to look bored and indifferent, and as if he didn't think much of the whole show. But really he was looking forward to the dancing and the supper, and he meant to watch the play from the garden through the window, even if he were not officially allowed among the audience. Absurd to let a perfectly good weapon against Robert and Ethel, that would probably do service for months and months, escape him like that.

The guests had all arrived. The music for the dancing had begun. William stood in the drawing-room, which had been 'turned out' for the dance and looked round him critically.

He slowly eliminated from his list of possible

partners a girl with red hair, another with a too long neck, another with the wrong shaped nose, and another with a slight cast in her eye.

Slowly, by a process of elimination, he determined on the prettiest girl in the room, and walked across to her, baring his teeth in what was meant to be an ingratiating smile. Just as he was a few yards from her, Robert came up and claimed her, and they both moved off without looking at him. William's smile died away. He looked round the room again.

Well, that girl wasn't bad – the one with curly hair and the yellow dress. William assumed the smile again and walked across to her. Just as he was approaching her a friend of Robert's came up, put his arm round her waist, and off they went together. William took off the smile. His face wore an expression of sardonic bitterness. All the girls seemed to be dancing now. No, there was the one with the wrong shaped nose still sitting by the window. William glared at her critically across the room. She wasn't so bad, really, if you didn't look at her sideways. William summoned up his painful grin and went across to her.

'May I—?' he began with excessive politeness.

A large man stepped in front of him, took the girl's hand, and led her off among the dancers.

William was boiling with fury. A nice set of people Robert and Ethel had invited. They didn't seem to

WELL, THE GIRL WASN'T TOO BAD, WILLIAM DECIDED –
THE ONE WITH CURLY HAIR AND THE YELLOW DRESS.

WILLIAM ASSUMED HIS SMILE AGAIN AND WALKED
ACROSS TO HER.

know how to *behave*. There was only the girl with the squint left. William looked at her for a long time with an intent frown. She wasn't really so bad, especially when she was looking at the ground. William bared his teeth again (his jaws were aching by this time) and walked up to her.

'Excuse me——' he began.

A man stepped up from the other side.

'Shall us?' he said to the girl, and off they went.

William stood, his hands in his pockets, leaning against the wall, a ferocious frown upon his polished face. Everyone was dancing now, except a few couples who were sitting in the alcove talking and laughing. Nice lot of *manners* they'd got, thought William bitterly. Simply no one taking the slightest notice of him.

Not that he *cared*, of course, but you'd have thought that *someone* would've wanted to dance with him. Nice thing when you wasted every Wednesday afternoon at a beastly dancing lesson, and then when you went to a dance no one wanted to dance with you. Nice thing going to all this trouble of washing and hair-brushing, and putting on your best suit, just to watch other people dancing. Huh!

William turned and went with scornful dignity from the room. The only thing that in his eyes spoilt the effect of his scornful exit was a definite and very well-founded suspicion that no one had noticed it.

He went to the side door, and looked out into the night. Ginger, Douglas and Henry were coming cautiously up the walk. Now, the Outlaws, though never encouraged socially by each other's families, yet took a great interest in the social activities of each other's families.

Whenever any of them gave a party the Outlaws would be there – uninvited and very unofficial guests – generally in the garden keeping a friendly eye on the affair through the windows. William was glad that his friends had only just arrived and had not witnessed his ignominious failure to secure a partner a few minutes ago. To his friends William exaggerated his own importance at his family's festivities.

'Hello!' whispered the Outlaws. 'How're you getting on?'

'Fine,' said William, with rather overdone enthusiasm.

'We thought p'raps you'd be dancing,' said Ginger.

'Oh, I got a bit tired of dancing,' said William airily, 'an' came out to get cool. Come round an' have a look at 'em.'

Glad to be with his friends once more, he led the Outlaws round to a part of the garden where they could see the drawing-room, and, hidden among the bushes, watched the festive scene within.

'Quite a lot of 'em,' said Ginger, impressed.

'Oh, yes,' said William, 'an' there's really a lot more than there looks.'

'Has Ethel got a new dress for it?' said Douglas.

'Oh, yes,' said William. 'Everyone's got new clothes for it. I'd better go in again soon. They don't want me to be away long.'

'Which one was you dancin' with?' said Henry.

William gave a short laugh.

'Goodness! I can't remember all the ones I was dancing with!' he said.

'Is there a good supper?' said Ginger.

'There just *is*!' said William. 'Come and look at it.'

They crept through the side door and into the dining-room. There William proudly pointed to the table, resplendent with ices and creams and fruit and trifles and jellies of every kind. The Outlaws licked their lips.

'*Crumbs!*' gasped Ginger. 'Doesn't it make you feel empty.'

'You can have a go at it when they've finished,' promised William generously. 'I'll tell you when they've all gone back. They're going to do a play afterwards.'

'*Crumbs!*' said Ginger again. 'Is it a good one?'

'I should just *think* so,' said William enthusiastically.

'Can we watch through the window?' said Henry.

'Cert'n'ly,' said William kindly, 'an' I'll come out and watch it with you. I don't suppose they'll notice I'm not sittin' with them in the room.'

'P'raps we'd better be goin' now,' said Henry, ''case they come. The music's stopped an' they're kind of movin' about.'

But it was too late. There came the sound of the opening of the drawing-room door, and an influx of guests into the hall.

'Get under the table, quick!' said William.

So the Outlaws got under the table – quick.

The guests entered. They found William apparently alone, an expression of mingled innocence and boredom and long enduring patience upon his frowning freckled face. He was engaged in arranging the chairs round the table.

'Here's the ubiquitous William,' said one of Robert's friends. William hoped that the look he received in return made him feel small. Ubiquitous, indeed. When he'd washed his face, and brushed his hair, and put on his best suit, and looked as smart as any of them.

They sat round the table. William was right at the corner, next to a tall, pale man who was suspected of cherishing a romantic passion for Ethel. The food was in the centre of the table, so the tall, pale man had to hand the dishes to William and keep him supplied. He tried at first to talk to William, but found this difficult.

'I suppose you've broken up?' he said.

'Yes,' said William, his voice and face equally devoid of expression.

'Do you like the holidays?'

'Yes,' said William in the same tone of voice.

'Are you fond of lessons?'

'No.'

'I expect you're looking forward to Christmas.'

William, considering this remark beneath contempt, vouchsafed no answer. The tall, thin man, crushed, transferred his attention to the lady on the other side of him.

Now William was painfully conscious of the presence of Ginger and Henry and Douglas beneath the table. He realised, too, that he had towards them the duties of a host. He could not eat in comfort with Ginger, Douglas and Henry cramped and uncomfortable and hungry in his so immediate vicinity. He took two bites at the sausage-roll with which the tall, thin man had supplied him, then, looking dreamily at the opposite wall, slipped his hand under the table.

There another hand, grateful and unseen, promptly relieved him of the rest of the sausage-roll. His plate was empty. The tall, thin man looked at it. Then he looked at William. William met his eyes with an aggressive stare.

The tall, thin man looked at William's plate again. It was true. This child really had consumed a large sausage-roll in less than a minute. He handed him the plate of sausage-rolls again.

Again William took one.

Again William took two small bites and handed the rest to his invisible friends beneath the table.

Again he turned his aggressive stare upon the tall, thin man.

Again the young man looked with rising horror from William to the empty plate in front of him, and then from the empty plate back to William.

He then took the whole dish of sausage-rolls, put them just in front of William, and turned to continue his conversation with his other neighbour. William felt cheered. This was just what he wanted. He took a roll on to his plate and looked round. No one was watching him. With a lightning movement he transferred the roll to his knee and held it out beneath the table. The unseen recipient grabbed it eagerly. William did the same with a second, a third, a fourth. He grew reckless. He put down a fifth, a sixth, a seventh. That was two each. He was doing them jolly well. There were three more on the dish. He'd given them those, too, and then he'd begin to eat something himself. One – two – three –

He twitched them all quickly from the dish to his

plate, from his plate to the unseen hand. No more were within his reach. He turned his aggressive stare upon the tall, thin man. As though hypnotised by the stare, the tall, thin man turned slowly to William. He looked at the empty plate and the empty dish in front of William and his jaw dropped open weakly.

He put his hand to his head, and pinched himself to make sure he was awake. He simply couldn't believe his eyes. It was like a dreadful nightmare. In a few seconds this child had eaten up a large dishful of enormous sausage-rolls – he must be suffering from some horrible disease. William did not speak, merely fixed him with that hungry, unflinching stare. The tall, thin man tried to say, 'And what can I pass you now?' but he couldn't. Words wouldn't come. The sight of that enormous empty dish had broken his nerve.

Just then a diversion occurred. A friend of Ethel's almost opposite had slipped off her shoe under the table, and a few minutes later reached out for it, and could not find it. She made a large circular sweep in search of it with her stockinged foot and just caught Ginger on the neck above his collar where he was most ticklish. Ginger dropped his half-eaten sausage roll and gave a loud yell. A sudden tense silence fell over the table. Had the proverbial pin been dropped, it would have been heard for miles. Then the girl who had tickled Ginger gave an embarrassed little giggle.

'I'm afraid I kicked your dog – or your cat – or something,' she said. She lifted up the table-cloth and grew pale. 'It's boys,' she said in a breathless whisper; 'ever so many of them!'

It was half-an-hour later. Ginger, Douglas and Henry had been ignominiously ejected. William had been despatched to spend the rest of the evening in his bedroom. The dining-room was empty. Only three pathetic half-eaten sausage-rolls beneath the table were left to tell the tale.

William leant out of his bedroom window. The shadowy forms of the Outlaws lurked in the bushes beneath.

'What're they doin' now?' whispered William.

'They're acting the play,' whispered Douglas, 'an' everyone is watching – maids an' all.'

'Well, go an' watch it,' whispered William, 'an' tell me about it tomorrow. Tell me about Robert an' Ethel – speshly if they do anythin' silly – An', I say—'

'Yes?' whispered the faithful Outlaws from the bushes.

'I'm awful hungry. I only had a few bites of roll – go an' see if there's anyone in the dining-room and if the stuff's still there.'

'There won't be anyone in the dining-room,' whispered Henry, ''cause everyone's in watching the play.'

'Well, go an' get a lot of grub,' ordered William in

a sibilant commanding whisper. 'Keep some for your-self an' put some in a basket, an' I'll throw down a rope to draw it up.'

This method of obtaining food appealed greatly to William's romance-loving soul.

The Outlaws departed and in a few minutes returned – very quickly.

'William,' said Ginger excitedly, 'there's a burglar in the dinin'-room.'

'What!' said William.

'A burglar with his bag of tools an' his bag of booty, an' everything. He's drinkin' wine or somethin' at the sideboard.'

In less than a minute William had joined the Outlaws in the garden, and together they all went round to the dining-room window. Yes, there he was – a real burglar in dingy clothes and shabby necktie, a cap pulled low over his eyes, his bag of tools and a half-filled sack by him. He was standing at the sideboard drinking a whisky and soda.

The Outlaws retired to the bushes to discuss their tactics.

'We'd better go'n tell your father,' said Douglas.

'No, we *won't*,' said William, 'we'll catch him ourselves. What's the fun of findin' a burglar an' lettin' someone else catch him?'

Henry and Ginger agreed with him. William

assumed the position of leader. There was an enormous curtain in a box upstairs. They'd used it for theatricals once. Robert and Ethel had got a new one for this year, but the old one would do nicely to catch the burglar in. It hadn't many holes.

'What'll we do with him, then?' said Ginger.

'We'll – we'll lock him up somewhere,' said William, as he went up to fetch the curtain.

In less than a minute he returned with it. It was certainly voluminous enough. The Outlaws laid their plans. They crept into the dining-room silently and, stealing up behind him, enveloped their prey, just as he was in the act of pouring out some more whisky. He was taken completely by surprise. He lost his footing and fell forward into a dusky mass of all-enveloping green serge. He was not a big man or a strong man. He tried to regain his footing and failed. In his green serge covering he was being dragged somewhere. He shouted.

It happened that in the morning-room (where the play was being held) Ethel, in her capacity of heroine, had just finished singing a song, which was greeted with frenzied applause by her loyal guests. The applause drowned the burglar's shouts. Douglas flung open the French windows that led from the dining-room to the garden, and panting, tugging and perspiring the Outlaws dragged their victim out into the night across the lawn. Douglas opened the green-house door. They hoisted the large green curtain, which still contained its straggling inhabitant, into the greenhouse, shut the door and turned the key in the lock. Then, still panting and purple-faced, the Outlaws went back to the house.

'Well, he *was* a weight!' commented Douglas.

'Shall we go an' tell 'em now?' said Ginger.

But William was still rent by the pangs of hunger.

'Oh, he's all right for a bit,' he said. 'He can't get out. Let's take a bit of food upstairs first. We can tell 'em after.'

The Outlaws approved of this. It was certainly a wise plan to make sure of the food. They returned to the dining-room, heaped several plates with dainties that particularly appealed to them, and crept silently upstairs to William's bedroom. There they sat on the floor munching happily and discussing their capture. They were just deciding that it would be rather fun to be policemen when they grew up, when Ginger pricked up his ears.

'Seems a sort of noise going on downstairs,' he said.

Very softly the Outlaws opened the door of William's bedroom and crept on to the landing. There was most certainly a sort of noise going on downstairs. Everyone seemed to be bustling about, and talking excitedly.

'Do be quiet a minute while I ring up his mother,' said Ethel's voice, distraught and tearful. 'Hello – hello – Is that Mrs Langley? *Has* Harold come home? *Hasn't he*? – No, he's completely disappeared – No one knows *where* he is – we got to the point in the play where he comes on – just after my song, you know – and I waited and *waited* and he never came, and I had to leave the stage without finishing the scene. My nerves had absolutely all gone. I'm still trembling all over, and everyone was hunting and *hunting* for him – and we had to stop the play,' tearfully; 'we couldn't go on without him. He was the burglar, you know – I do hope nothing awful's happened – I mean, I hope he didn't get so nervous he lost his memory, or – or – went out and had some awful accident or anything. We're all so distressed – it's quite spoilt the party, of course, and *ruined* the play. We only got to the song – I don't know when I've felt so awful.'

She was interrupted by Mrs Brown's voice, high and hysterical. 'Oh, Ethel, do fetch your father. It's too dark to see anything – but there's the most awful commotion going on in the garden. Someone's breaking all the glass in the greenhouse.'

The entire party sallied out excitedly into the garden. They were not there long, but during their absence two things happened. The Outlaws, acting with great presence of mind, seized their share of the food and fled like so many flashes of streaked lightning to their several homes. And William got into bed and went to sleep. He went to sleep with almost incredible rapidity. When his family entered his bedroom a few minutes later, demanding explanation, William lay red and breathless, but determinedly and unwakably asleep. The grimly set lines of his mouth and the frown on his brow testified to the intense and concentrated nature of his sleep.

'Oh, don't wake him,' pleaded Mrs Brown. 'It's so bad for children to be *startled* out of sleep.'

'Sleep!' said Robert sarcastically. 'Well, I don't mind. It can wait till tomorrow for all I care. The party's *ruined*, anyway.'

Fortunately, they did not look under the bed, or they would have seen a large plate piled with appetising dainties. They went away with threatening murmurs in which the word 'tomorrow' figured largely.

When they had gone William got out of bed with great caution and sat in the darkness munching iced cakes. That sleep idea had been jolly good. Of course, he knew it couldn't go on indefinitely. He couldn't go on sleeping for a month. He'd have to wake up tomorrow, but tomorrow was tomorrow, and when tonight holds an entire plate of iced cakes (many of them with layers of real cream inside), tomorrow is hardly worth serious consideration.

CHAPTER 13

REVENGE IS SWEET

THE Outlaws were agog with excitement, for the day of Hubert Lane's party was drawing near. This may sound as though the Outlaws were to be honoured guests at Hubert Lane's party, were to join in the cracker-pulling and cake-eating and dancing and parlour games that were being laboriously prepared for it by the Lane parents.

Far from it. For between the Outlaws and the Hubert Lanites a deadly feud waged, and tradition demanded that they should treat each other's parties with indifference and contempt. It was the Hubert Lanites who had broken that tradition. They had deliberately wrecked William's party the week before Christmas. They had gathered round the windows to jeer at the Outlaws disporting themselves within, and had dispersed miraculously in the darkness whenever a sally had been made from the house against them. They had, moreover, substituted a deceased cat (which Hubert had found in a ditch) for the rabbit which the conjuror had brought with him

303

and which was to appear miraculously from his hat.

Even the adult relations of the Outlaws had resented this outrage. But they had told the Outlaws that little gentlemen would regard the matter as beneath contempt. The Outlaws, however, did not regard the matter as beneath contempt. They were not out to prove themselves little gentlemen. They were out for revenge.

They were determined to wreck Hubert Lane's party as Hubert Lane had wrecked theirs. They wisely hid their resolve, however, from their elders and betters. Their elders and betters fondly imagined that the Outlaws had accepted the insult like little gentlemen.

But the Outlaws with silent determination were only biding their time. They were awaiting the day of Hubert Lane's party.

The news that Mr and Mrs Lane would be away for the party and that Hubert's Aunt Emmy would preside heartened the Outlaws considerably. Mr and Mrs Lane had flown to the sick bed of an aunt of Mr Lane's, of whom he had 'expectations', and against those 'expectations' the success of Hubert's party seemed a negligible matter. The Outlaws felt that Providence was on their side. The conviction was strengthened when they heard later that at sight of her nephew the sick aunt completely recovered and did not even offer to pay his railway fare.

Of course, Aunt Emmy in command simplified matters considerably for the Outlaws. The Outlaws had met Aunt Emmy. Anything vaguer, kinder, more shortsighted, and more devastatingly well-meaning than Aunt Emmy could scarcely be imagined. Aunt Emmy should not be difficult to deal with in any crisis.

The Outlaws had made no definite plans. They had simply decided that somehow or other they must gain admittance to the Hubert Lane mansion on the night of the party and then let things take their own course. William, the head of the Outlaws, like all the best generals, preferred not to draw up his own plan of action till he had ascertained the enemy's.

The party was to begin at seven. At half-past six, ten boys in single file might have been observed creeping through a hole in the fence that bordered the Lane garden. At the head crept William, his freckled face contorted into a scowl expressive of determination to do or die. Behind him came Ginger, behind him Henry and behind him Douglas, and behind Douglas came six anti-Lanites and supporters of the Outlaws.

A pear tree grew conveniently up the side of the Lane mansion, and it was possible with a certain amount of danger to life and limb (which it was beneath the Outlaws' dignity to consider) to climb up the pear tree and in at an attic window.

William led the way. The others followed with a

puffing and panting and a rustling and a cracking of twigs and muttered imprecations such as 'Coo!' and 'Crumbs!' and 'Golly!' which on a more normal night might have attracted the attention of the whole household. But tonight was not a normal night.

Hubert was in his bedroom at the other side of the house anxiously arraying himself in an Eton suit and shining pumps. The maids were in the kitchen giving the final touches to mountains of sandwiches and trifles and creams and cakes and jellies and blancmanges. Mr and Mrs Lane, whose bedroom was on the direct path of the pear tree, were at the bedside of the exasperatingly recuperative aunt, and Aunt Emmy was in the kitchen with the maids driving them to distraction by her well-meant efforts to 'help'.

She had already sprinkled salt over a trifle under the impression that it was sugar, and made a jug of 'coffee' out of knife powder, because she was too shortsighted to read the labels on the tins.

So there was no one to oppose or even notice the Outlaws as one by one they climbed up the perilous branches of the pear tree and in at the open attic window. There were a few minor casualties of the march, of course. Ginger, whose foot became firmly wedged in a fork of the branches, with great presence of mind undid his shoe and performed the rest of his journey without it. A small boy christened

'Marmaduke' by his parents and re-named 'Jam' by his contemporaries, who had insisted on joining the expedition, lost his footing and nerve just as he was about to leave the pear tree and clamber into the attic window, and uttered a yell that might have been heard a mile away, but William grabbed the youthful climber by his ear, Ginger grabbed him by the hair, and together they hauled him into safety.

Then they sat on the floor and looked at each other – collars and ties awry, jackets torn, knees scratched and dirty, trousers plentifully adorned with some white material that had evidently been used in a vain endeavour to beautify the Lane attic window-sills. Then William drew a deep breath and said: 'Coo! *That* was a climb and a half.'

'Yes,' panted Douglas, 'I went to a film thing on Mount Everest, and it jolly well wasn't *half* as steep as this ole pear tree.'

'Jam' was glowering at his rescuers. 'You needn't 've tore my ear'n hair out by the roots,' he muttered malevolently, nursing the injured organs with both hands. But no one listened to his lamentation. The army of bravos was busy by this time inspecting their eyrie. The Lane attics proved to consist of three fair-sized rooms packed with boxes of rubbish of all kinds, water cisterns, spiders' webs, and mysterious pipes. On the tiny landing outside was a small window leading straight out on to the roof. It was a boyhood's paradise.

The eyes of the Outlaws gleamed as they explored it. It said much for the general futility of Hubert Lane and his satellites that they never utilised this heaven-sent playground, but regarded it merely as an ordinary room in an ordinary house.

'I say, let's play robbers!' said Ginger in a hoarse whisper.

'No, let's be shipwrecked on a desert island,' said Henry, his eye roving about the scene and already picking out the outstanding features of the scene – the sea, the shore, the rock, the octopus, the log hut, the lagoon, the—

But William called the attention of his band to the immediate object of the expedition.

'We've not come here to play!' he hissed fiercely.

Henry had opened the little window and ventured out upon the roof. Two other daring explorers had climbed up to the water cistern. Others were balancing themselves upon pipes or clambering upon packing cases or rummaging inquisitively through huge boxes of rubbish.

'You'll have 'em *all* up,' said William angrily, 'an' *then* what'll you do?'

'Fight 'em,' responded 'Jam', who had by this time recovered his nerve and warlike spirit, and had fixed an old wicker plant pot upon his head in lieu of a helmet and was brandishing a bamboo curtain pole that he had found lying on the floor. '*Fight* 'em!' he repeated, drunk with valour.

But William's words had recalled his followers to a sense of the realities of life. They descended from pipes and packing cases and water cisterns and clustered round him.

William dropped his voice to a conspiratorial whisper.

'We've gotter creep out an' see what's happ'nin' first of all,' he said hoarsely, 'an' then – an' then we'll think what to do.'

Very creakingly on tiptoe the Outlaws crept out after him and hung over the banisters of the attic staircase.

Aunt Emmy's voice, dear and flute-like, arose from the hall.

'*That's* right, Hubert, darling. You look *very* nice, my cherub, very nice indeed. *Quite* a little man. Now I'm sure you know how to be a little host, don't you darling, and look after your little guests? You must think always of *their* pleasure and not your own.'

'Your hair's coming down, auntie,' said Hubert.

'Little boys mustn't make personal remarks, darling,' said Aunt Emmy.

The Outlaws were listening with silent rapture to

this. William, with frowning concentration, was storing up every word of the conversation in his mind for future use.

There came the sound of wheels on the gravel outside the front door, and the sound of the front door bell.

'The first guest, darling,' said Aunt Emmy. 'I'll open the door and you'd better stand just there to receive them – smile a little, darling, and remember to say "How d'you do?" nicely.'

Then came the sound of the arrival of fat Bertie Franks, the most odious of the Hubert Lanites next to Hubert himself. Arrivals followed fast and furious after that. The Hubert Lanites all bore a curious physical resemblance to Hubert, their leader. They were all pale and they were all fat. They rallied round Hubert chiefly because of his unlimited pocket-money, and, like Hubert, when anyone annoyed them, they told their fathers and their fathers wrote notes about it to the fathers of those who had annoyed them. The guests hung up coats and hats in the hall and changed into pumps and drifted into the drawing-room. A dismal, very-first-beginning-of-the-party silence reigned.

'Now, what shall we play at first?' said Aunt Emmy, with overdone brightness. 'Puss in the Corner?'

This suggestion was met with chilly silence.

'Postman's Knock?' went on Aunt Emmy, her brightness, becoming almost hysterical.

Silence again – something almost ominous in it this time.

'Hunt the Slipper?' quavered Aunt Emmy.

The silence this time was suggestive of fury.

'S-s-s-supper?' said Aunt Emmy, striving vainly after her first fine careless rapture of brightness.

She hadn't meant to have supper till much later, but she'd come to the end of all her other suggestions.

A murmur signified qualified approval.

One of the guests took the matter into his own hands.

'What about a game of Hide and Seek an' then supper?'

'Hide and Seek—' quavered Aunt Emmy; 'that's rather a *rough* game, isn't it?'

They assured her that it wasn't, and drew lots for who should be 'It'. The Outlaws, craning necks and ears over the attic staircase, gathered that Hubert was 'It'. The guests, led by Bertie Franks, swarmed upstairs in search of hiding places. They swarmed up the first floor and the second floor and began to swarm up to the attic. Meekly and devoid of initiative they simply followed Bertie Franks. The Outlaws withdrew hastily to their lair.

'Here's a little window,' squeaked a Hubert Lanite,

'goin' out on the roof. Let's go'n hide on the roof.'

'No,' said Bertie Franks earnestly. ''S dangerous. We don't want to go anywhere dangerous. We might hurt ourselves.'

'And we don't want to do anythin' to get our best clothes dirty,' said another Lanite.

They entered the attic opposite to the one where the Outlaws were concealed.

'We could all hide here,' said a Lanite, 'behind boxes an' things,'

The Lanites always followed meekly anyone who would take the lead.

'It's rather dusty,' said another Lanite with distaste.

'Never mind,' said a third, 'it's not for long.'

'Ugh! There's spiders an' things,' said a fourth disgustedly.

This conversation tells you all you need (and, I hope, want) to know about the Hubert Lanites.

'Let's shut the door so's he won't see us,' said Bertie Franks.

Someone shut the door and from within came sounds of Hubert Lanites settling into hiding places, moving boxes, clambering over obstacles and uttering exclamations of disgust as they did so.

Very quietly William slipped across and turned the key in the lock. Evidently no one heard him.

'Coming!' yelled Hubert Lane from downstairs.

'Don't shout so, darling,' said Aunt Emmy's flute-like voice. 'Say it quietly. Little gentlemen never raise their voices.'

Hubert Lane came slowly upstairs. He paused at each landing, but did not explore. Some instinct seemed to lead him straight up to the attic. He stopped at the open window that led out on to the roof. His orderly mind knew that that should be shut. And it was open. They must have gone out on to the roof.

After a moment's hesitation he got out of the window and began to explore the recesses of the chimney pots. Like a flash William, who was watching behind the door, streaked to the window, shut it and bolted it. Hubert turned in dismay and William had a vision of Hubert's fat pale face staring open-mouthed through the pane before, with admirable presence of mind, he moved two large table leaves that stood near, to shut out the sight. That disposed of Hubert. There was no real danger. The window gave on to a stretch of flat roof, bounded by a parapet and there was no fear of the cautious Hubert venturing even near the parapet.

The Outlaws streamed out of their hiding place to join their leader. It was evident that William had some plan.

'Come along,' he said tersely, 'an' do jus' what I do.'

They followed him trustfully on his bold course downstairs – right down to the hall where Aunt Emmy stood smiling painfully and pinning up her ever descending hair.

Very faintly from upstairs from behind the barrier of window pane and table leaves there came to them an indignant protesting 'Hi!' It was only just audible and fortunately Aunt Emmy, as well as being near-sighted, was what she called a '*leetle* short of hearing – not really *deaf*, you know'.

As to most of us, hens are just hens – though we realise that they must have distinguishing marks of feature and expression invisible to us whereby their nearest and dearest know them – so to Aunt Emmy boys were just boys.

About ten boys had ascended the stairs and now about ten boys descended. It did not occur to her that they might not be the same boys. Even had she been less short-sighted that possibility would not have occurred to her. She certainly did notice that their former spick and span appearance was sadly blurred, but she knew that there is no power on earth that can keep a boy tidy longer than five minutes. She knew that there is a powerful Law of Attraction between Boys and Dirt and that you cannot with impunity interfere with the Laws of Nature.

She threw a glance of distaste at the Outlaws'

WILLIAM HAD A VISION OF HUBERT'S FAT FACE STARING
OPEN-MOUTHED THROUGH THE WINDOW.

ruffled hair, crooked collars and suits covered with whiting and cobwebs. She closed her eyes for a minute at the sight as though enduring untold agony. Then she mastered her feelings and inquired faintly:

'Where's Hubert, dears? He should have conducted his little guests downstairs.'

William, his freckled face as expressionless as a mummy's, spoke in a mincingly polite tone of voice: 'Hubert said he was coming down in a minute and would we begin supper without him, please.'

Aunt Emmy was taken aback.

She went to the bottom of the staircase.

'Hubert, darling!' she called. Very, very faintly from the far away came the indignant protesting 'Hi!' of Hubert locked out upon the tiles. The real guests were still crouching behind packing cases in the attic waiting to be 'found'.

Hubert's 'Hi' was too faint to reach Aunt Emmy's short hearing. She might, of course, have gone on a voyage of discovery in search of the missing Hubert had not the sight of the 'guests' surging forthwith into the dining-room recalled her to the scene of action. She looked at them reproachfully.

'I think, perhaps, Hubert has gone to tidy himself,' she said, 'and I think, perhaps, it would be as well if you little boys did the same.'

The 'little boys' ignored this suggestion, and,

sitting down at the table, began to eat.

Aunt Emmy had always had a vague suspicion that she disliked boys, and the suspicion now grew to a certainty.

These boys might have made up their minds to consume all the most attractive food on the table in the shortest possible time. They refused sandwiches and bread and butter. They devoured iced cakes as fast as poor Aunt Emmy could hand them round. They demanded trifle and blancmange and creams. They ate ravenously as though it were some mighty task they had set themselves. They got through enormous quantities of food. They ate in silence, ignoring all Aunt Emmy's polite remarks about the weather and questions as to how they were getting on with their lessons at school. They worked like Trojans. The dish of iced cakes was empty. The trifle dish was empty. The cream dish was empty. The blancmange dish was empty.

Only plates of wholesome bread and butter, of sandwiches and of plain cake stood untouched.

Aunt Emmy looked round aghast.

Louder and more indignant grew the Hubertian 'Hi's!' from upstairs. And another sound had joined them – a sound of the pattering of many hands on a distant door. The real guests had evidently awakened to the fact that something had gone wrong somewhere.

'Do you hear a – a sort of *sound*?' said Aunt Emmy, doubtfully, putting her hand to her ear. William looked up as if straining his ears to catch the ever-growing racket.

'What sort of a sound?' he demanded, fixing Aunt Emmy with his stern unblinking gaze.

'I – I think I'll go and see whatever dear Hubert's doing,' said Aunt Emmy faintly, and, her hair coming down more

AUNT EMMY LOOKED
ROUND AGHAST.

violently than ever, she fled from the horrible spectacle of these ungentlemanly little boys eating like – well, like nothing Aunt Emmy had ever seen before.

William opened the dining-room window, and the Outlaws, their bodies sated with the joy of the Lanite feast, their souls sated with the joy of vengeance, crept out into the night. The Lanites had openly mocked them and spoilt their conjuring show. They had eaten the Lanites' supper. An eye for an eye, a tooth for a tooth – a supper for a dead cat. They were quits!

Aunt Emmy found and rescued the infuriated

THE DISH OF ICED CAKES WAS EMPTY. THE TRIFLE DISH
WAS EMPTY. THE CREAM-CAKE DISH WAS EMPTY. ONLY
WHOLESOME BREAD AND BUTTER AND PLAIN CAKE
REMAINED.

Lanites, brought them down to the relatively Spartan
fare left them by the Outlaws, and then went away to
have a nervous breakdown quietly by herself. Never
would she have anything to do with boys again –
never, never, *never*! She got through her nervous
breakdown as quickly as she could and then returned
to brighten up the victims of this terrible catastrophe.
But the gloom that had fallen over the proceedings was
too heavy to be lifted; even by Aunt Emmy's
brightness.

Mr Lane was not in the best of tempers when he returned home. He was taking a gloomy view of life generally. The vindictive cheerfulness and persistent healthiness of his aunt had had a very embittering effect on him. And the story of the Outlaws marauding expedition proved to be the last straw. So he sat down at once and wrote a very strong letter to the Outlaws' fathers.

The fathers of the Outlaws were quite accustomed to receiving strong letters from Mr Lane. Whenever a boy annoyed Hubert, Hubert's father wrote a strong letter to the boy's father. And quite often the father did nothing at all beyond dropping the strong letter into the waste-paper basket. But this was, of course, a serious matter. Verbal or even bodily insults, to Hubert Lane and his followers, might be, meta-phorically speaking, dropped into the waste-paper basket, but consuming vast quantities of Lane food uninvited, was, in the eyes of the adult world, a serious matter, and the heavy hand of parental retribution descended upon the Outlaws that night.

But the effect of the heavy hand of parental retribution is always short-lived.

The next morning the Outlaws sallied out to school undaunted even to bumptiousness. The Lanites looked gloomy and infuriated and they glowered ferociously at the Outlaws silently during school. After school the

Outlaws in a body approached the Lanites in a body.

'*You* jolly well caught it last night,' said Hubert derisively.

'Hush, darling!' said William, in a shrill falsetto. 'Say it quietly. Little gentlemen never raise their voices.'

'I'll tell my father,' said Hubert, in fury.

'Don't take any notice of them,' counselled Bertie Franks. 'My mother told me never to have anything to do with them.'

But the Outlaws now began to rub their hands round their stomachs in vulgar mock show of appreciation, smacking their lips and screwing up their faces.

'Cream cakes,' said William. 'Coo! *Jolly* good!'

'Trifle!' murmured Ginger rapturously.

'Sugar cakes!' said Ginger. 'Oh, crumbs!'

This was more than even the Hubert Lanites could stand. Unwarlike as they were, accustomed to take their stand behind Mr Lane's strong letters and avoid open conflict, they threw caution to the winds, and hurled themselves to mortal combat with the Outlaws.

It was a good fight and revealed unsuspected resources of courage and prowess in the Hubert Lanites.

It ended in a general mix-up of Outlaws and Lanites in a muddy ditch.

There Outlaws and Lanites sat up panting and covered with mud, and looked at each other.

And slowly over the faces of all dawned a grin of satisfaction.

'Go home and tell your father now,' said William to Hubert.

And Hubert, swelling with pride and joy after his first real fight, said: 'No, I won't. An' – an' we'll fight you again,' and added hastily (for though he'd enjoyed it he'd had quite enough for one day), 'tomorrow.'

JUST
WILLIAM

RICHMAL CROMPTON

WITH A FOREWORD BY SUE TOWNSEND

'He's mad,' said Mr Brown with conviction. *'Mad. It's the only explanation.'*

There's only one William Brown – better known as Just William. Whether he's trying to arrange a marriage for his sister or taking a job as a bootboy as step one in his grand plan to run away, William manages to cause chaos wherever he goes.

A selected list of titles available from Macmillan Children's Books

The prices shown below are correct at the time of going to press. However, Macmillan Publishers reserves the right to show new retail prices on covers, which may differ from those previously advertised.

Richmal Crompton

Just William	978-0-330-53534-2	£5.99
More William	978-0-330-53535-9	£5.99
William Again	978-0-330-54518-1	£5.99
William the Fourth	978-0-330-54517-4	£5.99
Still William	978-0-330-54470-2	£5.99

All Pan Macmillan titles can be ordered from our website, www.panmacmillan.com, or from your local bookshop and are also available by post from:

Bookpost, PO Box 29, Douglas, Isle of Man IM99 1BQ

Credit cards accepted. For details:
Telephone: 01624 677237
Fax: 01624 670923
Email: bookshop@enterprise.net
www.bookpost.co.uk

Free postage and packing in the United Kingdom